# The Colonel's Daughter

KARL-WERNER ANTRACK

CW01551827

UPFRONT PUBLISHING
LEICESTERSHIRE

The Colonel's Daughter
Copyright © Karl-Werner Antrack 2004

ISBN 1-84426-281-2

First published 2004 by
UPFRONT PUBLISHING LTD
Leicestershire

Printed by Lightning Source

# THE COLONEL'S DAUGHTER

# CHAPTER 1

Many years ago a small boy lived and was brought up in a tiny hamlet or village called Jückelberg, near Altenburg, Thüringen, Germany.

The town Altenburg is a very old community dating back from or before Roman times. It has a lovely castle built on a rock in the centre of the town and a church called 'the red church', (Die rote kirche). This church has two towers, one higher than the other, which is said to represent the beard of the old Emperor (Kaiser) Barbarossa, or Fredrick I. This Frederick I, before becoming emperor, lived in the castle and he had a red beard, which grew to be completely uneven, with one long and one short end. Thus this church is said to have been built in the emperor's honour, since he was proclaimed to have been the Emperor of the Holy Roman Empire and that is where the two different towers are said to originate.

He was born about 1124AD, belonged to the Hohenstaufen family and was chosen to be the German king in 1152, in succession of his uncle Conrad III, and was crowned Emperor of Rome in 1155: he eventually drowned in Asia Minor on June 10th 1190.

Legend however has it that he returned to his beloved country and settled down on the Kyffhäuser Mountain in a cave called the Barbarossa höhle. There in daytime he used to sit on a stone bench and table; he fell asleep and his beard grew through the table, from which it is said, he could never escape or get up again and died at this spot.

There are many black ravens still circling over the treetops high above this mountain, most likely in the hope of picking up a good meal.

All this was long before the young boy called Kiel Willy Aldorf could remember and all this was taught him at school, or he learned it from his parents.

His mother unfortunately died from stomach cancer at a very early age, very soon after seeing her young son settled in at his first school year in 1931. The young fellow with his brother, two years his senior, and his ferociously hard father had a tough time and used to go or sometimes live with a neighbouring farmer by the name Ivan and Flora Kirste and their family.

When he went to school for the very first time with his mum, he was introduced to a lovely little blonde girl named Gertrautel Müller, the daughter of one of the largest farmers in the village, where his mum had occasionally helped out.

This lovely, fair, curly haired young girl most certainly took his fancy, both being the same age and born in the same month and year. They both got on very well, especially later in singing, as both of them had good clear voices and were often picked for solo singing. These two always had to sing in the church choir at parties, weddings and many other special occasions.

The young boy often went round to the large farm and played with the little girl, especially after his dear mum had passed away. In the winter months, there was a nice swing hanging down from a large beam in the barn with plenty of straw or hay beneath for playing or rolling in.

These were some of the greatest memories the young man ever retained; this young girl was his early boyhood school girl friend, never to be forgotten.

The lovely name of the little hamlet or village, Jückelberg, is taken from the surrounding hills and beautiful valleys; it has a tiny stream flowing through it, which passes the small family house, still standing on its bank.

'Oh, Jückelberg, wie liegst Du, auf Berge-schön, so stolz?'
(Oh, Jückelberg, how can you lay on lovely hills so proud?')
By Ilka Jost, a good friend of the author and Orts-Chronistin
(area chronologist), who also tried to search out the origin of
the strange word and came up with a variety of names:
Guckilberg, recorded from the year 1336, Gokkelberg,
Juckwerk and Ygelsberg. After a great deal of thinking, the
author would personally go for the first, Guckilberg, or similar
and, possibly more appropriate, Guckelberg. This more than
likely arrived from an old local German word, gucken or
ausschauen, which in English would mean 'lookout', with berg
being a hill, since from the top of this hill one can see for miles
over the low lying areas.

Kiel carries on to Flemmingen, the next, slightly larger
village, where they all went to school and there were all the
shops as well as baker, tailor, saddler et cetera. This name
appears to come from the earlier days when it was a swamp
and seemingly the Flemish people from up north were
brought down with knowledge to drain the swamps.

Wherever this lovely name Jückelberg comes from, it was
this young boy's home for several happy and unhappy years
until after he left school.

The elder brother had already left home to go and work for
one of his uncles some miles away, to get away from their
loving, but at times very hard, lashing out father, and bad
times.

Yes, the very bad 1930s about which almost every one,
especially the elder people, know all about and will never
forget. The two boys had to struggle to keep themselves alive,
never mind happy or prosperous, there was no money
anywhere and little food or clothing.

That is why all, even the children, had to go and work on
neighbouring farms to help out in the hope of getting
something to eat and clothes to wear. They very often had to
pick up the leftovers, like small potatoes or corn, after

3

harvesting from fields, with the individual farmer's permission.

Some years later, Kiel left school and began to earn real money, when at first he worked on the little farm for the family Flora and Ivan Kirste, in conjunction with their two sons and two daughters. These sons and daughters were quite a few years older and taught him all the mischief there was to be learned.

They all had a great time, with the haymaking, harvesting, cattle herding, feeding, milking the cows and grooming the horse's et cetera.

Until one day the young man, Kiel, had to take Herr (or Mr) Kirste, who had a bad leg and could not walk very well, on a wagon with one horse to see the young family, who were busy working in the fields.

After they had a long chat, laughter and coffee, Mr. Kirste and young Kiel were on the way back to the farm again.

All of a sudden, the front wheel of the wagon slipped into a shallow ditch and Ivan Kirste was thrown off the wagon, the rear wheel running over his bad leg, and the other before young Kiel could stop the horse.

All his children, who were late teenagers or older, came running to help him back on to the wagon, since he was not badly hurt, only bruised. They gave Kiel a good telling off, which did not go down too well, especially when he did not think this having been his, but the horse's, fault.

After returning to the farm, the young fellow had to get Flora Kirste, the farmer's wife, to help get Ivan, her husband, off the wagon and into the house. She gave the young man a clip round the ears, the first time she had ever hurt him and he was more ashamed than hurt, but this was the last straw for Kiel.

The next day, early morning, the young man picked up his few belongings from home and went off on his bike to look for work elsewhere. He left the keys for the family house with an elderly lady who lived upstairs at the time, and without a word of where he was going, which he did not know himself, he disappeared round the corner and out of sight.

## The little House in the Valley

The little house stood in the valley,
Next to the crystal clear water, flowing brook.
The house stood near the crossroads,
Where he could see all goings on, by just a look.

This tiny stream next to the house,
Was full of water, coming from underneath a bridge.
Water collected from all fields and land around,
Which ran down from high upon the ridge.

The way down it was branched, through some farmers' ponds,
Which were full of carp and many other fish.
Further down it widened, where they could paddle or bathe,
And tickle blue trout under banks, along a tiny path.

This brook was called the Heidelbach or stream,
Well overgrown and in places, where it hardly could be seen.
This flowed down the valley and through the Heidelberg,
Joining up with other streams, before it flowed to Altenburg.

He remembered this stream and remembered it well,
Passed willow trees through grassy banks, the waters swell.
Looking back those years, walking along its banks,
All one could give this little brook was some sort of thanks.

The brook was still continually flowing,
Bringing water for the ponds to stay.
Carrying fresh water from the pump,
This seemed a cruel long way away!

K-WA

# CHAPTER 2

At first Kiel thought of going to seek out his elder brother, but cycling along the way he thought better of it, since there was very little friendship between the two after their mum had passed away, and his brother had left home rather suddenly. Kiel was only just over sixteen and always wanted to study and further improve his knowledge of the world around him. But how could he do this without having somewhere to live and put his head down in the first place?

Cycling along in the direction of his brother and uncle, he suddenly thought of another distant uncle whom he had not seen for years. Kiel knew that he lived and worked on a large estate, not very far from where his brother and other uncle were working. He had all the time in the world and thought he would go to this distant uncle first and find out where he and auntie lived and what they were doing.

Arriving at this large estate, the young man found someone to talk to and found out about the little house where uncle and auntie lived. They were living in a small cottage on the estate itself, as had been thought, which was quite common in these days, especially since uncle was the horse headman and had to get up very early in the mornings.

They were both naturally most surprised to see the young man Kiel, who they had seen only twice before, once as a baby and the second time when his mum had passed away. They were over the moon and could not cuddle him enough, which he himself had missed for a number of years.

He was starving hungry; he had not eaten since early morning, just before taking off from home.

The table was laden with all sorts of goodies and with a lot of explaining as to why he had suddenly come this way, the time went and it was beginning to get dark.

Without knowing the whole story but realising that there was something not quite right, they could not possibly allow him to cycle back home. They invited him to stay the night at least, which he gracefully accepted. Evening was stretching out and with a further cup of coffee and snack, the whole story had to be told.

They have never had any children and were only too delighted to put him up for as long as he wished. But he had to find a job and earn some money, so he asked his uncle, who in turn enquired the next morning with the estate manager and a job was found for Kiel. He had to help out with the cattle, feeding, milking and mucking out, which suited him fine, as he had been used to this hard work all his young life.

After meeting up with the estate manager himself, it was agreed that the young man's job should be arranged in such a way that he could attend college as well, which was fantastic and his eyes began to glimmer once again.

The Paul von Hindenburg College was in the town called Riesa, not far from a very large agricultural estate near the river Elbe where he was now living with his uncle and aunt, which could easily be reached by cycling that short way.

All the young man needed now was to go and see if he would be accepted for the next term since his school papers had not been too excellent, mostly owing to the loss of his dear mum's departure from life at his and her very young age. At home he often missed school and went for walks through the woods or fields, many times with Gertrautel, forgetting all timing and schooling, dreaming about his lost mum.

Although he had very good marks for arithmetic, history, geography and, of course, singing as well as drawing, which was one of his best subjects and that was why he wanted, hopefully, to be taught architecture.

After a few days he picked up the courage to try and see the head, who unfortunately was on holiday, but an appointment was made with his secretary for the following week.

Still shaking in his boots and soaked all over with sweat, the young man got back on his bike and returned to the large farm, or estate. This was so massive and extended from the main road almost to the little town of Strehla (where he had in fact been brought up the first few years of his life), right beside the large river Elbe. This large river was well known by now (in accordance to the first meeting of Russian and American troops in April 1945). The river Elbe rises in Czechoslovakia and flows all the way through Germany, via Dresden and up to Hamburg and further, into the North Sea.

Everyone was pleased to see this young fellow again even though nothing positive had been achieved. Most thought that he would not have the courage even to go and make himself known to either the college or the head, but by the time that he had arrived back he was all excited and everyone soon found out his new adventure.

He seemed overexcited as if he had already been accepted and naturally hoped for the very best, although his writing and reading was not really up to standard. These two subjects were, in fact, his worst, including the spelling, all of which he was very slow at, but he had great confidence and was indeed willing to listen and learn.

He did extremely well in his job with the cattle and was accepted by his uncle and auntie as their own son, he was very willing to help out wherever he could and noticed where some help was needed.

He especially loved the little calves and fed or played with them whenever he found time and all knew exactly where to find him if he could not be seen around. The young man was indeed an all-round animal lover and treated all, young or old, the same, looked after their food and welfare and soon learned how to clean, milk and feed them even very early in the mornings. Nothing seemed too much for him, early or late, even though he continually kept rubbing the sleep from his eyes.

One hot day the head milkman said, 'I know how to wake you up,' and sent him to a friend for a glass of cool fresh water from the distillery, from which they got all their sugar beet pulp for feeding to the cows in the winter months.

Kiel went into the distillery completely unsuspecting and asked the distillery foreman for this nice, cool, clear water. He was requested to wait a minute, which he did, admiring all the fine polished stainless steel cylinders and copper pipes. Very soon this gentleman returned with a metal cup half full of this seemingly nice cold water, or so he thought, until he took a mouthful and spat it straight out again.

This was horrible: the sharp and bitter, burning taste, which most certainly woke the poor little chap, this was not clear water, but clear 'schnapps' or alcohol. It was almost pure alcohol, which he had never drunk before and this was burning all the way down his throat. Everyone else was laughing at him.

They obviously wanted to teach him a lesson, not to keep walking about half asleep for the rest of his life and this most certainly did the trick. In fact it took many years, until he joined the army, when with others he began to take to this stuff again and began to quite like it on occasions.

## Drinking

There are many good reasons for drinking,
And one of them just entered my head.
If a fellow can't drink while he's living,
How on earth can he drink when he's dead?
K-WA


Coming back to the large farm or estate, at that time called the Rittergut, which belonged to Baron Colonel von Youngrock before and during the war years. After the war, when Germany was divided into two parts, East and West, this part was in the east and came under the control of the Russian forces and East German government, when all properties were taken over by the state.

This story, however, was from before or the beginning of the war in the late 1930s and early 1940s, when this young fellow was in his mid to late teens.

One day he noticed a well-polished black car with the hood down arriving at the large house, with all the servants seemingly dancing around taking out luggage and carrying it into the big house.

Among all the people he could make out the tall, fine, upstanding figure of the colonel in uniform, his wife and daughter, neither of whom he had seen previously and naturally the chauffeur and staff, some of which he had seen and met earlier.

It seemed that the colonel and his family now lived in Berlin; he was previously, after the First World War working with Field Marshall Paul von Hindenburg, later head of the German Republic and Democratic government at Weimar, Thüringen, Germany. The colonel, however now appeared to be one of Adolf Hitler's war cabinet, not coming to the estate very often and only spending a few days on the estate for holidays or recreational purposes, taking in the fresh country air whenever he possibly could.

At that time the young man Kiel had little chance of seeing a great deal of any of the family except for very short occasions, first when the colonel and his daughter came to the stables to take out two horses for riding and exercising.

The colonel's horse was a beautiful white and grey stallion. The young lady's horse was a spectacular shiny looking black mare very similar to Black Beauty (from a previous film most people know about), with the small white marking on the forehead.

Both horses had obviously been previously ordered, or was it known that these were required? They were both polished with feet blackened just like the horses on horse guard parade in London, with all leathers and saddles shining in the sunlight, as were the black boots of the riders.

That was the first time the young man Kiel had ever seen either of them close to and he lifted his cap in greetings, while both did the same and smiled.

The young man's eyes almost dropped out of their sockets when he admired this pretty young lady and she in turn smiled at him. He could not believe what he saw and hid himself behind a low wall, but could not take his eyes off this charming young girl, who seemed about a similar age. Even after they had gone, he would still keep on looking, which one of the workman noticed and told him not to forget his work; she was much too rich and charming to look at a farm labourer twice.

The next day the young lady came into the cowshed, saying 'hello', admiring the little calves, which he was feeding at that time and, to his amazement, she even came into the cubicles and stroked the little ones and allowed them to lick her hands and legs. She had this lovely gentle laugh or giggle when one of the calves tickled the sensitive skin on her arms or legs with it's little rough tongue.

It seems that they were both smiling and talking to each other, or at least Kiel himself had overstayed the time, when he was called away for other duties by the head cowman. They had been quite a long while talking to each other when she asked his name, which he gave as Kiel Willy Aldorf.

'Oh, I like Kiel, similar to the town up north, with the Kiel Kanal from the east to the North Sea,' she remarked, 'and that is what I shall call you form now on. My name is Secilia Maria, but everyone calls me Secilia, which comes from my Dad's grandmother, although I like Maria best.'

'I like Secilia,' Kiel said, 'it is quite a new name for me. I have never heard it before and that is what I shall be calling you from now on, unless you wish me to call you Maria?' he enquired?

'Oh, no, Secilia is fine,' she replied.

Before leaving, she shook his hand and gave him a little kiss on the cheek, which he was careful not to wash off for days. The boy rushed away waving his hands and arms after her, and left her with the calves, which she obviously liked.

He was warned not to get too familiar and forget his work in the process, and was told that the girl was the daughter of the colonel. The colonel was the owner of the estate, the one who paid the wages to work, not hang about talking to his daughter.

This sounded very fair, but where he came from, 'Everyone talked to each other, farmer or labourer and he was used to this,' he replied.

'This may have been the situation in a small village,' the elderly person said, and continued, telling him, 'this is not just a farm and the Colonel is not just a farmer; this is a large estate and the Colonel is a baron and gentleman, and his wife, the Baroness, a lady.'

This, the young man had forgotten and all he could think about was the young girl or lady and her gentle behaviour, especially towards his beloved calves. The young man carried on with his newly given duties but could not forget the lovely short time he has had and continually kept looking across to the calves and the girl.

All of a sudden the head cowman came and spoke to the young man and said, 'I think the calves need cleaning out as well, you had better do this before the young lady gets stuck.'

Kiel smiled, collected his tools and off he went to do just as he was told, getting into a conversation with the girl, saying 'It looks like you love little calves as much as I do.'

'Oh, yes,' she replied, 'I love all animals.'

'Yes, I could see that when you got onto the horse and went riding with your dad. I noticed you kept stroking the horse's neck, which not many people seem to do,' he replied.

She continued by saying, 'I love all animals, even the rabbits and hares in the fields and deer as well as pheasants and

12

others in the woods. Do you like all animals?' she wanted to know.

'Oh, yes,' he replied, 'especially the smaller ones, which cannot look after themselves. I have been with animals all my life,' he was saying and continued. 'We had some at home and when I worked on different farms.'

'That sounds great,' she replied, and carried on. 'You must tell me more about yourself when we get time. Have you been all over the estate and woods?' she asked.

'No, I have not been here very long,' he answered.

'I thought I had not seen you around before,' she said, 'but then we do not come here very often; only about once or twice a year for a short holiday.'

'I hope you come a little more often now that we have got to know each other and can talk. I like you and your little smile,' he pronounced.

'I quite like you, Kiel,' she said. 'One day when you have time off, I will take you round and show you the estate, but that will take quite a while,' she carried on saying.

'I don't mind how long it takes,' he replied and carried on with his job, which he had almost forgotten. 'Secilia, will you and your family be around for quite a while this time?' he asked, working and sweating at the same time.

'I am not sure,' she said and carried on, 'it all depends upon if Daddy has to go back quickly, but all being well, we should be here for a week or two.'

This obviously made the young man's eyes sparkle, when she asked, 'Why, would you like me to stay, or go back quickly?'

Almost stuttering and somewhat surprised, getting a little hot under the collar, he replied, 'No, no, no, I would love you to stay forever if you could.'

'Oh, that is nice to hear, but you do not have to get all red in the face, I will not harm you,' she laughed out merrily.

Poor Kiel did not quite know what to do for a moment, but recollected himself quite quickly and replied, 'I really mean this, I like you, it is easy to hold a conversation with you, you are of a similar age. How old are you, if I may ask?'

'You may ask,' she replied, 'but that does not mean that I have to tell you my real age; young ladies hardly ever do!'

The young man blushed again, not knowing quite how to get out of this, and smilingly said, 'I did not mean to be inquisitive, it just slipped out without thinking. I am sorry.'

'No, no, don't be sorry. I love you to be straight and ask any questions you like,' Secilia replied. 'How old are you, if I might ask?' she came back, and Kiel told her, 'I was sixteen in January this year.'

'Oh, that is nice,' the young lady said, 'I am going to be sixteen in June, or next month, so you were quite right in saying that we are of similar age.'

'This is really nice to know. When is your birthday? Oh, I am sorry, I should not have asked, please forgive me, it just came out again,' the young man said.

'No, I will not forgive you,' she replied, 'I shall be only too happy to tell you. My birthday is on the 19th of June, so you can send me a birthday card.'

'That is wonderful,' the young man almost shrieked out. 'That is the same day as my mum's birthday was; I shall never forget it.'

'Oh, that is nice,' Secilia announced. 'Where is your mum now? Will you go to her birthday or will you just send her a card?' she asked.

Kiel once again blushed and almost began to cry, when he had to tell Secilia that his mum had passed away a few years ago, but could not bring himself to repeat the whole story and quickly walked away.

Secilia followed, took Kiel by the hand and apologised for having asked, and said, 'You do not have to tell me all about your mum now, but I would like to know one day. Will you promise you will tell me?' She squeezed his hand and departed with a gentle peck on his cheek, which seemed to make all the difference. This made Kiel suddenly come back to life again.

14

He asked Secilia not to go unless she had to, and promised he would tell her the entire story one day.

It was getting to the time when Secilia had to go. She smiled, waved goodbye and departed, when suddenly his smile reappeared and he waved back at her, calling, 'Hope to see you again soon.' She turned with another smile.

That was a morning never to be forgotten; the young man had at long last found someone his own age to converse with and he was over the moon. Everyone could see that he was a different lad from this time on and all congratulated him for being able to talk with the young lady, who normally had hardly spoken to any of the staff on previous occasions.

She had gone now and disappeared into the large garden and big house to her parents, while the young man still had work to do, but soon went off to have his own breakfast with his uncle and aunt.

He certainly was more than over the moon and could not help thinking or talking about Secilia, and had to tell his aunt all about it, since she had no idea and had not heard or seen anything of this sudden meeting.

'You had better be careful, young man,' his auntie told him, and carried on, 'Secilia is a well brought up young lady and lives in a large city, not like you or us working folk.'

The boy listened carefully but could not really understand why people had to be different just because they had a better education or more money. There did not seem to be that difference in his little village or school, and he expressed his feelings.

'Yes, I quite understand what you are talking about Kiel, but life is very different, which you will find out as you get a little older. I am only giving you a little advice. You are quite right when you talk about a small village or while going to school, but the differences in humans do not show up until they get a little older, believe me,' she remarked. She followed on by saying, 'When I was a little girl, that is now some time ago, I thought exactly the same as you, but found out that life

15

is completely different to what one thinks or is made to believe as a child.'

In the meantime they both kept on washing up until they were ready and go and have a little rest before lunch, or the next shift of work came along.

Not that Kiel was all that keen on work, he just wanted to rush back in case the young lady would show up again, but he was unlucky.

Kiel now began to realise how the love and influence of his mother played a great part in his future life.

As with most people he had taken some hard knocks in his early life but had also had a great deal of fun, and his friendship with the colonel's daughter as a friend, was among one of his happiest memories.

# CHAPTER 3

The time and year was spring 1940, when most of the cattle were affected by foot and mouth disease and a lot of work had to be carried out to wash and care for all the affected beasts. Some of the worst affected had to be humanely killed and disposed off in deep dug out pits or graves and covered in a lot of lime before soil was placed back on top.

The least infected were treated by washing their mouths and feet with a mixture of a little vinegar and lots of water. One had to be very careful of the mixture and movements of the beasts themselves, since this was obviously burning the sore areas and only very gentle washing or tapping had to be done. Most of the young and strong managed to get over this dreadful disease, when even though at times they could hardly walk or eat. This was an experience he had never forgotten, which made all of them love animals even more thereafter.

Some, especially the younger animals, never caught the disease and were indeed very lucky, but when the people had to look after many hundreds, every hand on the estate, even the ladies, were required to help out. It took a long time to care for every one of these animals and all had to be kept inside, under cover on dry straw bedding most of the time, and as little moisture as possible had to be used for washing.

Perhaps better said tab the blisters or sore patches in mouth and around feet et cetera, when many of the cattle could hardly stand, walk or even feed themselves for several days.

Even milking was a most difficult task, since the udders and teats were sore with blisters and a soft cream with warm water was the only way one could bring relief to the pressure of milk build-up within.

Without having experienced such misery, no one could ever imagine the hardship some of these beasts and people had to endure for days and nights on end, but none of the animals were slaughtered unnecessarily.

Life, however, could be very tiring and all of us have had to experience difficulties we never thought of or thought possible to overcome.

Good times make up for all the bad and in the end only the good are normally remembered, which is just as well, or we would concern ourselves and worry all the time throughout life.

· The worst times were to get up in the early hours of the mornings around 4.30 a.m. to collect and bring in, feed and milk the cows every day, seven days a week. The good thing was that the horsemen had to get up even earlier at 3.30 a.m. to cut and collect the food for the cows, horses and other animals on the estate from the fields. That was when uncle always gave Kiel a knock on the door, which gave him plenty of time to get up, wash and dress, but he often dropped off again, only to be woken by the alarm at the last minute.

Although he had been allowed permission to take several hours off in the day to go and follow his schooling and studying, it was hard work. Very much better however, was the time he had been able to spend together with Secilia yesterday. He wondered if she was going to turn up again today?

He was naturally full of hope, but it was still early morning, when he was sitting with others under the cows, with the one-legged wooden stool tied around his hips. Everyone else had the same, for easy getting up and walking, without having to use one hand moving or carrying the stool all the time. This was quite an experience on its own and took a long time to get used to and get the balance, when many times he fell over backwards, especially when a cow moved a little, with the bucket of milk flowing down between his legs.

Both hands were needed for milking and some of the cows had such massive udders and large teats that it took all his time to get his fingers round them and fill the bucket standing or hanging between the knees.

Every now and again, one had a sweep round the ears from the cows' tails, which were often still quite moist and these were not always as clean as one would have wished. Often, especially in the summer when there were many flies around biting or stinging the beasts, one had to tie the tail to the cow's legs for safety. This was quite a good idea for us, but not the cows. They would often move and sometimes step on one's foot, which was not too comfortable, and black toenails were often received, with walking difficulties for a few days.

If one would continually think of all these problems, one would not have had time to enjoy life or have a laugh, which they all had when it happened to someone else and they certainly did when it happened to Kiel.

The cattle were allowed to go out to grass again after feeding and milking time was over and the cleaning up would once again begin.

All feeding was done in front of cows on long gangways with greens or hay with a through flowing trough all the way for the sugar beet pulp coming straight from the distillery still slightly warm, which the cows liked, especially in winter or cold mornings. These troughs and gangways always had to be cleaned and washed, ready for the next time, which was twice a day, morning and afternoon.

Thereafter, himself being still a youngster, learner or helper, had to get some milk to mix it up with cornmeal or bran, and take it to the young calves, which were already making a noise, being hungry and waiting.

Going along with two buckets or more in each hand half full of food for the youngsters, he spotted what he thought was Secilia coming out of the large house and garden gate. Obviously his eyes had not been fixed on where he was going, but followed his thoughts and hopes and he stumbled, spilling some of the milk and got told off.

True enough, while he was hanging the buckets into safe places for the young calves to drink and eat their food in safety, there she was coming towards the small compounds and animals again.

'Good morning, Secilia,' he called out, and back came the reply.

'Good morning, Kiel, how are you?'

'Oh, I am fine, how are you?' he replied. 'Where were you yesterday afternoon? I had hoped and was looking out to see you again then.' he asked.

'Yes, I had hoped to see you again, Kiel, to carry on with our conversation, but I went out to town with Mummy and Daddy. We did a little shopping and went for a cup of tea; it was quite nice and I enjoyed it. What did you do, Kiel?' she asked, stroking one of the calves.

'I was working most of the time, but did go for a short walk, just round the back of the fields,' he replied.

'Did you go down to the woods and the river?' she asked.

'No I did not; I have not been that far,' he mentioned.

'Oh, you must go and see, it is very nice there. I will take you, if you would like to come. What time will you finish today?' she asked.

'Yes, I would love to come. I shall finish as soon as I have fed the calves and had some breakfast,' he replied, 'which will be in about an hour. Will you be available by that time?' he enquired.

'Oh, yes, I will be, I have all morning,' Secilia replied. 'That will be nice. Would you like to come with me, Kiel?' She was keen to know and smiled.

'Yes, nothing will stop me, I would enjoy you showing me your dad's lovely estate,' he said, and carried on. 'I always wanted to know how big the estate was and how far it goes down to the river.'

'Can you swim, Secilia?' he asked.

'Oh, yes, I can,' she replied, and asked, 'Can you swim, Kiel?'

'Yes, I can; we were taught in the Hitler Youth and I also managed to get my gold medal for life-saving,' he replied.

'Oh, that is wonderful. I don't have to be afraid of going swimming with you in the river, but it might still be a little chilly this time of year,' she followed on saying.

'Yes, perhaps you are right; I shall not bring my swimming trunks. We probably won't have any time for swimming anyway,' he answered.

'Oh, you must bring yours, please, but I don't think I shall worry about my costume, but I would like to see you swimming if we have time,' she replied. 'I shall be in the yard, waiting for you,' Secilia called out.

'Yes okay, I shall not be too long,' he called back and ran off to do the rest of the cleaning.

After finishing and returning home, he had hardly time to swallow his breakfast, when auntie asked, 'What is the rush, are you going out somewhere?'

'Yes, I am going through the fields, down to the woods and river with Secilia,' he said.

She seemed to lower her eyebrows, a little which brought a smile to uncle's face.

'Did she ask you, or did you ask her?' she suddenly inquired in a deep voice, 'I hope you have not been too forward, my boy?'

'No, Auntie, Secilia asked me, or, better, told me to come with her, so that she could show me all the estate, the woods, animals and the river. I might even go for a short swim if we have time before lunch,' he replied.

'Well, do be careful as to what you get up to, don't drown yourself, and don't show off in front of Secilia,' she said, not knowing quite what she meant.

He ran upstairs to get his swimming trunks and called back, 'Please do not worry yourself, Auntie, I shall behave myself and won't show off; she is too much of a fine young lady.'

'That is right, my boy. Just remember that she is a nice young lady, whom we would love to see for many more years to come,' she called out after him.

'Yes, Auntie, I shall look after her. Please do not worry, I shall try to be a gentleman, whatever that is,' he called back while running to the door, where he could see Secilia already waiting and waving to him across from the far end of the yard.

She once again looked ravishingly beautiful, with her slightly dark skin under a flimsy silk dress and her dark, almost black, wavy hair with shining eyes and smiles.

### When the Grass is dry

I'd love to take you, darling, where the grass is dry,
But then, no doubt, you'd like to question why?
I find no special reason to explain,
But sunshine is much better than some rain.

The many flowers in the meadows green,
Produce a welcome with a sunshine beam.
We'll walk together, going hand in hand,
Which even God above would understand?

When all the farmers cut their grass for hay,
And all the people sit around and pray,
That harvest of the corn was just as good,
While all the poorest gather forest wood.

For fires when the grass is frosted or wet,
And at that time they'll sit and will forget,
What life was like without the darkened sky?
There is no need for anyone to question why.

I'll be around and wait for this fine sunny day,
If nothing else, I'll wait for you and pray.
God above please open up those massive clouds,
Of this, I'm certain and I have no doubts.

But will you come, as you have said before,
Or wait for me at home, behind your door?

No, you are here, now do let's go,
There's plenty time, so take it slow.

We'll walk along, among the grass so dry,
And both are wondering just why?
But we are happy holding hands,
Until we've reached the river's banks.

K-WA

# CHAPTER 4

'Hello Secilia,' he called out from the distance, almost running towards her. 'Have you been waiting long? I did not see you until I opened the door. Sorry about this, but I was looking for my swimming trunks.'

'Oh, did you bring them? I have only just come along, thinking that you would not be too long. I am glad you could make it. What did your uncle and auntie say?' she asked and smiled, stretching out her hand for a friendly shake.

'Yes, I did bring my trunks, just in case the water is nice. I love swimming. Oh, uncle and auntie just gave me a little talking to, but were quite happy for us to go,' he replied. He shook her hand, which was so very soft, small and gentle, and apologised for his being a little rough.

'Don't apologise, Kiel,' she said, 'I like a boy or man who has got a strong handshake, as long as you do not squeeze mine too hard,' she followed on.

'No, I shall be very careful and rather squeeze you,' he replied, getting a little red under the collar and, no doubt, the face.

Then she turned and said 'Now, now, Kiel, behave yourself and you don't have to be sorry for yourself or get red in the face. I have heard all these remarks before and love to be liked. Do you really like me that much, Kiel?' she asked.

'Yes, I do,' he replied, 'I think you are wonderful and kind to animals and you even talked to me, when I am just a farmhand, which I thought was very kind of you,' he followed on.

'Why should I not talk to you? You are about the same age as myself, and you are not only a farm worker, you are a student similar to me.' She continued. 'I liked you from the first time I saw you with the little calves, you seemed so kind and gentle with them.'

He appreciated every word and felt taller than he really was and so proud to have found this pretty young lady to walk with and chat to. He so much enjoyed her clear soft voice and speech as well as her gentle movements and lovely little smile. 'Oh, look at these lovely flowers,' he said pointing to a little shallow ditch along the small farm track as they were walking along.

'Yes aren't they beautiful, and of various colours?' she remarked.

He jumped into the shallow ditch and picked a small bunch, climbed back out and handed them to Secilia.

'Oh thank you,' she said. 'Are they for me?'

'Yes,' he replied.

'You shouldn't have, I could have gone to pick them myself; that is kind of you,' and she carried on, 'I shall take them home and put them in a vase, or dry them and place them in one of my books, which will always remind me of today and you, Kiel. Thank you,' she said and she gave him a soft peck on the cheek, which he more than appreciated.

Once again he was delightfully overwhelmed with her warm nature and kindness, and she, it seemed, appreciated the attention he gave her.

They walked along and kept on chatting about various things, when she suddenly called out and said, 'Look at these young deer, pheasants and partridges along the side of the wood, all eating and pecking away in the shade of the trees.'

It certainly was a wonderful sight and we tried to be as quiet and careful as we possibly could, and got quite near before they all turned and ran or flew away into the bushes and trees beyond.

We both had a slow and gentle walk through the wood and saw several more on their way, but it was a little too dark among the trees and bushes to see them all in their lovely true colours and so they continued slowly to the far end of the forest. Still holding hands occasionally and talking, we finally arrived at the edge of the river Elbe, which was quite a wide and large river coming all the way up from Czechoslovakia, with quite a number of large cruisers and boats floating up and down.

There was a lovely shallow type of grassy beach but no sand along this side of the riverbank. They sat down and dangled their feet into the water. This was nice and cool and with the sun overhead, it all seemed quite a pleasant experience.

Secilia looked absolutely beautiful with her hair glittering in the sunlight and her eyes shining like stars in the sky, her soft, slightly dark skin, and her curves in all the right places.

They sat there talking and enjoying themselves, and the gentle waves coming up their legs, when a boat went by, admiring the flow of the river with the occasional boat or cruiser.

'Are you going for a swim, Kiel?' Secilia asked.

'No, I think it is a little too chilly,' he replied.

'Go on, you coward, the water is quite nice and warm. I would have gone in if I had brought my swimming costume,' she stated.

He thought he would never be called a coward, so he began to undress and said, 'Why worry about a swimming costume? There is no one watching and I shall keep my eyes shut.'

'Yes, I quite believe you will keep your eyes shut, even underwater,' she replied and giggled. 'You couldn't keep your eyes shut for even one second, the way you keep looking me up and down. You little cheat; you are no better than any other boy or man. Oh, I just remembered I did not bring a towel to dry myself after a swim and I could not walk about naked with you around. That would not be right, would it?' she remarked.

'No, of course not. At least not out here in the open fields when people might be looking,' he replied. 'That reminds me, I did not bring a towel, so I better not go for a swim either.'

She looked absolutely divine lying there, and he certainly could not take his eyes off her, or so he thought, until he suddenly looked up and called out, 'Oh, look, there is your mum and dad galloping round the field on their horses. What shall we do?' he asked. 'It is a good job I did not go into the water, not having a towel to dry myself, with you sitting out here. Whatever would they have thought?' he enquired.

'Don't be silly, you would have looked fine, just as you do now,' she replied. 'We shall get up and wave to them; they knew I was coming out here for a walk with you.'

Secilia was an even greater pleasure to look at when she laughed outright and he could have cuddled her there and then, had it not been for those two horses and riders being so close with, no doubt, their eyes upon us both. Kiel took Secilia's hand and was helping this little gorgeous looking and sweet smelling, beautiful girl on her feet, when she slipped into his arms with a welcoming little hug.

We got up, waved and called. When they saw us, they turned the horses and came slowly closer; the lady was riding sidesaddle, which was common for ladies in those days.

The colonel was sitting on his Schimmel; a white and grey spotted well-groomed horse, straight and upright as an officer and gentleman would and both of them looked terrific.

The lady of the house rode the black horse that Secilia had been riding previously and looked very attractive. That was the first time Kiel had ever seen Her Ladyship so close. She seemed so tiny and petite sitting on her horse and looked very charming with her riding hat, off-white breeches and black polished boots, coat and black shiny hair, with hat and slightly brown skin.

'Hello, Secilia, hello, Kiel. What are you both up to, here by the riverside? Are you going to have a swim?' she asked, while

Kiel went round to stroke the horses' heads, and allowed Secilia to explain.

'You look beautiful my lady,' he pronounced.

She said, 'Thank you, Kiel, that is nice to hear; you look quite nice yourself.'

'Thank you, my lady,' he replied.

'Do you like horses, Kiel?' the colonel asked.

'Oh, yes, sir, I have been with horses all my life and I like all animals, especially horses, which I can ride,' he pronounced.

'Can you ride as well?' the colonel enquired.

'Oh, yes, sir, I have been riding for a long time, but mainly bareback, without a saddle,' he answered.

'That is nice to hear,' the colonel answered, and followed on by saying, 'I will make a note of this, then you can take our horses out for exercising, but do be careful,' he remarked, and continued 'I do not like to see them hurt.'

'No, sir, thank you, sir, I'd be delighted to take your horses for exercises and clean them thereafter; I love doing that,' came Kiel's reply.

'Good, that is settled. I shall leave word with the headman and give him my permission, but do be careful,' he pronounced again.

'Yes, sir, thank you, sir,' Kiel called back with a big smile on his face, when the Colonel saluted, touched his hat with his whip, turned his horse and slowly rode off.

Secilia had explained to her mum, in the meantime, why they could not go for a swim although they had both thought about it.

'Well, don't make a spectacle of yourselves, be good and behave,' she said, smiling to both of us, turning her horse to follow the colonel.

Once again touching their whips to their hats, they very slowly rode away, when the lady called back, 'Don't be too long,' and we waved with a smile.

'How did you know I keep looking you up and down? Did I make it that obvious, that I admire and love you?' Kiel asked.

'Do you really love me, Kiel?' she said, now fishing to know.

, 'Yes, I do. I think you are easy to talk and listen to and wonderful to look at,' he replied. 'I hope I have not offended you by these truthful remarks?' he requested to know.

'No, no, it's quite nice to be admired and spoken to in an open manner, and I hope it is truthful?' she asked.

'Yes, of course, I would never lie to you, Secilia,' he answered.

When she leant forward and gave him a kiss on his cheek, this he had never experienced, only from his young school friend girl some years ago.

Secilia most certainly was a remarkable girl and easy to get along with. 'I don't know what time it is,' he said, 'but perhaps we better get along on our way home for lunch?'

'Are you hungry already?' she enquired.

'No, no, I just thought that you might have to get back, according to your Mummy's remarks,' he replied. 'I could always eat you, if I was really hungry,' he said, and followed on by saying, 'I am sure you are sweet enough to eat.'

'Kiel, you are making a joke of me, you would not really eat me if you were very hungry would you?' she asked, and gave him a little punch in the ribs, looking somewhat distressful.

'No, of course, I would not eat you, my love, although I might take a little bite out of that sweet figure of yours,' and he gave her a little peck on her cheek, which she seemed to appreciate, but pushed him slightly away. 'When I say sweet figure, I really meant it,' he said, and looked at her.

She was gorgeous; Secilia had curves in all the right places, with beautiful wavy dark hair and beautiful sparkling eyes. But she could be a little irritating and most certainly had her own mind at times. 'Am I getting a little too friendly or cheeky when I said and did this?' he asked politely.

'No, no, I was just somewhat surprised you were open enough to say and do what you just did, which was rather nice of you. But perhaps you are right, we might just as well return slowly, so we do not get home too late,' she replied.

Secilia took his hand and they began to walk away from the river, back through the wood and along the little farm track towards the estate.

Suddenly she said, 'Oh, dear, I have forgotten all about the lovely flowers that you picked for me and left them by the riverside when we quickly got up to wave to my parents.'

'Never mind, I will pick some more on our way back if you would still like some,' he remarked with a smile.

'Oh, yes, please, Kiel, I would love to take some home with me, and I know Mummy would like them as well,' she replied quickly.

Still walking slowly hand in hand, they chatted about all sorts of things, like school and college et cetera.

He asked, 'What is the big city of Berlin like? Do you enjoy living there?'

'Yes, it is very nice. We have a large house; you will have to come and visit us one day. The school is very close and I have many good friends. We also have a cook and a housekeeper, but not very much garden to play in,' she replied.

'What do you do all day, after you come out of school or college, if you have no garden to play in or go for walks?' he asked.

'No, I have my own room and I like reading and playing with my dolls, then we have a large park not far away, where I take our little dog for walks,' she replied, and followed on. 'Sometimes I go alone and sometimes with Mummy or the housekeeper, but often I meet up with friends from school and we sit around or play a game,' she replied. 'If the weather is nice we often go to town or I go for a bicycle ride in the park or visit a friend of mine, of whom I have many; we all go to the same school,' she said. 'I never seem to get bored, although I do love coming out to the estate and fresh air, especially to see all the animals and go for a ride on Mummy's horse with Daddy, if I am allowed,' she remarked.

'You seemed to like the horse, when I saw you yesterday and the horse appeared to like you. Do you gallop like we saw your parents doing a moment ago, or do you take it easy?' he inquired.

'Oh, yes, we do gallop, which Daddy likes. He has been with horses all his life, even in the army; he was in the cavalry during the last war,' she said, and continued. 'I have been riding since I was about two years old and had a little pony here on the estate, some years ago,' she remarked and carried on. 'I also go to a riding school in Berlin once a week, which I enjoy. There we learn all the musical rides, but I am not too good at that; I prefer to ride out in the open fields,' she rattled on.

Secilia was a good talker as well as a good listener and never seemed to forget anything. Then we suddenly came to the place with lovely flowers along the side of the little farm track, in the shallow ditch.

'Oh, look, there are these gorgeous wild flowers, shall I go and pick a few more for you to take home?' he called out.

'Yes, please, I'll come with you and help you pick them,' she replied, and they both stepped into the shallow ditch together. She nearly stumbled and he caught her just in time, putting his arms around her. This he had looked forward to doing for quite a long time, but never dared, but she soon wriggled herself free again. He held her quite close for a few seconds, to allow her to catch her breath again, when she said, 'Thank you, Kiel. I could have got hurt; you are a real gentleman, but please don't do this too often.'

This made him blush a little, since he had hoped she would stumble, so that he could hold her in his arms for the first time. She was so amazingly soft, almost like a little rabbit, which one has to gently hold and care about or even stroke.

They sat down for a few minutes to admire the countryside and the lovely flowers around them. There seem to be just these few within a little circle either side; there must have been some special soil just in that area.

He remarked on this to Secilia, when she looked and said, 'Yes, Kiel, that does seem strange, I had not noticed or thought about this before, you are clever,' she remarked, and gave him another little peck on the cheek with a smile.

He never really knew what to make of her; one minute she seemed over enthusiastic and the next on the defence. Having been given the so-called cold shoulder, which surprised him a little, he was not sure if at any time he dared do it again and began to think.

But the sun was high in the clear blue sky and lying there in the little shallow ditch, where only God could see them, he tried to put his arm under her head, pulling it a little closer to him to make her more comfortable and gave her a little peck on her cheek in return, which seemed to work.

'Thank you, Kiel, you are good to me, and it seems you do love me just a little after all,' she whispered in his ear.

'Do you love me a little? I like and love you a lot, darling,' he remarked.

She turned her head towards him and said, 'Thank you, Kiel, that is the first time you have called me darling; did you really mean it?'

'Yes, of course I mean it,' and he pulled her just that little closer, when there was hardly room for fresh air to get between them and kissed her, this time on her lips, which she seemed to enjoy, and returned the kiss, saying, 'Thank you again.' He was a little puzzled; what exactly was in her mind?

They lay there for quite a while, not knowing quite what to do next, when she suddenly jumped up and said, 'We had better go and pick some of those flowers before it gets too late.'

This was probably just as well, or he might not have been able to control his emotions, which may have gone a little too far or he might have lost all he had gained in these last two days.

'Yes, darling, I think we should, and slowly go back home, or we shall be late for lunch and every one will wonder what has happened to us,' he mentioned.

'Nothing will happen to us with you around, Kiel, I am sure you will look after me all the time we are together, but please remember not to call me darling on the estate or in front of anyone else, or I shall be very embarrassed,' she mentioned.

'No, darling, I shall remember and will call you Secilia every time I see you and I hope that will be quite often. What are you going to do this afternoon?' he asked politely.

'I am not quite sure if we are going out; if not, I shall be coming over to see you and the little calves again, I hope. Would you mind?' she enquired to know.

'Mind, darling, no, of course I do not mind. I would love you to come again and see my other little darlings.'

'Oh, you have got some more?' she quickly enquired.

'Oh, yes, I have got all these small calves, which I call my darlings; do you mind?' he asked.

'Now you are teasing me,' she said and hit him and ran away.

He quickly caught up with her, pulled her close, gave her a little kiss and said, 'I call everyone I love "my darling", even my auntie sometimes for a joke.'

'Oh, so you say it for a joke but don't really mean it,' she called out.

'No, you are twisting my words. Of course I mean it with you, and the little calves. I cannot really call my auntie, "my darling" and so I do this for a joke,' he repeated. 'Come here, my little darling,' he called out and embraced her, gave her a little kiss, took her hand again and, while walking, he said, 'Now I hope you know I mean it.'

'Yes, darling, I know you do, I was just kidding you,' and she laughed as she spoke. That was the first time she called him darling, which he appreciated and remarked upon, while they both walked close, hand in hand with each other.

# CHAPTER 5

They soon reached the entrance gate to the estate. She gave him a little peck on the cheek and said, 'We better let go of each other or people might see us and begin to talk, which my parents would not appreciate.'

'Yes, of course, my love, I fully agree with you.'

He squeezed her hand and tried to let it go.

'Oh, now I am your Love,' she said. 'Things get better all the time,' she said and squeezed his hand once more and with a sweet smile allowed him to walk her to her garden gate.

They said goodbye to each other without another thought but a smile; he left her and ran home quickly, since the time was getting on.

Auntie was delighted to see him and gave him a cuddle, which was greatly appreciated and he had to tell her and uncle all about their adventure (after a wash and scrub up) over lunch.

They both seemed exited and listened with great interest to all his stories, about the birds and the bees as well as the river and meeting up with his Lord and Her Ladyship.

'I did not go for a swim, the water was still a little chilly and I had forgotten to take a towel for changing and drying myself afterwards,' he said.

'That was just as well,' auntie replied, and followed on, 'the young lady would not have appreciated you standing there naked and soaking wet.'

'Yes, you are quite right, mother,' uncle said and spoke in between, 'that would have been a sight for sore eyes,' and laughed.

Kiel was not amused. 'I am a fine figure of a young man,' he pronounced, 'and I have just behaved myself as I should or have been taught.'

'Yes, of course, my boy.' Uncle spoke again and followed on by saying, 'I was only joking, Kiel, you must not take everything so seriously.'

Then auntie stepped in and said, 'And you, father, should not take the mickey out of young lads. They are not all as clever as you and all have to learn as they go along. Never forget this. You did not know all before you got to your age,' she said, and seemed quite sharp.

Kiel told and showed him that he did not really mind and knew that he was just trying to ruffle his feathers.

'Good for you, Kiel,' she carried on, 'don't take any notice of his silly remarks, he does not really mean them.'

'No, auntie, I quite understand, but first I thought uncle meant something completely different. I would never try to upset Secilia or her parents, and she knows that. We have talked about it; she is quite broadminded, really,' he pronounced.

'Is she really?' auntie replied, 'I had better keep an eye on the two of you, so you don't get up to any mischief.'

'You don't have to worry about us two, auntie,' he said and carried on, 'we are both still young but we do like each other and hope to go for another walk again.'

'Well, we'll see about that,' she replied and this made him think of his dad; he was just as cautious as his auntie, which must be inbred in the elder people, he thought, and did not reply.

He had about an hour or so left and went upstairs to lie down for a while, reading a book and thinking of Secilia, who he could not get out of his mind. She was absolutely gorgeous and so friendly, ready to talk about any and everything; she was quite well educated, not a bit like him, who had missed a great deal of schooling after his mum had suddenly passed away, the first year after he started school.

He must have dozed off when he heard auntie calling. He looked at the alarm clock and got such a surprise that he quickly jumped off his bed, put on his working clothes shot downstairs and across the yard, when he heard auntie calling, 'Don't kill yourself, boy!'

By the time he arrived, the cows had already been collected and tied up, ready for feeding and milking. It was Saturday and every one wanted to go out in the evening, which he had completely forgotten and apologised to the headman, who in turn said, 'If you were not spending all your time with young ladies, you would be wanting to go out in the evenings, too.'

'No, thank you,' he replied and continued, 'I am much too tired in the evenings to go out and I do not like drinking or dancing either, I am too young.'

The headman laughed and said, 'Well, you had better get on with your work, so that the others can enjoy themselves when we have all finished.'

'Yes, sir,' he replied. He collected his bucket and milking stool to start cleaning and milking while the others were still feeding.

The warm sugar beet pulp running along the large troughs in front of the cows smelt nice with some sort of Schnapps aroma; no wonder all the cows like it, especially in the cold or cooler mornings. There never appeared to be any left to clear up and all troughs were licked smooth and clean. Even the green fodder on the gangways in front of the cows were always empty and clean; the cow's tongues appeared to go even in the smallest corners or crevices.

After milking had once again been finished and all the cows led out to the fresh green fields, he had to do his daily task of feeding the ever increasing number of little calves.

Before he had got all the buckets ready with milk mixed with bran from the corn to give these little ones something to chew and build up their muscles, Secilia was already waiting.

'Hello, Secilia,' he called out, being very careful not to call her darling, 'How are you? I am glad you managed to come and give me a hand. With more and more calves being born, I shall need you every day,' he called out.

'Oh, will you? I shall have to see and have a talk with my parents, who may not be too keen on the idea. They want me to carry on going to college and university later,' she replied.

'We can go to college together here in Riesa and you can help me with my lessons, when in time I shall be as clever as you,' he said.

'I don't think my parents would agree, although I would love to go to college with you and help you, but you are quite clever yourself, or so it seems,' she announced, and followed on by saying, 'we shall have to talk about this later. The calves are waiting for their food, please come.'

Secilia helped him with the carrying of the buckets and by the time they got there, all the little calves were waiting and crying out for their food, poor things. We placed the buckets in the little retainers, so that they could help themselves, but the tiny ones or last comers had to be helped to find out by placing one's hand in their mouth and guiding them into the bucket, while sucking our fingers. This they would do all the time, even when getting older, which they had learned themselves when sucking after birth from their mums', similar to babies. They loved doing this and they both enjoyed it, since they kept tickling our fingers with their rough tongues.

But they would get hold of anything, even one's trousers, shirt or blouse, and Secilia would run away if they became too close to her tiny, but well-developed and protruding chest.

Kiel had to laugh and said, 'I would not mind being a little calf myself at times.'

She seemed to get a little red in her face, and replied, 'I am sure you would not, but you had better keep your eyes on your work and do not talk too loud.'

'I am sorry. I did not mean to upset you or make you blush; the remark just came into my head without thinking,' he said, and apologised again.

'Well, in future you will have to think first before speaking, especially when there are other people about,' she remarked, and seemingly he became red in his face. She noticed it and continued, 'Now you know what it is like when one gets shamed and humiliated in front of others,' and giggled. She came back to continue with the feeding and stroking of the dear little calves.

'Have I really annoyed or shamed you?' he asked.

She turned to him and said, 'No, of course not, but you must be more careful when speaking to me with other men around,' she replied.

'Yes, of course. I am truly sorry and should not have made such a remark. It just seemed so joyful the way you turned and ran away from this little fellow; I won't do it again,' he remarked, apologetically.

'Will you come over again tomorrow?' he asked.

'Maybe tomorrow morning, if I am allowed, but we do have guests and relations coming for lunch and coffee, and I may not be able or allowed to come in the afternoon,' she mentioned. 'What about this evening? Would you like to take a little walk with me? It is a nice day and we are not going anywhere,' she asked.

'Yes, please, if I may, after I've had a bath and some supper. What about seven thirty?' he enquired.

'That would be fine, as long as I am allowed out, but I think so, for about an hour. I shall look for you,' she replied. 'But if I am not there waiting, do not worry, I might come later or I will let you know over the garden wall, or give you a sign and wave from the window overlooking the yard,' she said.

He was once again over the moon, although he had not thought of this himself, but he never realised that she would be allowed to come out in the evening, and was overjoyed to hear her asking.

She went off saying 'Goodbye,' and waving her hand, disappeared through the door and across the road into the large garden near the big house.

He could not get the cleaning up done quick enough and nearly fell over his own two feet, when the headman called out, 'Don't be in too much of a hurry and hopefully you can get up in time in the morning, which you have not managed this afternoon.'

'Yes, sure, I will, or at least I will do my very best, and set my alarm, which I did not do earlier this afternoon,' he replied and laughed.

He finished his jobs even faster than he had ever done before and was congratulated by the headman for having been very thorough and good, which was very much appreciated. He called out 'goodbye,' and rushed off for his supper.

When he got across the yard to the little cottage, auntie called out, 'What is the rush? You have done nothing wrong I hope, and nothing is spoiling, supper is not quite ready.'

'No, auntie, I hope supper won't be too late; I want to go out, so I had better go to wash and change first,' he called out, and ran upstairs as fast as his legs would allow him.

'Yes, all right my boy, but don't be too long, supper will soon be on the table,' auntie called out, 'and don't forget to wash behind your ears,' she called up the stairs.

'I always wash behind my ears,' he thought, 'what is she on about?'

She may have realised that he was going out with Secilia and meant to make absolutely sure, which he did and looked into the mirror close up while combing his hair, of which he was always very proud.

Running or nearly falling downstairs, he was met by auntie, who again called out, 'Steady on boy, what's the rush? No one has died, I hope?'

'No, no, auntie, I thought you were both waiting for me, since it took a little longer than expected,' he replied.

'No, you are all right, boy, sit yourself down with uncle and I will dish up,' she said and carried on. 'Are you going anywhere nice? You are not going to see Secilia again, are you?' she asked quietly.

'Yes, as a matter of fact I am. We are going for a little walk; since the weather is so nice, she asked me if I wanted to,' he replied.

'Oh, that is nice, are you sure she asked you and not the other way round?' she requested to know.

'Yes, I am sure,' he replied and went on. 'I would not have had that cheek after we have already been out this morning and had such a lovely time. She is really nice, auntie, I like her outgoing nature and beautiful smile.'

'Yes, I can see that,' uncle butted in. 'Can't you ask Secilia if she would like to go out with someone a little more knowledgeable, like me for instance?' he asked and laughed.

Auntie shot in between and said, 'Don't you dare, my boy, he is just an old man and jealous, but jealousy will get him nowhere. You take her out by yourself,' she said. 'I just hope you have a great time together, but as I have said before and will say it again, be careful, my boy, and do not take chances. She is a nice young lady,' she continued.

'Yes, auntie, I will,' he replied while getting on with his supper and hoped that they would both be quiet and not keep on.

After they had all finished, cleared the table and started with the washing up, auntie said, 'You had better be off, my lad or Secilia will have gone by herself. I saw her waiting outside for you a minute ago.'

'Did you really?' he questioned, and virtually shot out of the front door, waving to Secilia and running across the yard towards her.

'Slow down,' Secilia called out, 'or you will fall over and hurt yourself, then we cannot go for our long walk and I shall have to carry you back home,' she continued.

Completely out of breath, he grabbed her hand and said, 'I did not want you to wait too long or go without me, that's why I rushed.'

'Oh, that was nice of you, but you do not have to fall over to get to me that quickly,' she said and laughed, following on by saying, 'I think your auntie is watching us from the front door.'

He turned, saw her and waved, as they slowly walked along through the big gate at the rear of the estate, which was still open for late workmen to get back in with their horses.

'Where shall we go, up to the wood or along the river?' Secilia asked, and followed on by saying, 'It's not much good going on the main road.'

'No, there will be too much dust and traffic. You are quite right, as always,' he replied.

'Let's go up to the woods and see if we can spot more of those lovely animals, which should be feeding around this time, before going to their beds to sleep.'

'Yes, that is what I thought,' Secilia replied, and followed on by saying, 'I must not be too late, Mummy told me to be back by half past nine.'

It had only just gone seven thirty, so they had nearly two hours, which was nice and quite long enough to have a slow walk.

'I'm glad you managed to come, Secilia, I thought perhaps you would not be allowed out again, since you had permission to go with me this morning,' he remarked.

'Oh, yes,' she replied, and carried on saying, 'Mummy and Daddy are quite good. That gives them a little rest from all my continuous questions, they keep saying.'

Walking along hand in hand, seeing the horsemen still working in the fields all around them, Kiel said, 'You can question me as long as you like. I might not be able to answer all, but I'll try. I like being with you.'

'Do you really, Kiel?' she wanted to know, and carried on, 'I like you; you always seemed to be so friendly and cheerful and full of smiles. I like that,' Secilia said. 'Oh, look, there are the deer with babies outside on the edge of the wood again feeding to their heart's content,' she called out.

'Don't they look lovely?' We had better sit down for a minute and be very quiet, so as not to disturb them,' he spoke quietly. 'And there are quite a lot of pheasants and partridges among them, pecking away, further out. They do look nice and peaceful, without a care in the world,' he remarked.

'Yes until there is the shooting time and then they get killed for the table. Isn't that a shame?' she said, and carried on, 'Although I like eating them, I cannot bring myself to see them get killed, poor things.'

'No, I don't like this either, but then we have to eat and we have always been asked and went with the guns and dogs, beating the bushes,' he replied. 'What makes us do things like this, without even thinking?' he spoke and enquired.

'I don't know, Kiel,' she replied, and carried on. 'I have never, ever been asked or I would not have gone, but then I am a girl, I suppose,' she said.

They sat there close to each other, admiring the lively animals and birds, feeding without taking any notice of the surroundings or us, or so it seemed, until there was the slightest different noise and off they ran or flew into the woods for cover.

They both were quite content sitting or half lying there in a shallow ditch beside the little farm track, picking a few small flowers around them, when she reached out too far, suddenly slipped and fell almost on top of him. She suddenly shrieked out, jumped up and tried to run away, when he quickly got hold of her and pulled her back into his arms asking, 'What brought on this sudden fright?'

Secilia apologised, said sorry and curled back in his arms again. She was so soft and gentle that he hardly realised, apart from her charming smell and soft hair falling around his face.

She spluttered out, 'I have just placed my hand onto a small snake, which slipped through my fingers.' This he had not seen or felt either.

'Please, don't apologise,' he said. 'It was lovely to hold you, you can do this as often as you like,' he replied.

But she did not seem to be amused and still looked shocked and frightened, wiping her hand against his shirt. Holding her gentle figure in his hands, and persuading her that this more than likely was just a little baby grass snake, which are harmless.

She slowly got up, looking all over, making sure there were no more, in a still fearful manner. He soon managed to calm her down again and even made her smile, when a few feet away they found the tiny little thing still crawling away, and he picked it up just to show her that they were completely harmless. Still in his arms, she began to smile again, but was not completely assured, and not prepared to touch the slippery little thing.

This brought him to think of a joke he had heard some time ago but did not know what it meant at the time.

An elderly fellow told him, 'I slipped and fell on a young lady today in the market square.' When he apologised, the young lady replied, 'don't apologise old man, if everything on you is as hard as your elbow, you can fall on me any time.'

This he could not possibly tell the little girl beside him, and so he just smiled to himself, thinking of what this above-mentioned young lady had in mind, which stirred a few muscles in his own body.

'What are you smiling about?' Secilia asked quietly, 'Are you making fun of me?'

'No, darling, of course not. You are lying there so nice and quiet and I do love you,' he replied.

'Do you really love me?' she enquired.'

'Yes, my darling, I do,' he confirmed. 'I just thought of this little poem I have in my mind,' and told her.

## Your Shining Hair

The shining waves within your hair,
This you look after with great care.
Your skin is brown and clear, so fine,
Your body feels so close to mine.

Your lips like cherry blossoms glow,
Your eyes are shining like the stars.
The heaving bosom on your chest,
Belongs to no one but the best.

For this lovely most inviting place,
You have dressed with delight.
Which should have told me from your face,
To feel this female's beating heart,
Takes more than just a gentle start.

Your temperament is like my own,
The time too short and soon we part.
You are so great, I should have known,
I'll have to treat you with a loving heart.

No one will ever give to you, my pet,
The love you so deserve.
Promises I'll make are few,
 But darling, let me come to you.

I'll wait for you all through my life,
And this will not decline.
If you don't wish to be my wife,
To have you near me is just fine.

K-WA


'Oh, thank you, Kiel, do you really mean it?' she said, rolled over and gave him one of her soft kisses on the cheek.

'Oh, yes, I mean every word of it,' he replied. At that time he got hold of her petite little figure and kissed her back on her lips, which seemed to be appreciated and this certainly took his breath away, as well as, seemingly, his brain.

He tried to undo one of her silky blouse buttons, wherein some two tiny little soft, yet firm bosoms appeared to be moving in his direction.

She suddenly pulled away and said, 'No, Kiel, not here and certainly not yet. There are still people in the field not too far away and we can be overlooked from the big house and cottages down the estate.' She seemed a little upset and frustrated with him.

'Oh, I am sorry,' he said and carried on, 'I did not mean to upset you, I was looking at this very pretty button,' and withdrew his hand.

She smiled again and said, 'Oh, yes, and no doubt all of which is behind this button and blouse, you cheat? You always have an answer for everything,' she pronounced.

'I must admit I was a little curious, and thought to go by the old saying, 'those who never try, will never succeed,' but I must apologise for even thinking that you would allow me to try. Please don't be cross,' he begged.

'I am not cross with you, Kiel, just a little surprised, and yet perhaps not even that, since I was expecting you to try something sooner or later, as we were getting on so fine. All young boys seem to be inquisitive,' she pointed out.

'Oh, I am not the only nosy or inquisitive person around you?' he asked and continued, 'I just wanted to have the same chance or better than the little calves, who wanted to have a bit of a nibble.'

'You are even more cheeky than I thought,' she pronounced, and followed on by saying, 'We had better get up and be on our way home. What time is it?'

'It must be getting quite late since the sun has set behind the horizon and the moon is up in the sky.' she remarked.

'I'm not sure. I don't have a watch, but perhaps you are right, you always are, you little coward,' he proclaimed, and made him think of another little joke.

★

There was a young boy, who heard noises in his mum and dad's bedroom.

· He opened the door, when his dad asked, 'What do you want?'

The little boy replied, 'I want a watch.'

'Okay,' his dad said, 'go out and shut the door; I will get you one in the morning.'

Going to school, he showed his friend and told him the story.

That evening this boy goes into his parents bedroom and says, 'I want a watch.'

His dad turned round and said, 'Okay stand in the corner and be quiet.'

★

When he told her, she seemed back to normal, laughed out loud and said, 'Is that what you did when you were little? By the way I am not a little coward, just careful. I know what crawly things and boys are like; we have got some of them in Berlin, when we go to the park,' she replied.

'Oh, have you? I had better not let you go back, but keep you here for me only,' he commented, and carried on. 'You are my little darling from now on and only I have the right to play with you.'

'As long as you mean playing and do not go too far, I would like to be your little darling, but I have to do what Daddy and Mummy want or agree to, I am still too young to decide for myself,' she informed him.

She looked gorgeous in the shimmer of the silvery moon, with her dark hair shining and her gorgeous smile, the petite, well-shaped figure and her silky, almost see-through blouse.

'I am old enough and I will look after you, you don't have to ask Mummy and Daddy every time,' he said.

'What with no money and nowhere to live?' she replied and continued, 'You are a fine one; we could not even eat, let alone live or sleep somewhere.'

'Who is talking about sleeping? We shall have too much to do and very little time for sleeping,' he replied.

'Oh, yes, you are right, of course you are right, my dear, how could I be so foolish as not to think of all those things first?' she pronounced, and said, 'I hope you're joking. I tell you why you are in love, and older people always say, when in love you forget who you are and lose your appetite,' she politely announced.

'I never lose my appetite for you, my little precious; in fact it is getting bigger and better all the time,' he replied.

'I can see and feel that, Kiel, the way you keep on pressing my hand, but is this not meant to be the appetite for love?' she enquired.

'Could this be your appetite for food, perhaps? Have you lost your appetite for love already?' she asked.

'I most certainly have not lost either; in fact, I could bite into you right now, I am so starving,' he grabbed her hand tighter and smiled.

'I don't think I can trust you any more, Kiel, you are getting very naughty, but I like you. Let's sit down and have another little talk,' she commented, and virtually pushed him into the shallow ditch beside the drive, not giving another thought about any more snakes or other weird creatures, with her rolling virtually on top of him.

'Now who cannot be trusted?' he called out. 'Not so loud,' Secilia said, and continued, 'We are almost near the gate and people might hear us.'

'Okay Darling,' he quietly whispered, when she nearly hit him and really pushed him down into the short green grass.

The moon overhead was so full and virtually a crystal clear circle, shining almost like the sun, with a big smile on his face so that one could see almost every little flower around. Most of them, however, had by now gone to sleep.

Secilia looked like a little princess, her hair shining or glittering in the moonlight as if she was wearing a crown on her pretty head. He pulled her close, embraced her tightly and gently kissed these sparkling, shining lips of hers with great passion.

She responded and, no doubt or hopefully, had the very same feelings for him, which he had for her, but respect had to be deeply considered, especially since she had made it quite clear, so far and no further. She seemed to allow him to touch her tiny but firm breasts without interference and, seemed to move her tender body somewhat closer to his, which he more than enjoyed, and felt all the small curves against his body.

It all seemed like a dream come true, and he must have smiled a little, when she asked, 'What are you smiling about, Kiel? What is on your mind this time?'

'Oh, nothing special, really, apart from you,' he replied.

'Apart from me?' Secilia asked once again. 'Come on, tell me, I know there is something tickling your brain, if you still got one?' and she laughed out fairly loud.

He placed his hand over her lips and said, 'I hope you won't hit me again when I tell you. Like you told me last time, not so loud.'

'No, I won't, depending on what you really have on your mind,' she replied.

'I was just wondering if you are as pretty and dark halfway down as you are on your head,' he curiously asked, and she rolled him off her with some surprise.

'You are very naughty,' she said, and gave him a little touch on the head, saying, 'I think your head needs examining. You should not even think of such things. Where do you get your ideas from?'

'Why don't you tell me, then I won't have to wonder or get ideas any more. I bet you look in your mirror every night admiring your own lovely body,' he commented.

'No, I don't,' she replied. 'Is that what you do every night?' she enquired to know and was quite inquisitive about it.

'No, I don't, or can't, my mirror is too high up,' he replied and he began to laugh out again.

'What are you laughing about now?' she enquired.

I just thought of a small joke some elderly fellow told me once, and he repeated it to her.

★

'When I was a young man, it looked up and watched me shave. Now that I am old, it just looks down and watches me clean my shoes.'

★

'What is 'it?' she enquired, and suddenly caught on, when she began to jump up and said, 'I think we better go home, or you will get some more ideas into your head.'

'I am sorry, Secilia. Don't be cross with me; I can't help it if people tell me those sorts of jokes,' he almost called out, grabbed her hand and apologised.

'There is nothing to apologise for,' she said. 'I am getting more and more surprised about you. I hope you will never get old,' she said and laughed again. 'It is, however, getting late and I don't want to be told off, or we shall never be allowed to meet and go for a walk again and you wouldn't like that, would you, Kiel?' Secilia asked.

'No, I certainly would not like this to happen. Would you come out with me again, Secilia? I thought perhaps I had upset you a little?' he said and squeezed her tiny hand.

She leaned over and gave him a peck on the cheek and said, 'No, my dear, you could not offend or upset me, when I am learning something new every day. You carry on the way you are and we shall be great friends for life,' she replied.

That put his heartbeat back into rhythm and continued the circulation, which he almost thought he had lost, or had it gone too fast to be recognised?

By that time they had got as far as the large farm gate, which was still open, when he asked, 'May I take you to your garden gate to say goodbye, or would you rather walk across the yard yourself?'

'No,' she replied and continued in a somewhat stern voice. 'As a gentleman, you have taken me out, so you must be prepared to take me back home, unless of course you wish to leave me and run away. Remember, we might not meet up tomorrow.' This made him almost shake in his boots.

'Oh, no, I would love to take you all the way, like I did this morning and not let you walk on your own, but I did not want to embarrass you, in case your mum and dad are waiting for you.' he replied.

'Well, if they are waiting for me, you will have to explain all we have been up to. We have not done anything wrong, have we?' she asked and smiled again.

Her little smiles always made his blood flow faster, and looking at her he said, 'No of course we haven't. At least I haven't,' he remarked and pulled her closer to him.

'Be careful now,' Secilia remarked, 'someone might be watching through the curtains and we do not wish to bring suspicion upon ourselves, do we?' Then she squeezed his hand and smiled again, staring in to his eyes.

By that time they had arrived at the small garden gate. Sure enough, as she had assumed, there was her mum, opening the gate for them.

'Hello, I saw you both coming across the yard, are you coming in for a cup of coffee, Kiel? We would love you to come,' she enquired in her gentle voice.

It came as such a surprise, he did not really know what to do or say, then Secilia smiled at him and replied, 'Yes, I am sure he would love to come in, wouldn't you, Kiel?'

That was as good an invite as he expected and said, 'Thank you, my lady, I would love to accept your invitation.'

He followed them both into the lit up garden house, where the colonel was already seated, with newspaper and a beer next to him on a small table.

Luckily, they had managed to clean themselves up a little before walking home, but Kiel noticed a piece of grass in Secilia's hair and pulled it away quickly, which she felt and said, 'Oh did I bring a piece of grass back from when we were sitting down admiring the animals near the wood?' she remarked and no one seemed to take any notice. 'I'll just quickly go and wash my hands. Would you like to wash yours, Kiel?' Secilia enquired with her usual smile.

'Oh, yes, please, if I may. We have, after all, been sitting down on the grass and ground,' he remarked and followed her into the house.

He thought perhaps she wanted to ask or say something to him, but no, she showed him a little washbasin, just inside the door and ran off.

He had never been in this big house before and this was only the entrance hall, his eyes nearly popping out of their sockets, when another young lady, obviously a servant arrived with a clean towel, and said, 'Please help yourself, Secilia won't be long.'

'Thank you,' he called after her, but she disappeared almost as quickly as she had shown herself.

As luck would have it, there was a toilet where he was able to allow himself a quick wee before washing his hands.

He was in a complete shemozzle and did not really know what to do first, but managed to sort himself out before Secilia called out, 'Are you stuck in there, Kiel?'

'No, thank you, I am on my way,' and opened the door with the towel still in his hands.

'You had better leave this behind,' she remarked, took it out of his hands and threw it back in the room.

'Come on, the coffee is getting cold,' she said and took him by the hand.

As mentioned before, the colonel was sitting inside the summer house smoking a cigar, when Kiel went towards him, bowing his head and stretching out his hand saying 'Good evening, sir.'

He took my hand and said, 'Good evening, Kiel, have you had a great time? Where did you go and what did you see?' He carried on. 'Secilia tells me you have only just come to the estate and have not been round to see it all until now.'

'That is correct, sir, this is the very first time I have been outside the rear gate. I only arrived here a few days ago,' Kiel replied.

They got into a real conversation and he had forgotten all about the coffee, while Secilia and the Lady herself, both listened with intense interest.

Being a big talker himself, Kiel just carried on telling where he came from and how he managed to get there, hoping to go to college et cetera, which took a little of the nervousness away, albeit Kiel still did not feel very comfortable.

No doubt Secilia noticed and asked him, 'Do you want to have a quick walk round the garden, before it gets too dark?'

'Oh, yes, please,' he almost called out, drank his coffee quickly and tried to disappear out in the fresh air with Secilia, when the Lady spoke and asked politely, 'May I come with you both to get a little exercise and fresh air? Would you mind?'

'Oh, no, of course not, we would love you to come, my lady,' he pronounced, offering his hand to guide her down the one step.

'You are very kind, Kiel, thank you,' she said, and took the lead.

They all looked at and admired all the roses and other different flowers on the way, when the Lady suddenly asked, 'Do you have a garden at home, Kiel?'

'Yes, my lady,' he replied, 'but not as nice or large as this, we had mostly vegetables and berries in ours,' he replied.

'Oh, how nice,' she remarked, 'we do not have a garden in Berlin, and I do miss it so much when we go back.'

52

'This is a lovely large garden here, all the hedges trimmed nicely with trees and flowers everywhere and neatly laid out with stone slab footpaths all round. There is quite a lot of work for your gardener, and no doubt yourself, my lady,' he remarked.

'Yes, we do help when we are here, and we love gardening, don't we, Secilia?' she replied.

Secilia, butting in between, 'Yes Mummy, or at least you do and know more about it than I do.'

They continued walking, with Secilia hardly speaking at all, and Kiel seemed quite at ease with Her Ladyship, who was short and dainty, with dark wavy hair and slightly darker skin, seemingly of Mediterranean stock.

Not knowing quite which smelled nicer, the ladies or the flowers all around them, they continued walking, when Kiel suddenly thought and asked, 'When are you going back to Berlin, my lady?'

'This we are never sure of, Kiel,' she replied and continued, 'hopefully not for a week or two, but the colonel often gets called back in a hurry and we just have to leave everything and go along.'

'I would love you to stay for a little while. I like talking to you and Secilia.'

Secilia butted in and said, 'Kiel's mother passed away a few years ago and he has no sisters, and only one brother who lives not far from here, and his dad is working away from home most of the time.'

'Oh, I am sorry to hear about your mother.' Tears came back into his eyes, which she obviously noticed and changed the subject quickly by saying, 'Oh, look at these gorgeous lilies. But I would love to hear all about your mum one day,' she enquired.

It was beginning to get dark, so he quickly butted in and said, 'I had better get back to auntie and uncle, they will be wondering what has happened to me,' since he did not really want to talk anymore, although he thought a lot about his mum.

'Yes, Kiel, I quite understand. You had better take him back to the gate, Secilia. I hope to see you again,' the Lady called after him.

'Yes, my lady,' he returned the call and turning, he took a few steps back shook her hand and saying goodbye, and thanking them for the coffee and their kindness.'

'Thank you for staying, Kiel,' she replied.

When they both returned, walking back to the little gate he said, 'I would like to kiss you goodbye, Secilia, but I daren't.'

'Oh, but you must,' she gave him a little peck on the cheek, which he returned, said goodbye, waved his hand and disappeared round the corner without looking back.

What a lucky fellow I am, he thought to himself, and rushed through the door calling out, hello to his uncle and auntie, on his way in.

'Come and sit yourself down, my boy, you are all puffed out. Where have you been all this time?' aunty asked. Naturally he had to tell them all about their walk and his new adventure, which they could hardly believe. 'I hope you've behaved yourself,' she pronounced.

'Oh, yes, auntie. I have been asked to go again, and I will go again all being well,' he replied.

'That is nice to hear. I think you have been the only one who has ever been asked into the big house and their lovely garden, apart from people working there,' she remarked. 'I have seen it over the wall, and I have been inside helping,' she remarked, and continued, 'you have been very fortunate in the short time you've been here, Kiel,' to which he agreed with a smile.

### The Lovely Sun

This lovely sun has disappeared
Behind the darkened clouds and sky.
This happens often in the year,
With people asking why?

Why are we so frustrated when it rains;
Or the lovely sun burns our skins?
Is it because at these particular times,
We can't relax but remember our sins?

K-WA


'Yes, I know,' he replied and continued, 'but I shall not see Secilia tomorrow, they have guests coming for lunch and tea.'

'Oh, that's a shame,' his auntie said and carried on. 'Never mind, you may have some more time with her in the next week or two, while they are here.'

'I hope so, and will certainly look forward to that,' he replied sleepily, and said goodnight to both of them.

He went to bed, but could not go to sleep and kept tossing and turning in bed until late into the night, when in the end tiredness must have overtaken his thoughts and mind.

# CHAPTER 6

Next morning he jumped out of bed when the alarm went off, since he had not heard his uncle's knock on the door or call earlier, unless he'd forgotten. His eyes still closed, he ran around washing and dressing all at the same time and rushed downstairs to get to work just in time as the headman arrived.

'Good morning, Kiel,' came his call with a big smile.

'Good morning, sir,' Kiel replied, not quite knowing where he was, with the eyes still half closed. He had forgotten to comb his hair, and no doubt looked a bit scruffy.

'Did you get up in a rush again? Your hair is all over the place. Or have you lost your comb, or perhaps you have given it to Secilia?' the headman called out.

'No, sir, yes sir, sorry, sir, I did wake rather late and completely forgot to look into the mirror, sir,' he answered in a somewhat uncertain way, and feeling completely flustered.

'What's the matter with you this morning, Kiel? Have you had a bad night, or perhaps a bad evening out with the young lady? I hope you behaved yourself and did not upset her,' the headman continued.

'Oh, no, sir, we had a lovely time, but I could not get to sleep very early and got up in a bit of a rush,' he replied, being completely uncertain about every thing now.

'That is quite understandable, my boy, we all get our bad nights, especially after going out with a young lady.'

Kiel must have blushed. He continued, 'There is no need to blush, my boy, this happens to all of us, especially when young.'

Kiel tried to get away and rushed for his stool and bucket to start milking, when he called after him, 'I want to know all about it later, don't forget.'

Kiel did not really feel like talking about it at all, or to anyone, and yet he had that deep desire to let them all know how lucky he had been to get invited into the big house and garden, by Her Ladyship and have coffee with all of them, which made him think about last evening and getting up late this morning.

## Life and Love

Life and love is not a bed of roses,
 A bunch of flowers or chocolates each day.
It's not all smiles and cuddles,
For all above, one has to pay.

With sometimes sweaty and hard labour,
Which bring money in the purse.
Another day, there's nothing,
Which is even worse.

But that's no way to think of life,
The sun will always shine.
That is the time to hold on tight and smile,
When you can say, all this is mine.

When you are smiling and you smile a while,
And that smile of yours is true.
The sun, the moon, your dear friends,
And the whole world smiles with you.

That's when you buy some roses and you say,
I will bring you from now on, chocolates each and every day.
That's when life and love will flourish,
For all of us continuing to nourish.

K-WA

Settling down under a cow with the bucket in between the knees and his head resting against the lovely warmth of the cow's skin, he fell asleep and soon was woken by the cow moving and the milk and bucket with him once again on the floor. With everyone looking as to what had happened and the noise, the cow had moved and stepped on his foot and hurt it, all of which woke him so quickly, that he never, ever went to sleep under a cow again.

This reminded him of a little joke he had heard some years ago, when someone said.

'A man got killed by drinking milk.' When one asked, 'Oh, how could that happen?'

'The cow laid itself down on top of him,' was the reply.

Even Kiel had to laugh again, looked at the others and said, 'Sorry, I slipped.' No one would believe him and they kept on all day about him falling asleep under a cow, which needled him at first but after a while he had to laugh about it himself and told the joke to the rest.

Every now and again he kept looking towards the little calf enclosure, hoping Secilia might slip in for just a moment, but no such luck.

Nothing happened even when he went to feed the tiny things; there was no sign of the young lady anywhere. While feeding and cleaning out these little mites, he kept looking across to the big house and garden, but there was no sign of anyone or anything, although it was not easy to see over the high brick wall.

It seemed a dull and dreary morning although there was plenty to do. All he wanted was to see Secilia, if only just for one moment, to cheer him up a little and open his eyes completely, but this was not to happen.

After finishing the work and taking the cattle out to pastures green, they all went for a good breakfast and by golly they were ready for it.

Uncle and auntie kept talking about Secilia, trying to keep on fishing and teasing him in the process, but for some reason or other he managed to keep quiet and just smiled to keep them thinking.

Uncle in the end piped out, 'No doubt you will see her sometime today when you will get back to normal.

'You have been dreaming about her all morning boy,' auntie called out.

'No, I haven't,' he spouted out in a somewhat testy manner, and ran upstairs to lie down.

Within a few minutes he went off to sleep without another glance or word and did not wake up until auntie knocked on the door and called out, 'Lunch is ready, are you coming down?'

'Yes, auntie, I won't be a minute,' he replied, jumped out of bed, had a quick wash and combed his hair this time round, so as not to be reminded of it again and stumbled down the stairs.

'Sorry uncle, sorry auntie,' he called out, and continued by saying 'I must have been tired and fell into a deep sleep almost straightaway.'

'That's all right, my boy, we hope it has done you a lot of good, we all need a good sleep now and again,' uncle pronounced.

Auntie dished up the lunch, which smelled terrific. 'We have Sauerbraten und Klöse (dumplings) today,' his auntie said, and carried on, 'I hope you like it?'

'Like it?' he replied, and continued, 'that is my favourite dinner. I'll just love it, almost as much as Secilia.'

'Well, now, take it steady boy, you cannot eat her, even though you might think that way sometimes, but you just be satisfied with your lunch,' his auntie spluttered out.

That was a great and enjoyable meal, with the gravy running down the side of his lips, showing that he really enjoyed it.

This must have been noticed, for his auntie said, 'Take it steady, my boy, there is plenty of it, and if you want any more, just ask.'

'Yes, thank you, auntie,' he replied and asked for another helping.

Uncle always had a glass of beer with his meal while auntie and he were satisfied with a glass of water, but this time he asked uncle. 'May I try a drop of your beer, uncle? You seem to like it.'

'Yes, of course you can, my boy, but don't drink too much the first time or you will fall off to sleep again,' his uncle remarked and poured him a drop into a new glass.

'No, I won't, I just want to try; perhaps I won't even like it,' he replied, and took a mouthful.

'Oh, no, that's bitter and takes all the lovely taste away. Thank you, I would rather stick with water,' he pronounced.

While his auntie said, 'I don't blame you boy, that stuff is for old men.'

After the meal he was so full and could hardly get up from the table. He offered to wash up, but auntie said, 'No, my boy, you go out for a little walk. I notice you keep on looking out of the window, and washing up is your uncle's job on a Sunday.'

# CHAPTER 7

Kiel was really glad and stumbled across the yard in the lovely sunshine, when he heard a lot of talking and laughing coming from the big house with its bottom windows open, of which he could only see the top of their heads over the wall. He stood and listened for a moment, but could not make out what they were all saying, but he could smell the cigar smoke and assumed that they must have finished dinner.

All of a sudden he heard a slight whisper, and looking round, saw Secilia standing or leaning out of an upstairs window and waving.

He waved back, without daring to speak; he returned her gorgeous smile, then she disappeared behind the curtains, still waving.

That was the best part of his day and made it all worthwhile, when he thought of a song:

'I could have danced all night, I could have danced for you' and nearly did, but he retreated slowly out through the back gate. Looking back he saw her once again giving a quick wave and smile, which he returned. She seemed to look so very happy.

Dreaming once again, he proceeded along the rear of the outbuildings alongside the field, where they both had been the day before. All of a sudden Secilia appeared round the corner and he ran back quickly to meet her for a little kiss and cuddle, with an exchange of a few words.

They quickly embraced with a little kiss, when she said, 'I must go back; I just came to say hello, since I saw you coming out this way. We have got a houseful of guests.'

'You look gorgeous, like always.' he said and gave her another peck on her cheek.

'Oh thank you, Kiel, you are kind', she replied, turned away and ran back to the house, with a quick wave.

He nearly ran after her but had to consider the other guests and her parents, who most likely did not even know that she had come out to see him, and so he continued his walk, fully awake this time. He never thought that he would see Secilia today, although he naturally hoped he would and his dream and thought became a reality.

She looked so tremendously radiant, and ravishingly beautiful, just like a little princess, which filled his head with a great deal of thoughts again, and wondering if he would ever be good or desirable enough for such an outstanding young beauty?

In front of him were acres and acres of fruit orchards, with all kinds of fruit growing, but not ripe enough to eat, although he was still full from the wonderful lunch. That is where his auntie and the other ladies helped out with fruit picking et cetera.

This fruit was mainly picked for resale. Many baskets, or even tons, of fallen or overripe fruit would find their way to the distillery for Schnapps making, which is, he found out later, a rather nice drink or a chaser with beer, similar to vodka, gin or whiskey.

At that time, he had no taste for any of these strong alcoholic drinks and was completely put off by that first time, when it was given to him for fresh cool water. Later in life, however, he like everyone else began to learn and was often persuaded to take undesirables and sometimes one finds these to one's satisfaction or even a pleasure, especially when getting a little older.

After walking around for about an hour, he thought it best to return ready for the afternoon shift and naturally hoped to spot the young lady Secilia again on the way.

He returned slowly and coming through the rear gate, he noticed two or three, black limousines standing along side the road or garden wall, but no little girls or his precious young lady Secilia.

He heard a few voices with laughter, seemingly coming from the garden, passing by the wall, even though he kept looking and listening there was none of the expected sound from the house or from behind the garden wall.

He returned home, 'Hello auntie, hello uncle,' he called out.

Auntie replied, ' You are just in time for coffee, would you like a cup?'

'Yes, please,' he returned the call. 'I'll be back down soon,' and ran upstairs for a quick wash and back down again.

Auntie and uncle were sitting at the table enjoying their cup of coffee and piece of cake, even though still full from lunch, when he saw that cake he suddenly seemed to be hungry once more.

Uncle spoke first and said, 'Sit yourself down, boy, and tell us all about you meeting up with Secilia again? We saw her running across the yard and out the rear gate following you, did you meet up together?'

'Yes, uncle, we did, but only for just a few minutes. She had to get back to her parents and guests, she just came to say hello,' he replied and said, 'You don't miss much do you?'

'No, we don't,' uncle butted in, 'that was nice of her.'

' She must be quite fond of you, to leave her family just to say hello,' auntie remarked and continued. 'Would you like a cup of coffee and a piece of cake, Kiel?'

'Yes, please,' he replied, with his eyes on the cake.

'Would you like a large or a small piece? How hungry are you?'

'Oh, a large piece, please. I am starving after my long walk,' he answered. He wasn't really but it looked so appetising.

'You must have a large tummy, boy,' uncle announced. 'You have had quite a large lunch and now you want a large piece of cake. All that will make you grow, lad,' he continued.

'Oh, leave the boy alone, I can remember when you had a large tummy and would eat almost anything that came on the table,' auntie remarked, and at the same time asked, 'Do you like cake, Kiel?'

'Oh, yes, I love it. I still remember Mum used to bake nearly every day when I was still young and she was alive, but dad did not have a lot of time, and I was no good at it, although I often tried, but it mostly fell down and turned out heavy.'

'I would think you were always too quick and nosy to open the oven door for a sniff before it was really cooked,' she remarked, and carried on. 'One must give cake time to cook through before opening the oven door.'

That was something else he had learned, although he remembered his dad kept telling him this many times over the years, but how does one know if the cake has cooked through without opening the oven door? He had asked dad and now again his auntie but none of them knew, and just said, 'That is a matter of experience and guesswork. You will find out if you do a lot more cooking.'

It is all very well for the elders to keep telling the young these things, but from where does one get all that experience? He presumed everything was trial and error, and the more errors one makes, the more one has to keep on trying, to learn perfection in the end.

It was time to get away from the table and get changed for work. 'Thank you, auntie, thank you, uncle. Would you please excuse me, I have got to get ready for work.'

'Yes, of course, boy,' they both spoke almost simultaneously. He went upstairs to change into his working clothes and came down again, calling out 'bye-bye,' and virtually flew through the door.

Running across the yard, he heard a whispered call of 'Kiel' and by instinct looked round towards the big house and saw

Secilia up in the window, waving again and quickly disappearing out of sight with her pretty smile.

He waved back, but doubt that she even saw him doing it. She must have been waiting and had to get back quickly. But he was delighted to have seen her once again and hoped that she would turn up later at the tiny calves for feeding time.

Getting on with his work and helping others, time soon passed by, especially at weekends when everyone would work just that little harder to get finished quicker for more time off in the evening.

After all the other jobs had been done, he, as usual, went to feed the little calves and kept looking and hoping, but there was no sign of Secilia.

Finishing off all the cleaning after the cattle had been allowed to go out to pastures green, they were at last ready to wash their hands and faces to return for supper, which after all this hard work was once again quite welcome.

It was a gorgeous day with the sun still shining, so after a proper clean up and supper, he decided to go out for another stroll. He nearly decided to take a bike ride and have a look over the garden wall from the entrance road, but thought better of it.

Although he would have loved to see Secilia again, he did not really fancy being seen or even invited to join a lot of highly educated people. Albeit he was at ease with most folk, he always felt just that little hemmed in or overcrowded at parties, especially of higher society.

He felt a great deal happier with animals, which did not ask a lot of questions, and yet he liked talking. Perhaps he did not like listening and yet he was nosy to a point, when he wanted to know almost everything. In fact, he was happiest on his own or with just one person around him which he liked and appreciated, especially female company. That could be why he was still very much attached to his dear mum and could never get her kindness and attention out of his mind.

He wandered along the side of the fields singing and whistling, which were his favourite pastimes, especially whistling to or with the birds, or a song; whatever came into his head and seemed convenient at the time.

The sun was still quite hot and he took his shirt off still walking along when he got near the wood and spotted some deer grazing on the outside. He sat down on almost the very spot they had been sitting together admiring all the birds and animals in the distance. Being very quiet and just laying there with his eyes well open and listening, he heard some horses galloping in the distance, and looking up, who would it be but Secilia with another young lady friend.

He was not quite sure what to do or how to behave, lying there without a shirt, but they had already spotted him and came his way.

He quickly put his shirt on over his trousers, got up, and waved, as they came nearer.

'Hello Kiel,' came the call from Secilia and almost at the same time from the other young lady, who was introduced to him as her cousin, Juliet, or so he thought.

'You did not have to rush and put your shirt on,' Secilia called out and continued. 'We have been watching you for quite some time, soon after you came out of the gate. We have been for an after supper ride, to the far end of the estate and down near the river. It is a lovely evening, is it not?' Secilia asked.

'Yes,' he replied and walked over, stroking both horses. These seemed a little moist, and he said, 'You have not chased these poor horses too much, I hope? They are quite moist.'

· 'No, Kiel', came the answer from both, 'but we have been out quite a while and it is nice and warm.'

Juliet was a nice little blonde. He said little, but looking at her on the horse she seemed taller than him, but appeared to be quite young and very attractive.

Both had that sincere soft smile, and one could see some resemblance in their manner if not in looks, but not in the colours of their hair or skin. Juliet seemed to have much paler skin than Secilia, who seemed slightly darker and with her black hair this seemed to fit perfectly, similar to Juliet's, who was blonde and seemed paler.

'We had better go now and give the horses a little rest and some cool water,' said Secilia, and Juliet nodded her head in agreement.

'Yes, of course, that is a good idea.' he agreed and carried on by saying 'I shall come and give them both a good brush down in a little while.'

'Oh, that is nice of you to offer, Kiel,' Secilia replied, 'but we shall be doing this ourselves as soon as we have taken off the saddle and leathers.' They both answered almost simultaneously again and smiled, 'Thank you, Kiel.' They called out and trotted off gently, waving goodbye when turning round again.

He waved back and called out, 'Please be careful, hope to see you soon.' Then they both touched their whips to their hats in salute and rode off smiling.

He was once again in a land of dreams and could not believe what he had just seen. That young lady cousin Juliet or, for that matter, both were absolutely gorgeous and he would have loved to have had more time to talk and get to know them both a little better. He was over the moon once again and could not believe that anything like this could have happened to him or was all of this just a dream?

Slowly he walked back and fully intended to go and look after the two horses, when the two young ladies came out of the stables and, just as previously hoped and wished, they met up again.

Secilia spoke first and said, 'We did tell you we would look after the horses; dry and clean them down and give them water and food, and we did. Come and have a look?'

They took him inside to show that they had both made a good job of the two horses, when he thanked them and said, 'I didn't think you would have time,' and continued, 'you are both wonderful and kind. I am glad you did such a good job,' he said, and continued, 'although I knew in my own heart that you would not neglect these horses, the way you Secilia look after all the other animals with great care, but we all make mistakes at times.'

'Is Secilia good at looking after all the other animals?' Juliet asked, and carried on to say, 'and what about you? Does she look after you, as well, Kiel?'

He did not quite know what to say and must have got a little red in the face, when she turned to him again and said, 'You don't have to blush, Kiel, Secilia told me all about you and I think she likes you just a little, if not a lot.'

'Thank you,' he replied and carried on, 'you are both very kind, or are you taking the mickey?'

'No, no,' Juliet replied, 'you seem to be a nice and kind young man, I would like to get to know you a little better.'

They both departed with a smile. He realised that she must be a little older than Secilia and appeared slightly taller.

They both waved, and Secilia called back, 'Hope to see you tomorrow, Kiel, bye-bye.'

He returned the wave with a no doubt broad smile on his face and called out, 'I hope so and I look forward to it.'

He followed with his eyes as they both disappeared through the little garden gate and both waved again, to his amazement.

He was overjoyed and seemingly sitting high, like riding on a horse himself. What have I done to deserve all this? He thought and dreamily walked to the little cottage with auntie and uncle, who saw them and were waiting for him.

'Have you had a nice time, my boy?' his Auntie asked, without giving his uncle a chance, and said, 'We saw all of you near the stable door talking to each other and laughing.'

'What are the horses like? Are they wet, dirty or sweaty?' Uncle asked like a horseman would.

'No, they are fine,' he replied, and continued, 'they have been rubbed and cleaned down and given fresh water and food.'

'That sounds good,' uncle remarked, and carried on, 'I had better go across the yard and find out for myself, but I'll wait a little while. Especially since you confirmed their condition and I am sure you would not tell me this if it was not true. I know you better than that.'

'No, uncle, they really are fine. I was going to wipe them down and clean them and told Secilia this when we met up in the field, but they promised to look after them and showed me that they did,' he replied.

'That is good,' uncle remarked, and said 'Secilia is like her dad, always quite good with horses or animals, but when two young girls get together with a young man, one never knows, and I always go and check every evening.'

'You can take my word for it, uncle, I would have done it before coming in but they certainly have been looked after very well,' he repeated.

'I believe you, my boy,' he replied, and followed on. 'It is in my nature to make sure and check that all is fine, every evening before I go to bed, or I could not relax and go to sleep before satisfying myself.'

All this went on while they had their last cup of coffee, after which he declared, 'I had better go to bed myself. I have had a long and lovely day. Goodnight, uncle, goodnight, auntie,' and off he went.

'Goodnight, Kiel,' they both called out, almost together, as he was already climbing the stairs to his bedroom.

The moon was once again shining through the undrawn curtained windows, and looking out it seemed as silvery as the previous night and was almost full moon, with his usual sinister smile looking down to earth. Kiel drew the curtains, undressed and jumped into bed, when once again he began to think of Secilia and her cousin Juliet, both of whom he thought were absolutely gorgeous and pleasant to talk to, hoping that he would meet both of them again.

He must have gone off to sleep very soon, since he did not hear his uncle and auntie coming up the stairs to bed, unless they came late.

# CHAPTER 8

Next morning he heard uncle knock on the door and he called out, 'Yes thank you,' and turned round again, but not to sleep this time, but thinking about all the lovely times he had since coming here.

Going to work that morning he looked at the big house on the way, but all was quiet and peaceful there. Since it was still early, they probably were all still asleep.

He carried on with his work and was recommended by the headman for being awake for once, 'Yes, sir,' he returned the remark, and carried on, 'I had a lovely night and woke up bright and early this morning.'

'Oh, well done, my boy, you are getting used to the early mornings? I hope to see you like this every day,' he replied.

'I hope so, sir,' he called back quickly, and carried on with his job of cleaning and milking.

'It has come to my notice that you had two lovely young girls to look after yesterday. It seems that you have all the luck,' he carried on and smiled, sitting under the next cow.

'Yes, sir' Kiel replied and carried on, 'it was Secilia and her cousin Juliet. They were both out riding and met me in the field, where I had gone for a walk.'

'You are a very lucky young man,' he answered, and continued, 'you had better be careful and don't overstep the mark.'

Kiel was not quite sure what he meant by that remark, but he took it as not getting too close to Secilia, since her dad was, after all, the paymaster to all of them.

'No, sir,' I'll try to do my best not to upset either and to be careful,' he answered back, still continuing with his work, as best he could.

'Are you going to town today to find out about the college?' the headman enquired, which Kiel had forgotten all about and said so.

'You are a good one,' he said and enlarged, 'these girls are getting into your head. Don't let them overtake your studying, will you?'

'No, sir,' Kiel replied, and continued, 'I will try not to let this interfere with my schooling and maybe will go and find out if it will be possible for me to attend college, which will start again next week, I believe.'

After milking was finished he once again began to get the food and milk ready to feed his little darling calves, which were already waiting and making a noise. There were quite a number of them now and to get the food ready for each and every one in time was beginning to be quite a job when he hoped that Secilia would soon be coming to give him a helping hand.

He kept looking and listening, but nothing seemed to be happening; then the headman came along helping him and said, 'There is no need to look out for Secilia this morning or any other time now. They went back to Berlin early this morning.'

These remarks dropped like a bombshell, since nothing like this had been expected. Although he knew it could happen any day, it was far from his mind at that time.

'Are you sure?' he said, being completely surprised and full of emotions.

'Yes, I am quite sure,' he replied, 'the estate manager came to inform me and others earlier.'

She, or better said Secilia seemingly went off while they were still milking, but did not come or perhaps was not allowed to come and say good-bye.

Tears must have almost run down his face, when the headman said, 'Don't worry too much about Secilia, these things will happen many times in your life, but with some luck they will be back in late summer.'

This cheered him up just a little and was something to look forward to. It was such a short meeting and having had the chance to talk to both Secilia and Juliet the evening before was still sticking in his mind, and their smiles he would never forget.

This was a Monday morning and the day, seemed to drag on forever, with his thoughts wandering through the last few days, when so many things were left unspoken.

He had hoped that she might have left an address for him to send her a birthday card this coming month and when time was available he went to the big house and spoke to the lady in charge.

There was nothing to be handed over or for him to collect, and the address she said, 'This could not be given for security reasons.'

That was probably why Secilia had not given him her address earlier, although he had never asked for it, when no doubt he would have been informed, but how can he possibly send a birthday card without an address he thought to himself?.

There were so many things floating through his head, some of which could not be explained or found answers to, but the day went by, with a great many people seemingly feeling sorry for him, which did not help at all.

Evening came, when he just had to go for a walk and retrace all the steps they had taken together, recalling the many memories still in his head torturing him at this time.

## That lovely Smile

That smile of yours, so beautiful, sincere;
But you are there and I am stuck right here.
It looks that I will have to wait a while,
To greet and see again that lovely smile.

Those earrings in you ears, which I would like again to hold,
They weren't just brass, but shining solid gold.
These rosy lips, and those delightful curves,
To kiss these, is a great deal more than one deserves.

Those sparkling eyes, which brightly shone those days,
Were just like stars, reflecting in the water's waves.
So soft your curls, your stylish nose,
Both scented like some autumn rose.

These shining waves within your dark brown hair,
I'd dearly like them near me once again to share.
These joyful cheeks with little dimples show,
That you're still young, but older you will grow.

Your gentle curves, so beautifully firm and strong,
I've found out and know I am very seldom wrong.
This slender long and straight up neck,
I'd love to touch again and further check.

You'll have to come again, to investigate some more,
But being careful, or I'll be shown the door.
Which would not, the nicest thing to be,
Or I'd have lost my wish, to have you close to me.

So dream I must, and wait, to carry on and find,
What's underneath this blouse or close behind?
These curves which show there's something covered there,
Which I would dearly love to bare.

Now once again I'll have to slow down and restrain,
Which is much more than just a little pain.
There is covered by that long dark skirt,
I cannot help myself by being just a flirt.

Your legs don't show, but surely they are just as nice,
As all the rest of you, like in good food, the spice.
When you have time and nothing else to do,
Please come into my arms, before I've had a few.

I'll hold you tight and never let you go again,
If lying in dry grass or indoors, shelt'ring from the rain.
So darling bear with me for just a little while,
While in the meantime, please retain your lovely smile.

I'll be around for you, right through these coming years,
When we can share our smiles or sometimes wipe the tears.
We'll fly around the clear blue sky like any dove,
And show the world that we are deep in love.

Being alone he took a lonely walk round this large estate,
Until it got quite dark and late.
Thinking back the moon was shining when they had a date,
Returning he looked at the garden gate.

But there was not the slightest move,
Even though his eyes looked through the tiniest groove.
He looked up to the windows in the place,
But even there was not a smiling face.

He was forlorn;
His mind was not with him at all,
But walked as if he was quite tall.
Even though he was quite short and small.

K-W A

# CHAPTER 9

Although he had previously been to town and college to see if he would be accepted, and was interviewed by the head, who seemed to know the colonel and family quite well, having gone to school with the colonel several years ago.

He asked many questions, especially in regard to Secilia, whom he had not seen since she was very young, having gone to her christening and seeing her and the family again later.

They both had quite a chat and he had been informed the his school reports were not really up to standard but since he was a friend of the colonel and family, to Kiel's greatest surprise, he was given the chance of a trial period for one year, as long as he could manage to pay his fees on a weekly basis.

He promised faithfully to do that, was given a chance to start the following Thursday, to find his place among the rest of the class and get to know the teachers.

This, at that time, put him in an extremely good mood for a little while and he was overjoyed going home and telling everyone, and all were pleased for him. However, by the time evening came he had forgotten this excitement and was full of dreams about Secilia, as before mentioned.

It was a very difficult time to overcome, at least until Thursday, when he went back to school or college again for the first time, since leaving school two years previously.

There he met a number of different boys and girls and soon began to talk about different things, which eased his mind, although he never forgot the great times he had with Secilia.

From then on he had a hectic period and very little time for himself, rushing to work and cycling to college and back to work, trying to learn at both places, with his poor head going round in circles. Even the evenings did not seem long enough anymore for walks, or very seldom and then only for an hour or so.

It was studying and learning all the time; where there was a small space left in the head this had to be filled with all sorts. God only knows where it all went, but most of it appeared to have been stored, as in a computer. It is amazing how much one can remember in just a short period of time, but then there is a lifetime in front of all and every day more has to be gathered, to complete a picture.

The time seemed to go so very slow, even though he always appeared to be in a hurry. His head was still full of memories of the few days he had with Secilia, which were probably the most enjoyable he'd had for a very long time.

Even though he had very enjoyable days with his previous school friend Gertrautel back home, this recent one seemed to have been a quite different relationship.

While at a young age, one loves playing games and going for little walks, even hand in hand, having great laughs and enjoying oneself in quite a different way with the smallest of pleasures. Once one gets just that little older, a slightly more senior relationship appears to develop quite unexpectedly.

As with conversations, while in the young innocent years one talks and giggles about anything, even a small insect wobbling along the ground, or autumn leaves falling off the trees and bushes. Being just that little older one appreciates the animals, crawling creatures or autumn leaves and colours as well as many other things in a more grown up way.

Time goes on and days go past, without realising how fast, and when Secilia's birthday came round in June, he did not know quite what to do. Since Secilia had not given him their address in Berlin, sending a card seemed impossible.

He took courage and went to the big house and rang the bell, when the lady in charge of the house came to the door. He was a little shy and tongue-tied but enquired if a birthday message could be forwarded by phone? The elderly lady seemed somewhat surprised that he asked such a question, but agreed to do so as long as he was prepared to pay for the phone call, which he did and the message was transferred.

A few days later he received a card from Secilia, forwarding her thanks, with a short note informing him that they would be back again in August, all being well.

He jumped for joy and had to show the card to nearly everyone on the estate, including his friends at the college. This cheered him up again, with everyone saying how lucky he was to receive a card from Berlin and the colonel's daughter. His auntie and uncle remarked the very same and could see that he was a different young man again from that day on.

Auntie asked, 'How did you manage to send birthday greetings to Secilia when you don't have her address?'

'Oh, that is quite simple, Auntie,' he replied, and told her about going to the big house and asking the lady in charge if she would be kind enough to phone a message through on his behalf.

'Well, I never,' auntie came out with, and continued, 'he has got the cheek of the devil, hasn't he, uncle?' she pronounced.

'Yes, he certainly has got some courage. I would never have dared to do this, or even thought of it,' uncle replied and carried on saying, 'He must be in love, mother. We shall have to congratulate him on his cheek and thoughts. What about a little drink to celebrate?' uncle asked.

'No, thank you,' he declined, and carried on. 'I know what your little drinks would be like; I don't like the stuff, it's similar to what I was given at the distillery earlier.'

'No,' auntie butted in, 'you leave him to his little Schnapps and beer. We'll have a small sherry, you will like this.'

She poured out something into two small glasses and gave one to him, which was a little sweeter, but not quite like orange or lemonade, which he would have preferred.

'Do you like this better?' she remarked.

I had another little sip, 'Yes a little better,' he replied, and drank the lot. 'But it still has a sharp taste, I think I prefer water or orange,' he remarked.

'You can have water or orange every day, my boy,' she said, and continued, 'on a special occasion one has got to have something a little special. All these things you will find out a little later in life. You will always be asked to have a little sherry if you go to parties or social gatherings later. Or even when you are asked to go to the big house again at some time,' she told him.

This he thought to be good advice, which he appreciated, and asked if he could have another little sip?

'This little fellow has got a cheek, as you can see, uncle,' auntie replied, and said, 'Yes, of course you may. You might even get to like it, and I will have to hide the bottle from you.'

'No, you won't have to worry about that, auntie,' he replied.

'No, I think I know you better than that, boy; this was just a little joke. I have to hide all bottles from uncle or he would drink the lot in one go,' auntie remarked.

'Now, now, my girl,' uncle announced and carried on, 'I am not as bad as all that, just because I like a little drop now and again does not mean I am a boozer, drinking everything that comes to hand.'

'No, dear,' auntie remarked, 'but if there was a bottle in your way you would rather drink the contents then put it away for another day, would you not?' she asked.

'Well, if you put it that way, perhaps you are right. I would rather drink it than let it spoil,' he replied.

'Nothing will ever spoil in our household,' auntie remarked, 'because you like your food and drink too much,' she said when he just smiled.

Kiel liked them both; they were a lovely couple and always seemed to understand each other, even if one or the other would grumble for a little while. They seemed to find some way to talk themselves out of it without a lot of shouting or bad temper.

He was the brother of his real uncle's wife, who still lived in Strehla, Saxony, not very far from this estate, which he would soon have to go and see, since they and his two little girl cousins do not even know he was in this area.

They were all born in this little town with the castle on the hill and the large river Elbe down below. They all lived together in one large house belonging to grandad, until he and grandma decided that they wanted to sell up and move into the Bavarian hills and mountains, when they all had to move.

Kiel's parents found a house and work in Jückelberg, Thüringen, which is a completely different county, adjoining Sachsen. This they began to love just as much as Strehla, Saxony or Sachsen, and had the Thüringer forest and other woods not all that far from home. There they often used to go mushrooming or collecting berries with mum and dad, when mum was still alive and the two boys were still young.

Thüringen is a beautiful county like most others, but this used to be a free state or another kingdom until Germany as a whole was united, back in the eighteenth century.

Both counties lying next to each other are mostly agricultural with lots of forests, rivers and lakes; there are or were a few open brown coal mines and some industry, but not like the centre or west counties of Germany.

Although Kiel loved it there and got to know all the different people, Kiel did not miss it as much as he missed Secilia right now.

But life had to go on and, with his new studies and plenty of work on the estate, there was little time left to even think or worry about one's own problems.

Kiel did like the college and friends. They all got on well and the learning of drawing and historical old buildings was just up his street and he enjoyed every minute of it. The teachers were brilliant, or so it seemed to him at least. He particularly liked to look at and admire the old Roman and Gothic style churches, cathedrals and galleries.

He liked most of all going on day trips to different cities not far from away, with all the lovely old buildings, including the royal palaces, magnificent libraries and museums, et cetera.

Some towns or cities are on the banks of the great river Elbe with beautiful green woods and grassy banks on the either side and pleasure cruisers going up and down all day long.

Work was hard, but even harder was the getting up in the mornings, even though the sun always seemed to be up before them, unless of course it rained, which did happen occasionally and made work even harder, at least fetching in and taking out the cows.

Although they were dry in the stables, rubber boots were advised to be worn almost every day, when feet washing was always the first priority or smelly and sore toes, or socks on feet could not be avoided.

The days went by with the sun reaching ever-greater heights, and getting more powerful by the day. Harvest was in full progress and dust was flying around everywhere. So were the little tiny black corn or harvest flies, which got under one's collar or into the hair or wherever and were most aggravating. Even the larger flies were irritating the cattle and one had to be very careful of the slightest movement or one was knocked over, or got the dirty tails round the ears and head.

Most evenings Kiel went swimming in the river with a number of other youngsters, or met up with older people from the estate. One had to be very careful not to swim too far out or to get in the way of vessels sailing up and down the river or get caught in the wash created by the larger boats, which at times swelled over the riverbanks.

They all had a great time and lots of fun, sometimes until late evening or into the night, especially when the moon was shining brightly making the waves shimmer in the moonlight.

At times Kiel almost forgot Secilia, especially when there were other girls of the same age around and when they found out that he was friendly with Secilia. They would then try and take the mickey. This always reminded him of the great times Secilia and he had together.

Time was passing quite quickly and he was very much looking forward to the return of the colonel, Her Ladyship and, naturally, Secilia for their annual summer break.

No one, however, seemed to know when exactly this was going to be and by the time mid-August came around, his eyes were continually looking in the direction of the big house.

By that time, college had already broken up for the summer holidays, but a great deal of homework was still to be carried out in preparation for the new term in the autumn.

It was a lovely summer with the sun high up in the sky most days and quite warm enough to work and walk about without a shirt.

The days went by and not a sign of movement around the big house, apart from the gardener and one of the housemaids or lady cook occasionally. Kiel knew the gardener quite well and often wanted to ask him for a job in the garden, but then thinking about it, and realising it would mean working all day with no time off for college, was not quite what was required.

All considered Kiel was quite well situated and by now got used to the early mornings, animals and his little friends, the calves.

He loved the occasional riding and exercising of the colonel's and Her Ladyship's horses, but in particular he liked the schimmel, the colonel's horse.

This horse loved galloping and jumping. At one time, when frightened by the blow of a horn from a boat, Kiel nearly shot over the top of the horse's head, but managed to hang on to his ears and neck. This most certainly scared him a little and his heart began to beat faster than before, although the horse did not seem to mind and carried on, by continually talking to it, albeit it blew its nostrils once or twice and pricked up his ears. They both managed to return safely to the stables, but the horse seemed slightly moist when Kiel had to give him a good rubdown.

Kiel groomed both horses almost every day, so they got to know him well. Every time he came into the stables they seemed to recognise his movements and responded by whinnying and looking round.

They just loved a good brush down, which they had every day from his uncle, who was in charge, and one of the horsemen, looking after and using most horses every day.

These two riding horses, however, were mostly out in the field just grazing and running around and were not used for farm work. They seem to have the best of both worlds and loved their freedom of roaming in the fields or meadows.

They had a foal almost a year old running around with them. He was quite a strange, but very pleasant, colour, mostly black with white markings, and was no doubt kept especially for Secilia to ride when it was a little older. This little chap was a tiny champion and would come running to meet Kiel every time Kiel walked towards the field or better-said, green meadow. This was fenced off with wooden railings, too high for any horse to jump, but the little one would poke his head through the railings to lick his hands, or looking to receive something special.

Following, the two parent horses would come along for a while to see if there was anything for them and to have their foreheads and necks stroked, especially after Kiel had climbed over or through the wooden railings to be with the small foal.

Sometimes Kiel would sit on top of the fence with bare feet when the little chap would lick and try to chew his toes, but this was a little dangerous when the two bigger horses came along and tried to knock him off with their heads.

Then, thereafter, they would both turn, kick up their heels and shoot off with the little one following, kicking his little legs and running all the way through the green grass until they all come to a halt again in the distance.

They were a marvellous sight to see and watch and sometimes Kiel would sit on one or the other for a short bareback ride or gallop when without halters. They would go where they liked and often tried with some kicks to throw him off. With his short legs, it was often quite a job to tighten his grip as one had to be very careful not to tickle them under their bellies, or they most certainly would throw one off.

Luckily, Kiel had been taught and ridden horses from a very early age and knew that if one treated a horse right and it got to know one, it would very seldom throw one, unless scared or it made a wrong landing after a jump. Kiel was taught always to allow the horse to make the judgement and never try to force it to do what it did not want or was not capable of doing. Any horse likes jumping once trained to do so but, like people, the height of a fence or surroundings sometimes confuses it.

It is an old saying, 'You can take a horse to water but you can never make it drink.' If this is remembered, all will turn out well. This goes with any animal. Trying to force them to do something they do not wish to do of their own free will is wrong and should be avoided, if at all possible.

Horses, like any other animals, including birds or fish or any wildlife, have always been important to him from a very early age. This, however, refers to the time or earlier years, when animals were of very much greater importance.

These days one presumes that in most cases it is machinery or motor transport one relies upon, since almost everyone appears to own one or the other. However, at that time back in the late 1930s to 40s, cars were actually owned only by the very wealthy people, industry or state.

Naturally, horses and other animals were of much greater importance and played a major part, especially in agricultural life. Tractors and cars were only just about coming in sight. Although the estate had two of these tractors, horses were still in daily use working the fields.

# CHAPTER 10

Writing about horses, their use and Kiel exercising the colonel's schimmel one fine day, what would he see but a car with the colonel, chauffeur and the two ladies in the rear, just turning in from the main road into the estate. What a surprise. He quickly turned the horse, waved his hands and arms, almost scaring the horse, and greeted all of them with a salute just like the colonel and Her Ladyship did to him and Secilia earlier in the year.

Secilia appeared to be really excited and waved back, standing upright in the open-topped rear of the car, while the colonel and Her Ladyship just politely acknowledged his greetings by raising their hands, waving and smiling.

By the time Kiel got back with the horse to the stables, Secilia was already waiting to say, 'Hello, and thank you,' for the good wishes he had forwarded for her birthday. She followed on to say, 'Please don't put the horse out to grass, Daddy wants to have a good ride, after we have had lunch.'

'Oh, have you not had lunch yet?' he asked politely, and carried on saying, 'We've had ours some time ago.'

'Have you really Kiel?' she asked and carried on saying, 'We have been travelling since early morning from Berlin.' She continued, 'Our lunch will soon be ready and on the table, I had better go and will see you later.'

'Yes, Secilia, you had better go,' he replied.

'Oh, you want me to go, just after I have got here,' she said and smiled, pulled him into the stables and gave him a little peck on the cheek. 'I hope you have behaved yourself, while I was not here looking after you?' Secilia pronounced in a somewhat stern voice, with her forehead slightly wrinkled and her pretty head upright, staring him straight in the face.

'Yes, of course I have, darling, I have been working hard and going to college every day, which left me no time for anything else,' he remarked.

He took her in his arms gave her a gentle kiss on the cheek and said, 'I had better clean down and polish the schimmel and the leathers for your dad, or he will not allow me to ride his horse again.'

'Oh, the horse seems more important to you than me now,' Secilia remarked, smiling and continued, 'I had better be off or they will be wondering where I have got to.'

She called back 'bye-bye', waved her hand and disappeared from the stables and across the yard.

Kiel quickly returned to the stable door and looked, to see her just about to enter the garden gate. There she waved again, which he returned by waving both his hands, with brush and cloth.

He returned and continued wiping down the horse, and was so happy that he was even singing a song while doing the cleaning and polishing.

## In Love

The lovely lass with jet black hair,
By God she had a lovely pair.
The pair I'd like to hold right in my hands,
And rolling with her in the sands.
The water's blue with sun above,
By golly I must be in love.
K-WA

Yes, he was once again himself, on top of the moon, full of admiration, affection and Love.

After finishing the jobs he thought necessary to do, he ran back home full of excitement, cuddling auntie in the process.

She wondered what on earth had come over him, but said, 'I know what has happened to you, my boy, I saw you with Secilia outside the stables, she then asked, 'She is back then, is she?'

'Yes, auntie,' he called out full of joy and kissed her.

'Hold on, boy, you nearly had me on the floor there. I am not as young and strong as you youngsters are,' she pronounced.

That was when uncle butted in and asked, 'Have you made a good job of Schimmel, my boy?' And continued, 'The colonel wants to take him out for a ride after lunch, I had better go and make sure.'

'There is no need, uncle,' he mentioned, and followed on by saying, 'I have rubbed and polished him, the leathers and saddle, painted Schimmel's hooves and given him some water and oats. Everything is fine, I promise, you uncle,' he replied and continued, 'I have been informed by Secilia that the colonel might want to go out for a ride, and I would not allow myself to get into trouble, would I?'

'No, of course not, my boy. I quite believe you, but I am in charge of the horses and thus I will have to make sure, since it is me and not you who will get into trouble if everything is not to his lordship's satisfaction. He is after all very proud of his horse and wants him to look his best when he goes out riding in case he is meeting up with someone. There is always someone he seems to run into on his way and perfection is in his blood as an officer,' uncle continued.

'Yes, I am sure you are right. There may have been something I have overlooked, but I don't think so. Please tell me if I have, so I do not to make the same mistake again,' he answered.

'I am sure you have done very well, Kiel,' auntie butted in and followed on by saying, 'Uncle has been here a long while and would like to keep his job, which he is very good at, so you must forgive him for being specially careful.'

'Yes, auntie, I fully understand, and in the excitement I might have overlooked something, but I don't think so, or at least I hope not. Uncle will soon let me know if I have,' he replied.

By then it was time for tea and uncle returned with a broad smile on his face, saying, 'You have done really well, boy. There was nothing I could find wrong and hopefully the colonel will not find anything either when he goes to get his favourite horse.'

We all sat down for coffee and a piece of auntie's lovely cake, which he could eat at any time, even though he felt still full from her lovely dinner.

Continuing to talk about the horse or horses, uncle asked him all about the knowledge he had gained in his earlier life and commented on his perfection.

This, of course, pleased him to hear uncle say this, and Kiel's halo grew ever larger. He replied, 'Thank you, uncle. It is nice of you to say so. I thought perhaps that you did not agree with my actions and looking after horses.'

'No, my boy; you are doing very well and hopefully you will continue to do so,' he said.

This made him very proud and he almost jumped for joy as he went up the stairs to get ready for the afternoon shift. Grinning all over his face, he changed into his working clothes, looked into the mirror to comb his hair, just in case Secilia would show her face again when feeding the calves.

He ran downstairs to shout cheerio, shot out of the door and across the yard, keeping his eyes on the big house and windows, but there was no sign of anyone.

He was the first one in the cowshed apart from the headman, who always seemed to be there, whatever the time.

Kiel had the cheek to ask him, 'Do you live and sleep with the cows? You always seem to be here any time of day.'

'No, you cheeky boy. You know I don't, but I like to keep an eye on the place, just like your uncle with the horses,' he replied. He followed on, 'We are a little older than you but no doubt you will do the same later in life, since you seem to like animals.'

'Yes, sir, I do, but I would not like to sleep with them. I would rather sleep with Secilia,' he answered back.

'No doubt you would, but I doubt that will ever happen,' he replied and carried on. 'You must not get carried away, my boy. Just because she talks to you or even likes you does not mean she wishes to sleep with you.'

'No, I know that. All I was saying is that I would rather sleep with Secilia than with the cows,' he replied and laughed.

'You had better come and help me get the cows in before you get too cheeky,' he said, and they walked out towards the field, where the cows were already waiting to come in.

No doubt their milk udders were full and heavy to carry around and they looked forward to some relief. Many were losing milk, by just walking along with the udders touching the legs. They were so full and had obviously had a good meal.

Cows or goats very much rely on time and once the udders are overfull the milk will just dribble out, which makes milking easy, but unfortunately is painful for the animals.

Kiel was quite happy and cheerful, chatting away to the headman, who always seemed to be in a reasonably good frame of mind. He never appeared to get hassled or rushed over anything and he just took his time and thought before he acted. Kiel was the complete opposite and ran his head against the wall rather than think, which is wrong and he knew it, but hoped that he would get calmer and more relaxed as he got older.

There never seemed to be time to relax or be calm. There are so many things to do and so much he wanted to do, but falling over one's own feet seemed not the answer.

While sitting under the cows drawing away the milk from their overfull udders to give these poor things some relief, many things went through his mind and head, most of all, naturally, Secilia. Will he see her again later?

But most of all, what would he say, how should he behave? It had been such a long time, or so it seemed, since she was here last, although it was only just a few weeks earlier.

Had she perhaps changed in those few weeks back in Berlin? She seemed okay, when seeing her earlier in the stables, and she waved madly when arriving by car. He thought she was still the same and feels the same as he did, but how can one be certain?

Milking was soon over and his next job, as always, was to get the food and milk ready for the little calves, which were surely waiting. While sorting out the different buckets for the older calves and getting ready to attend to the tiny ones, who would come running across the yard, but Secilia?

This cheered him up tremendously, especially when she called out 'Hello, Kiel, how are you?' This brought him into quite a happy mood; he waved his arms and went to greet her.

'I'm fine, thank you, how are you?' he replied and continued, 'I was hoping you could come and I have been looking out for you all afternoon.'

'That is nice. Why, have you missed me that much?' she requested to know and continued. 'I have certainly missed you, Kiel, and all the nice walks we had before we suddenly had to leave.'

'Yes, that was rather sudden. I had been looking out for you until I was told that you and your family had gone back to Berlin,' he managed to say, when she suddenly gave him a little peck on the cheek. This certainly made it all better and he said, 'You can come every day and night several times to do that.'

'Now don't you get cheeky again as soon as I have arrived. I shall turn straight round and go back to allow you to cool down. I would not have thought you would ask me to do this, although I would love to come and do this more often,' she replied.

'I would love you to do this to me, and would have loved and kissed you on arrival, but I had my hands full and you always said to be careful, or other people might talk,' he answered cheekily.

'Yes, that is quite true, but giving a little peck on the cheek or kissing each other is quite a different thing altogether,' she remarked, and smiled. 'Anyway, I came straight away to see you and give you a peck on the cheek when you were putting the horse away,' she remarked.

He knew from that very moment that he was back in her good books and obviously the colonel and her mum had not prevented her from meeting up with him again.

Secilia took one bucket out of his hands and entered the enclosure to help him feed one of the tiny calves with her hand in the little calf's mouth and the bucket of milk in the other, when she began to giggle.

'What is the matter?' he called out and laughed, knowing what it feels like for them to suck the milk through one's fingers.

'Doesn't this feel funny when they keep licking the fingers and draw up milk through them at the same time?' she answered and smiled.

'Yes, it does feel a little funny when you do it for the first time, I suppose, but I have been feeding little tiny calves for a long time and have got used to it, although I still enjoy their little tongues licking round and in between the fingers, 'he replied. 'What are you going to do this evening?' he asked and wanted to know.

'Nothing in particular, why?' she replied and questioned, 'What are you going to do, Kiel?'

'I'm not sure yet I had nothing planned until you suddenly arrived, but now I hoped we might go for a little walk, if that is okay with you?' he replied.

'Okay with me? Yes of course that is all right with me, I would love to go for a walk, but I have to ask my parents first and I will let you know, or wait for you as before,' Secilia remarked.

'That is fine. I can see you through the window from our cottage, or if you cannot make it you can let me know through your bedroom window, as before,' he replied.

'Oh, but that is not my bedroom window from which you saw me wave last time, that is the upper passage window. My bedroom is the other side overlooking the garden,' she remarked.

'I am glad you told me that or I might have climbed up the wrong window to come and see you one fine night,' he responded.

'Don't you dare,' she pronounced and was quite taken aback, or so it seemed at that time, but she smiled, as if to say, 'yes, please.'

'No, of course I would not do this without asking you first, that was just a joke,' he said.

'Yes, I should have known by now that you don't always mean what you say, from last time, but you will have to be more careful in future,' she replied.

'It certainly seems that I shall have to be more careful in future about what I am saying, 'or you won't believe me anymore,' he suggested and smiled.

'Yes, my boy' she said, and followed on by saying; 'You are getting carried away with your thoughts, when facts are more important and you'll have to get them right in future.'

'I just noticed you called me "boy", which is probably right, but you have never done this before. Is that all I am, from now on?' he requested to know.

'No, don't be silly, Kiel, that just slipped out as a matter of speech. You are a young man and I am proud of you, and it looks that I have to be a little more careful as well.' She carried on, 'It looks like we all do or say silly things at times without thinking and have to forgive each other,' she replied. 'I had better run now, but I will try to see you later, Kiel. Don't work too hard while I'm away,' she called out and ran through the yard and the little gate into the garden and disappeared out of sight.

He was still busy cleaning out the calves' compound and following, cleaning the buckets and cows' troughs before he could run for his coffee break, although he was quite peckish himself.

Secilia seemed to have run away rather quickly after their little controversy or slips of the tongue and he began to wonder why. Had he really upset her just that little bit, or was he imagining things again? He was not quite sure and kept telling himself not to be so silly, but it would not go out of his head, since upsetting her would have been the last thing he wanted to do. Uncertainty seemed to creep into his thoughts while going across the yard and back to the cottage.

He kept looking at the windows of the big house almost all the time, but there was no sign of anything or Secilia, which appeared to make it worse.

Entering the cottage, auntie noticed that he was not quite himself and in a wandering mood, when she asked, 'What is the matter, boy, (and she used this word all the time) you seem to be dreaming about something?'

'No, it's nothing, auntie, only Secilia seemed to have gone home so very quickly, which made me wonder if I had upset her in any way,' he replied.

'I hope you haven't my lad. What have you been doing or saying to her?' auntie wanted to know.

'Nothing really, auntie, we seemed to have a small misunderstanding just before she left and she appeared to leave rather quickly, that's all,' he remarked, and carried on, 'but we shall soon know, since we have decided to go for a walk later.'

'Oh, have you? Well, you had better go up for a quick wash and change. Supper will be ready when you come down,' auntie remarked, and up those stairs he disappeared, with a little more enthusiasm, than he had earlier.

After a good wash, brush up and a change of clothes, he felt a great deal better and was looking forward to their meeting and short walk.

He sprang down the stairs, when uncle, who had just come in through the door, caught him, 'Steady on, boy, are you in a rush? Where are you going?' he asked.

'Nowhere, uncle,' he replied, 'I just come down for coffee, and thought perhaps you were both waiting for me.'

'No, I have only just come in, I am a little late. I had to clean and rub down Schimmel after the colonel seemed to have had a good ride and made him sweat. You will have to wait a short while for me to have a quick wash and change,' he said.

'Well, hurry up, Dad,' auntie called out, 'coffee will soon be ready and we are waiting.'

'Okay,' came the reply, with the old wooden steps creaking as he marched up the stairs.

While having their supper, Kiel kept his eyes on the window and the yard beyond.

Auntie remarked, 'You don't have to keep turning your head, boy, I shall see Secilia if and when she comes along or is waiting for you. I will tell you, so you don't miss the chance,' auntie remarked. Uncle smiled and said, 'He'll never miss that chance; I would not have done at his age, my dear.'

'Why don't you both stop needling me? Just think back of your young years. I doubt that Secilia is coming, I think I upset her earlier,' he butted in.

'Why, what have you done, boy? You better not have upset her?' uncle remarked. Auntie almost shouted, 'Stop you two, look who is there waiting.'

Turning round and looking he saw Secilia coming towards the cottage, waving her hand. She must have seen us through the window, looking out for her.

He jumped up from the chair behind the table and out of the door, hardly having time to wipe his mouth and hands, all of which went on the handkerchief quickly, to shake her hand.

'Hello, Secilia,' he called out, and continued, 'I thought perhaps I had upset you a little and you might not be coming.'

'What ever made you think that?' she enquired, and appeared to look a little puzzled.

'You seemed to have rushed off from the little calves in such a hurry and we did have a slight difference of opinion before you left,' he remarked.

'Oh, don't be so silly, Kiel,' she replied, and went on, 'I just had to rush to the toilet and did not have much time. Once you start talking there is little time to get a word in edgeways.'

'In future, you have to keep your legs crossed, like this,' he demonstrated, when she laughed and tried the very same but nearly fell over without great success.

'No, I don't think this to be a very good idea. I would rather rush to the loo than try this again,' she remarked, and asked, 'What do you do if you have got to go quickly?'

'I'll have to run like you, with my legs crossed,' he replied and laughed. 'But you had better not do that too often, my love, or I shall have my work cut out to pick you up after falling over each time,' he remarked.

'Oh, it's my love again now. That is the first time I have heard you say that since we came back,' she said.

'I thought perhaps you had forgotten the word and, by the way, I think you would just love to uncross my legs, would you not?' she remarked.

'Well, I had better not answer this in a hurry, or you will perhaps smack my face again like you did last time?' he replied.

'I did not smack your face last time, surely, did I?' she questioned.

'Well, you did not really smack my face, just poked my ribs, which was nearly as bad. I have still got the marks,' he said.

'Have you really?' she asked, and carried on 'I have had my marks for a long time from when you poked me, and mum wanted to know where these came from?' she replied.

I told her, 'It must have been some lumps in the ground when we sat down to pick some flowers. Oh, you must show

95

me later, so I can do it again and your mum will know in future where they came from,' he replied.

By that time they had walked quite a way up the little farm track towards the woods, without even asking or remarking as to where they wanted to go.

Kiel spotted some small autumn flowers in or near the tiny ditch and jumped in to pick them.

Secilia followed and they sat down for a while, chatting about all sorts of things they had been doing in the few weeks apart, when Kiel suddenly realised he had not brought his swimming trucks or a towel and told Secilia.

'I did not bring mine either, since we had not mentioned or talked about it earlier. I did not know how much time you had before you have to get back, Kiel?' she remarked.

'Oh, I have got all the time in the world and do not need to get back till late. Auntie and uncle won't mind,' he announced.

'I am not in a great hurry either, but I do not want to be back too late, since we have had a long journey and got up early this morning. Mummy and Daddy might want to go to bed a little earlier,' Secilia replied. Then he grabbed her as they had a little roll, kiss and a quick cuddle. All seemed to be back to normal, and both of them appreciated that nearness for a few seconds, when Secilia suddenly said, 'Let's take a walk through the woods.'

**Golden Autumn Leaves**

The autumn leaves are turning,
From green to golden-brown,
And in the slightest breeze of air or wind,
They are coming down.

From tiny trees and from high above,
The very tall,
They all turn pretty colours,
Before they begin to fall.

They're all lying there,
Like a carpet on the ground,
And as they fall,
They'll make a whispering sound.

To lie upon appears so very soft and cool,
But lie too long,
Many people think,
You'd be a fool.

The ground below is damp and could give one a chill,
But everyone is surely doing what they wish and will.
If the sun is shining and is high up in the sky,
Those gorgeous golden leaves are quite warm and dry.

I like going through a forest,
With the trees quite high up there,
When this lovely sun shines through the branches,
Nearly bare.

Then after walking,
lying down and take a little rest,
With these tall forest trees around,
which at that time is best.

A few more leaves come gliding down,
And shower us with gold,
There is no way that I
Would do exactly as I'm told.

Especially with somebody,
After walking hand in hand,
Since after all that time,
She surely is by now a friend.

When most golden leaves have fallen,
And lie there from the trees,
It's really soft and warm,
like a lovely bedspread right beneath.

Lying there on brown and golden leaves,
Without giving a hoot,
Does all, not only us,
A little more than good.

May these golden leaves be falling,
From high upon the trees?
After all these poor things need a rest
So once again they'll breath.

The cool and good fresh air,
Which should be all around,
And see their golden leaves,
Lying down upon the ground.

A cover for the mushrooms,
So be careful where you lie or tread,
There is no need for planting,
Since its own spawn will spread.

A creation from the ancient early days and our world around,
One has to wonder why and where they had first been found?

K-WA


Walking though these lovely woods, it was late August with a wet spring and very dry summer behind them. The leaves on the trees had begun to change their colour and looked absolutely glorious in the still brilliant evening sunshine.

As they were quietly lying there they saw some little fox cubs playing in the streams of glaring sunshine through the high up branches. These were so lovely to watch, one could easily go and pick them up to play with oneself. Having such gorgeous colours with their white chests and feet, these baby foxes looked more like toys rather than wild animals. Until they grow up and savagely kill most of the chickens and ducks et cetera on farms or other households.

All tiny, newly born animals or, for that matter babies seem or look like little toys to play with, especially to small children. Some of them, however, can turn nasty even in their young age and are best to be watched from the distance and not handled by the inexperienced.

There were small and large deer, pheasants, partridges and many other animals and birds running or fluttering around, all seemingly enjoying themselves and the food they found. Every now and again they would prick up their ears, listen and look for strange sounds, noises or movements, even the slight falling of leaves they seem to see or hear. We both enjoyed every moment, and kept as quiet as we could, by just whispering in each other's ear or pointing in certain directions, when seeing something new.

The sun was gradually beginning to go under when the animals and birds seem to slowly disappear into the depth of the forest and no doubt went to their nests, beds or below ground into their lairs.

After a little while longer, the moon was already beginning to shine its silvery glimmer, when they both decided it was time for them to make a move and return home. They had a great time and both enjoyed the moments when lying on those lovely golden-brown leaves below the tall trees admiring the animals and birds.

Kiel gave Secilia a little kiss on the cheek, helped her up and slowly they walked hand in hand back to the entrance gate.

Suddenly she drew him near to her, just before they got to edge of the wood, kissed him again and said, 'Thank you for the lovely evening. I really love to be with you, you are so kind and gentle.'

'Thank you for those kind words, and you are so very pretty and soft to touch as well as nice to talk and listen to,' he remarked and returned the kiss, pulling her even closer to him once again.

Hand in hand they strolled down the little grass-covered road or track, talking about little things they remembered from their last, or, better said, the first time they met, with the silvery moon shining down on her sparkling dark hair. Secilia looked delightful in her flowery dress, well shaped and these gorgeous legs, her eyes shining in the moonlight like crystals or the stars above.

He squeezed her hand a little tighter and told her just what he had in his mind and saw with his own eyes, when she said, 'You must not sit me on a high stool as if I were a princess, which I am not. I like you to say nice things but don't make me blush.'

'Oh, I am sorry, I don't want to hurt you,' he replied and carried on, 'but you are and look like a little princess to me. I would like to treat you like one; the only thing is I do not have the money to buy you all the nice things you deserve,' he remarked.

'The only thing I deserve is you, Kiel' and I have got you here near me. I do not wish you to have a lot of money and pretty things. I love you as you are and hope we shall be able to stay together forever and ever,' she replied, smiled and gave him another peck on the cheek.

This made him feel like a king, never mind a prince, and naturally hoped for the very same, and told her so.

'But you are a king, the way you treat me and take me for walks. I would not want anything better,' she remarked and squeezed his hand again.

Walking along slowly, they got as far as the large gate and buildings, when he pulled her close to him once more, gave her a peck on the cheek, and said, 'Thank you, darling we shall have to do this more often.'

Secilia returned the kiss and asked, 'Are you not taking me back to the house, now you have been so very nice to me?'

'Oh, yes, of course I will take you all the way home, and even put you to bed, if you let me. I only thought it might be best not to be too open with our relationship,' he mentioned.

'That is nice of you, Kiel. You seem to think of everything, even putting me to bed, but I think I can just about manage that on my own, although I would not mind. But we had better leave this until some later date, you might find that too hard,' she remarked and laughed.

He nearly said something naughty but managed to restrain himself and they walked across the estate yard to the small garden gate, where he pulled her gently closer again and gave her another peck on the cheek.

He said, 'Goodnight, hope to see you again in the morning,' which they both said almost simultaneously before he turned to go to the little cottage.

This little peck on the cheek she repeated and disappeared through the gate and garden. There was no one waiting for them this time, which he was quite glad of, since it was getting late and no doubt the Baron and Baroness wanted an early night.

He returned to the little cottage, where uncle and auntie were still awake, waiting for him to return home.

'Have you had a great time with Secilia? Where did you go?' uncle asked almost as soon as Kiel got into the door, with both of them waiting for a reply.

'Sit yourself down, my boy, and have a late snack. We were just having a cup of coffee; would you like one?' auntie asked.

'Yes, please.' He began to tell them all about their little walk and how they sat in the woods watching the small animals and birds.

'Are you sure you were sitting and not lying down?' uncle wanted to know.

'Well, both of it at times, I suppose, since we did not want to disrupt the animals or birds and their feeding. There were several little foxes playing about and small as well as large deer to be seen as well as partridges and pheasants almost all around us,' he said and continued. 'We really had a great time, with the sun still shining, the golden-brown leaves falling from the trees almost covering us, and later the moon coming out in a silvery glow. All of it was fantastic and we hope to do it again,' he explained.

Both uncle and auntie seemed absolutely overjoyed with his story; delighted, and listened full of enthusiasm while he was talking. He enjoyed telling them all the details and felt as if he was still there with Secilia.

We all sat there drinking our coffee and he had a piece of auntie's delicious cake, then she asked, 'Would you like another piece, Kiel? I only baked it today and it is nice and fresh.'

He certainly did not need asking twice, especially as he was starving hungry after their long walk, and replied 'Yes please, auntie, if I may,' with his eyes almost popping out of their sockets, still licking his fingers.

'You really like cake and seem to enjoy almost any type, or do you have any preference?' auntie asked and continued, 'Please tell me, so that I can bake whatever you like best?'

'I don't mind, really, I just love all cakes you bake auntie. You are just like my mum used to be (which seemed to please her, and she smiled), they all taste terrific,' he replied.

'That is kind of you do say so, but you surely must have a preference. Like uncle, he likes a nice dry cake, so he does not get his hands sticky,' she remarked.

'I do not really mind, but if it comes to preference, perhaps I like most of all plum or cheese cake, which I can eat until it comes out of my ears,' he replied.

'Well, we don't want it coming out of your ears, but I most certainly will make some plum and cheese cake next time I bake, if just a little one of each to satisfy your appetite,' she said.

'You are most kind, auntie,' he remarked and said, 'but now I must go upstairs and to bed, or I shall not be able to get up in the morning again.'

He asked to be allowed to leave the table and wished both goodnight before leaving.

He had a quick peep through his bedroom window, hoping that he could see something of Secilia in the big house or at the windows not far away, but there seemed to be only light downstairs, with just a glimmer of the hall light showing at the upper level.

After having a wash and cleaning his teeth, he jumped into bed and must have gone off to sleep almost immediately.

# CHAPTER 11

The next thing he heard was a bang on the door from uncle, to tell him it was time to wake up. He heard him going down the stairs and out of the door to work. Kiel must have slept very deeply and had a great night without any dreams that he could remember, and had to turn round for a few more minutes to really wake. He had almost another hour before he needed to get out of bed, but uncle always gave him a knock so he would not oversleep too often.

Many times he fell back to sleep again and woke only when the alarm clock went off, if he heard it at all. Often auntie had to wake him, since she always seemed to be awake, apart from in the evenings, when she often settled in her chair for a short forty winks or more.

Does it not seem strange that young people seem to be awake all day long and require a lot of sleep in the mornings when it is time to get up, while older people seem to be dozing all day and are awake most of the night, or early morning?

Kiel most certainly could keep going all day and evening without feeling tired at all, but by the time morning and getting up time came along; he could have carried on sleeping for hours. He presumes we are all different and many folk need more sleep or rest than others do; that is what makes the world go round.

The sun or moon are not always as awake or shining as one likes them to be, or at least one cannot always see them and they make excuses for being hidden by the clouds, but is this always true? No one will ever be able to tell us, unless someone is staying awake above the clouds forever, like the angels.

Is it not strange, that the sun and moon can be seen from different parts of this earth at different times, since they continually travel round and round? They always bring this golden or silvery glow from the sky, which delights the folk below, similar to stars.

And why is the sun always full and round, while the moon appears to be changing in size every month?

This we have all been taught at school, without having taken much notice, and it can be read or studied from books, but it will always be some sort of mystery and excitement to see it increase or decrease.

It is most important in life to have some sort of mystery, fantasy or excitement to try and actually find out. It is not always the best to see or know all, right from the start. The not knowing and trying to find out what hides behind some hidden mystery or fantasy creates the excitement and makes life worth living.

He seemed fully awake after the knock or call from uncle and was looking forward going to work and hopefully seeing his little girl Secilia again. Although he liked his work, his head seemed to be more controlled by the thought of Secilia and her shapely figure.

After a good wash with cold water he began to wake up completely and realised that the world does not necessarily turn around love all the time, which he had been informed on so many occasions, but will this ever sink into the head of anyone in love?

Going downstairs and walking across the yard in the early hours of the morning, his head automatically turned towards the big house and windows, but once again there was or seemed no life around this early time of day.

The sun was only just rising with a little light glow over the horizon, but it seemed quite light with lovely fresh air all around, once again a beautiful late summer's day.

The first thing after saying good morning to everyone was to go and collect the cattle or cows as normal, which were already waiting with theirs udders full of milk again and could hardly walk without milk spilling around their legs.

After all the feeding, cleaning and milking, which seemed to go on for hours, it was time once again to sort out all the different buckets and mix the calves' food with fresh milk. Buckets clattering and making a noise, they began to start shouting and waiting for their breakfast.

One never had time even to think, never mind dream or even look, although by that time his eyes were fully open.

He suddenly felt a scratch on his back and, looking round, who would stand there but his long looked forward to pretty little Secilia.

'Hello, good morning, Kiel. I thought I had better come and see you for a short while,' Secilia, said and laughed. 'We are having a small garden party this afternoon and evening while the weather is so nice. Would you like to come round and see us? Juliet and her family will be there,' she asked.

'Oh, yes, I would love to, but I have to work this afternoon,' he replied, and continued, 'perhaps I could come round for a short while this evening after I have had a wash and change.'

'That will be lovely. Don't eat or drink too much before coming, there will be lots; we are having a barbecue as well as plenty of tea, coffee and cake, beer, wine and champagne,' she carried on saying.

His mouth was watering already by just listening and he could hardly wait to see it all.

'All that sounds marvellous, but I don't have anything much to wear,' he suddenly remembered, and told Secilia.

'Oh, you must not worry about that, Kiel, it is a garden party not a dress up or dance party. You must come just as you feel, as long as you change out of your smelly working clothes,' she pronounced. 'You always look smart when we go out for walks and that will be just fine,' she said and carried on, 'I am sure you will look very smart when you turn up,' which made him feel a great deal better.

'What about your mum and dad? Did you ask them, or don't they know anything about me turning up?' he asked.

'Oh, yes, they told me to ask you. I could not possibly make such a request without them knowing all about it or asking their permission,' she replied.

'Darling, I could kiss you right here and now,' he cheerfully said.

'You had better not here, or this evening. You will have to control yourself, and make sure you do not call me darling too loud now or this evening, or I shall be very embarrassed,' she replied.

'No, darling, I won't. I will just think it, and quietly blow it in your ear when no one is looking or listening,' he remarked.

'Don't be so cheeky, or I shall call off the invitation and see if I can find someone with a little more upbringing and respect,' she said and stepped a short distance away.

After a second or so she looked back with a smile on her face, when he knew she did not mean what she had implied and he called her 'a tease.' For a moment he thought she had really meant it, since it was often very difficult to detect her true feelings, although he thought he knew her extremely well.

Secilia seemed to give that cheeky, undetectable rejection, which he should have known by now, but he had always been told that one should never trust a female further than one can see or reach. Or better the old saying, 'Don't trust any one further than you can throw them,' but very often one cannot even pick them up to hold her tight, although, he would have loved to have picked her up just then. But, like always, he had to restrain himself, especially here with other people around, who would only love to watch and see what would happen.

She soon departed, saying, 'Bye-bye, hope to see you later,' in her cheeky way, and disappeared across the yard into the garden of the big house.

Looking across, there seemed to be a great deal of activity going on, but he had too much work to catch up on and was possibly also too excited to take a lot of notice.

Kiel carried on with his work until all had been thoroughly cleaned and put in its place, ready for next time, when thereafter we were allowed to go for our own breakfast.

By that time there were lots of people busy moving things into the garden and putting up a large tent on the lawn. He was almost keen enough to go and have a good look, but his stomach persuaded him to go and have breakfast first and not be too nosy.

Telling uncle and auntie all about what was going on and his invitation, they could hardly believe him and kept asking silly questions, which he himself was not able to answer, or at least not just then.

He failed to ask what Secilia was going to do this morning and she did not tell, so he naturally presumed that she would be busy in the house and garden, or maybe waiting for the guests to arrive.

After breakfast he asked to be excused, went upstairs to lay down for a while and catch up with his sleep. This, however, was not to happen and he kept twisting and turning, jumping up to have a look as to what to wear that evening, but could not make up his mind and would lay down again for a few seconds. Even though this was to no avail, the twisting and turning continued, until he went to the window and had a good look towards the big house, but there again was nothing that could really be seen.

The big house and wall obstructed most of the vision of the garden and there was no one in the windows.

He seemed lost and forlorn and did not really know what to do, then suddenly he heard his auntie calling; 'Lunch is ready, you two. You had better come down before it gets cold.'

Meeting uncle on the landing, not knowing that he had decided to have forty winks as well, he called out, 'Hello, Kiel, are you okay?'

'Yes, uncle, but I could not get off to sleep for thinking of what to wear this evening,' he replied.

'You must not worry about that, my boy. As long as you are clean and tidy, as you always are, you'll be okay, I am sure,' he said, and we both walked downstairs together.

What a gorgeous smell. As soon as we opened the door, 'What is it, auntie? That smells terrific,' I asked.

'*Rolladen* with dumplings and red cabbage,' she replied and placed all the dishes on the table next to the warmed up plates.

*Rolladen,* a dish known also as 'Beef Olives', dished up with gravy and as above mentioned, a meal you can lick your fingers after, and even the plate if you dare.

He once again enjoyed this meal and had a second helping, which astounded both uncle and auntie again.

Uncle spoke up and said, 'Your food must go straight down into your legs; the amount you manage to put away is almost unbelievable.'

'Leave the boy alone,' auntie once again admonished, and followed on by saying, 'I am glad he likes my food, that makes cooking more of a pleasure,' auntie said.

'I enjoy seeing him and other people putting it away. You used to do the same when you were younger, some years ago, Dad,' she carried on.

'Yes, I know,' uncle replied and continued, 'that is quite a while back and I like seeing the boy enjoying it. It just seems so incredible; I surely did not manage to eat that much?' uncle asked auntie.

'Oh, yes, you did, you have just forgotten. You always used to have two helpings when we were first married and you worked hard in these days,' auntie mentioned.

'You just help yourself, my boy, and lick the plate if you like. It makes me feel good to see you enjoying my cooking. You will work it all off again in a few hours time, if you can still move,' auntie remarked.

As usual we had a couple of hours before going back to work, so he took his bicycle and had a tour round the big house and garden, just to see what was going on. He was most astounded to see a massive tent in the garden with cars standing outside the garden wall and in the entrance to the house. He heard people talking, but could not see.

Rather than being seen by Secilia or others, he kept his head down and returned, cycling out through the rear gates of the estate and up towards the woods for some exercise, to allow his big dinner to settle.

There he saw some deer in the distance, and got off the bike and walked slowly towards them, looking for any sign of movement and there they were again. The pheasants, partridges, rabbits, hares and foxes sniffing around to catch one or the other, but one sudden move and they all scattered into the air or wood away to hide.

After a little while it was nearly teatime and following work again, not yet having a watch to tell the time, he thought it would be better to return before it got too late.

He hoped he would run into Secilia and, by golly, there she was just coming out of the gate to look for him.

'Hello, Kiel, I saw you earlier, cycling through the yard,' she said and carried on, 'but you were too quick and I did not want to shout after you. Where did you go?' she asked.

'I did not see you, Secilia, so I just went for a ride up towards the woods and saw quite a lot of the animals grazing along the edge,' he replied.

'I did see you cycling around the yard, Kiel, and later I waved through the top floor window, but by that time you were already on your way through the gates,' Secilia remarked.

'Yes, I did look for you, Secilia, and saw that large tent in your garden with a few cars outside, so I did not want to make a fool of myself and went for a ride and enjoyed it. It is a lovely day for your party; have you got many guests coming?' he asked.

'There are quite a few here already and others will be arriving later. I hope you will come, Kiel?' Secilia enquired.

'I will certainly try, if nothing gets into my way, but I don't know what to wear,' he said.

'Don't be so silly, Kiel, you can come as you are now. As I told you earlier, this is just a garden party and nothing fancy is expected. I am wearing just an ordinary dress as you can see,' she said and gave him a little peck on the cheek. 'I must go back now, Kiel, since everyone will be looking out for me, and I or we hope to see you later,' she called as she ran away.

She looked terrific and well shaped in her tight fitting, silky, dress, coloured with flowers.

'Thank you. Bye-bye, I shall be looking out for you later,' he returned the call and waved.

He was still a little hot under the collar, seeing her here completely unexpected, and thinking about her later, and so he returned home.

Uncle and auntie were already expecting him and had seen them both through the curtains, with Secilia running away.

'You are just in time, boy,' auntie called out and continued. We saw you both having a chat; has Secilia told you not to turn up later?' They both wanted to know.

'No, no, on the contrary, she asked me again not to forget and to come in what I am wearing now, if I wished. It is only a garden party and nothing fancy is expected, she told me.'

'There you are, that's what we told you, but you must put something nice on before you go, since they will all look at you and want to know who you are,' auntie remarked. 'Come and sit yourself down, Kiel, I have baked your favourite plum cake,' auntie said while she was pouring out the coffee.

'Oh, that is lovely, I can smell it already, but I must not eat too much or I shall have no room for food tonight,' he replied.

'Help yourself to another piece if you want, and don't be so silly, you will have worn all that off working this afternoon, before you even think of going to the garden party,' uncle mentioned. 'When I was your age, I used to have about half a dozen of those pieces in the afternoon, didn't I, Mother?' he continued.

'Yes, you surely did, Dad,' auntie said, nodding her head and carrying on. 'Let the boy have what he wants and don't interfere. You can have half a dozen now if you wish, I can soon make some more. There are plenty of plums this year. What other fresh fruit cakes do you like, Kiel?' she asked.

'Oh, I like all of them; gooseberries, raspberries, cherries and apples, but I am not too keen on the latter,' he replied while eating and drinking.

'He is a bit like me,' uncle butted in and continued, 'he has a little of a sweet tooth, just like I had, and still have.'

'Yes, the boy is very much like you in many ways and we hope he stays with us for a little while, don't we, Father?'

Kiel certainly enjoyed myself and said, 'I hope I shall be able to stay a few years; and with your cooking, baking and Secilia being around, what better could a man wish for?'

'Oh, you're a man now,' said auntie smiling all over her face, obviously liking what he had said.

Kiel spluttered out, 'Well not quite, auntie, but with you looking after me, it won't be long.'

They both laughed.

It was high time for him to get away from the table and get ready for the afternoon shift, so he excused himself to get up and go upstairs to change.

They both gave their approval by nodding their heads and saying, 'Yes, of course,' while they continued drinking their coffee and taking things slowly.

He had a lot of work to do with others, so there was no time for him to take things slowly or easy; he would have been too late for the festivities.

He just could not forget this party and all the people who might be there, including Secilia and Juliet, whom he had met before and knew. But what about all the others, especially the guests, how should he have to behave himself and what should he talk about? This made him all anxious again.

Once he got changed and ran across the yard to the cows and calves all had slipped out of his head and mind and he carried on as normal.

By the time it came to feed the calves, he naturally kept looking across the yard in the hope that Secilia would come and give him a hand. But there was no such luck and he began to worry again, although he should have known by now she could not possibly come.

Luckily they managed to finish quite early. Everything went very well, almost like clockwork, after which he said, goodbye to the head cowman and shot off across the yard.

'Hello, auntie, hello, uncle,' he called as he flew upstairs to get washed and changed, to come down again for supper.

They were both sitting near the table waiting for him. Uncle always seemed to be earlier, but then he did have to go back again later to check out the horses before nightfall.

'Come on and sit yourself down, boy,' auntie called out while pouring the coffee, uncle was already feeding his face, helping himself to the lovely German sausage slices to place on his buttered bread.

All of it looked so very inviting, but he told himself not to eat too much since he was sure there would be plenty of food at the party and he would have to eat something there.

'What's the matter, boy, aren't you very hungry, or are you still worried about going over to the big house later?' auntie asked.

Following, uncle remarked, 'I think he is suddenly afraid to go.'

'No, I am not afraid and I am quite hungry, but I shall have to eat something when I go over there and so I have to restrain myself now, although everything looks very nice,' he replied.

He had a cup of coffee and a slice of bread spread it with butter and covered it with some of the lovely looking freshly sliced sausage.

'Yes, of course you must be careful, boy, but do have some more of this nice fresh sausage, that will not hurt you, since you may not get anything but a glass of sherry the very first moment you get there, and at your age you can always eat,' said auntie.

He followed on with some of that lovely liver sausage and *Thüringer Fleischwurst*, which looked so tempting, with another slice of bread and a cup of coffee, to keep both of them happy, and both seemed to appreciate his appetite. He had more sausage than bread and, by golly that really tasted terrific. He nearly had another slice, but I had to be firm and excused himself from the table to go upstairs and change for the evening.

He had thought a great deal about what to put on and laid everything out on the bed, which was not a lot or much to choose from. He only had one suit, which he thought was a little over done, so he chose the dark suit trousers, black shoes, a dark shirt with a cream coloured tie and off-white jacket. Looking in the mirror when he thought he looked quite tidy, he combed his hair with the little wave in front and went downstairs.

'Look at you. Come and have a look, uncle,' auntie called out, and continued saying, 'You do look very smart. I wouldn't mind coming with you and I won't have to be afraid or worry about you anymore.'

Uncle seemed to agree by nodding his head, still eating, which made Kiel feel a great deal better and more at ease.

He stepped over to kiss auntie, which she seemed to appreciate, said goodbye, to both of them, looked at himself in the hall mirror again and went to the door. They both called out, 'Goodbye, have a great time. Don't worry about the time, we shall both still be up to let you in,' and off he went, after giving auntie another kiss on the cheek.

Going across the yard, he was wondering what he should do when he got there, but once again he did not have to concern himself. Secilia and Juliet were already waiting at the garden gate to greet him.

They took him into the garden and introduced him to most of the guests, and to greet the Colonel and the Lady. Every one remarked on how smart he looked, which made him feel almost a little embarrassed but all that was soon rectified.

Secilia called over the girl with a tray of glasses full with a variety of drinks who asked, 'What would you like, sir?' holding the tray towards him.

By golly, she called me 'sir', and with Secilia and Juliet standing around he almost felt like one and asked for a glass of pale sherry, took it and had a small sip, which was great.

'Do you like sherry?' Juliet asked and carried on. 'There are other drinks like beer or Schnapps, cups of tea or coffee, whichever you prefer.'

'You will just have to say or help yourself, Kiel. Don't be afraid, just follow the rest of us or ask.'

'Thank you, my lady,' he replied very politely.

They both began to giggle, and Juliet said, 'You don't have to call me "my lady". I would prefer you to call me by my name, Juliet, and I will do the same to you, Kiel. After all, we are all friends, aren't we?'

This cheered him up no end and he began to relax even more, while the three all of a similar age walked around the garden chatting away as if they had known each other for years. No one seemed to care and all seemed very friendly. He began to feel at ease, or more like at home among friends of the family, although he still had to be a little careful what to say when being asked silly questions.

There was plenty of food around and everyone appeared to help themselves, when Secilia suddenly spoke and asked, 'Would you like something to eat, Kiel? There is plenty and all you do is pick what you want or like.'

'Thank you, Secilia,' he replied and all three of us walked across to the large platform tables to pick up a small plate and proceeded to walk round taking whatever took our fancy.

By the time they had walked round choosing from these delicious snacks, he had almost filled his plate and they all began to eat away to their heart's content and continued walking, and naturally, talking about all sorts of things.

Juliet and Secilia mostly asked him questions about his earlier life and where he actually came from, while he wanted to know a great deal more about theirs, and then they all sat down near a table. Both of the girls or young ladies looked absolutely charming and seemed so friendly, as if we were brother and sisters.

These were lovely little snacks, and one could easily talk and help oneself much easier than holding a sandwich in one's hands. But there was also a barbecue with hot chicken, and rabbit portions as well as the well known *Thüringer roast-brat würstchen'*, known better as roasted sausages, of which he had thought of having one with mustard and a glass of beer, in a minute, since his plate and hands were full at that moment.

This would make a real party for him and they all had a great time, when suddenly the coloured lights came on and a band began to play. There was a small dance floor just inside the tent, the sides of which were rolled up, since it was a glorious warm evening with the sun gently going down in the distance like a beautiful red golden ball, still glowing.

Continuing to walk again, Secilia asked him out of the blue, 'Can you dance, Kiel? I would love to have a dance with you. Would you, please?'

'Oh, dear, Secilia, I can't dance. We did have a few short lessons at school, but that was some time ago and I have forgotten the steps,' he replied in a somewhat surprised voice.

'Don't be so shy, Kiel,' Secilia and Juliet spoke almost simultaneously and continued, 'come on, we'll teach you,' they said.

He didn't know what to do, and what can one do with two females or young ladies almost dragging one onto the dance floor.

'I am sure I will step on your feet,' he said, and tried to get out of it, but there was no escape when Secilia got hold of his hand and virtually pulled him to go with her.

He once again followed like a little dog on the lead, getting very hot under the collar. Placing his right hand around her slender waist, holding her right hand in his left, just as they had been taught, but that was just about the only thing he could still remember.

Luckily it was a waltz, *The Blue Danube*, which was his mum's favourite, and she sometimes got hold of him in his younger years and pulled him round the floor with her.

The music alone made one move in the right direction, but he was very foot-tied and stiff.

'Relax and you'll be fine,' Secilia said in a quiet voice, trying very hard to quieten him down and guide him round the floor.

Having her in his arms with her soft dark, almost black, hair gently weaving as she kept turning her head from one side to the other and her soft body in his shaking hands, when she spoke and said again, 'Relax, Kiel; you don't shake when we are alone.'

She was trying to pull him round from one side to the other. He began to ease up and all went fine, apart from nearly stepping on to her feet once or twice.

The music stopped and he quickly pulled her away from the floor, when she said, 'Steady on, Kiel, you have done very well; we shall have to do this again.'

He was flabbergasted and did not know what to reply, apart from, 'Thank you, Secilia, but I am sure you only say this to make me feel better. I am really no good,' he replied.

'Oh, but you are, Kiel, if only you allow yourself to relax and not to worry. No one takes any notice, they all have to watch their own feet,' she said, and Juliet seemed to agree.

The music started again and Juliet took his hand and pulled him onto the floor, saying, 'Now it is my turn to get my feet trodden on, but be careful. My toes are sticking out at the end of my shoes and I do not like black toenails.' This once again scared him just a little and she realised what she had said and spoke quietly, 'Don't worry, I will not cry out,' and smiled.

He began or tried to relax again, holding her soft slender figure in his right hand and her right hand in his left. They began to glide around the room with the rest of the guests all seeming to watch them as they were dancing or sitting and standing around.

This once again made him freeze up a little and she appeared to notice his tension, and whispered in his ear, pulled him close to her, saying, 'Relax, Kiel, just relax.'

Juliet was slightly taller than himself and his nose was almost lost in her low-cut dress, which did him more than good and relax he did, in more ways than one.

It was a great night from then on and he had several more dances with Secilia and Juliet, the latter being just that little older and more experienced, allowing him to relax easier, or was this really true?

Her long soft blonde hair flowing down over her well curved shoulders often brushed in his eyes and nose. When moving it off he, completely unaware, touched her tiny breasts and apologised, but she did not seem to mind and just smiled. Maybe some of it was a little intentional, which she no doubt realised, and he quite enjoyed the gentle touches now and again, when she just smiled gracefully. She may even possibly have enjoyed the little tickles herself? He most certainly did, not only touching but also admiring these beautifully formed curves.

He relaxed more and more, talking almost all the time until the music stopped and they had to return to join Secilia sitting at the table having a cup of coffee, but no doubt watching all of them throughout.

'You are getting better and better, Kiel. You seem to be a lot more relaxed,' Secilia said, and asked almost at the same time, 'Would you both like a cup of coffee?'

'Yes, please,' Juliet replied and Kiel agreed, fancying a piece of these enormous cream cakes standing right next to them on the table and he helped myself.

Sitting at the table near Secilia, Juliet asked, 'Where do you put it all, Kiel? You don't seem to have grown any taller since we saw you last.'

He must have blushed just a little, because she continued speaking and said, 'You don't have to blush, Kiel, all best things come in small parcels, and I do like small parcels.'

He was not quite sure what she meant by this but it made him feel better. He remarked, 'I am similar to Secilia, she is just as small as myself,' and they all had a giggle.

'Yes, but she might be growing yet; look at her dad, and she is still very young. Are your parents tall?' she asked.

'No, my mum was fairly short and so is my dad and I presume I shall be like them,' he replied.

'Oh, what about your mum? You just said she was short? said Juliet.' Secilia butted in and told Juliet that his mum had passed away, and his eyes must have become moist as usual and she followed on by saying, 'Oh, I am sorry to hear that, you must tell me all about it one day.'

He was in no mood to talk about his mum's departure form life and let it spoil this party, so as usual he replied, 'Maybe some other time. I have not yet told Secilia or her mum.'

He quickly asked Secilia for another dance just to get out of this unfortunate situation and he told Secilia, 'I will tell you one day when the time is convenient and right, and then you can inform the others.'

'Yes, Kiel, I quite understand. These things just seem to slip out at the most inconvenient moments, when one does not quite know what to do or say, but Juliet will understand,' she replied and squeezed his hand.

Secilia seemed so understanding and gorgeous to dance with, when he pulled her a little closer and thanked her. She smiled and they carried on talking, changing the subject.

They passed her mum and dad and Kiel nodded his head while Secilia waved her hand, said 'hello' and smiled, continuing to dance. Kiel asked, 'Do you think I ought to ask your mum for a dance? I would like to do so but I am a little too shy,' he continued.

'Yes, I think you should. She'll like that. You are getting quite good,' Secilia replied, 'and Mum loves dancing.'

This made his halo appear to shine even more and closing up they had a little swirl on the floor, which Secilia seemed to enjoy.

She pulled him even closer and they went round again, turning continually to the right.

'Shall we try and turn to the left next time, which one should do every now and again, especially at a waltz?' she asked.

'Oh, dear, I don't know, I have never turned to the left. We shall more than likely find ourselves lying on the floor,' he remarked.

'No, silly, I'll hold you. Are you prepared to try? We first take a swirl to the right and following, a swirl to the left, and you'll see it is quite easy, Kiel,' she said.

'Okay, I'll let you know when I am ready by pulling you close to me,' he replied, and they managed it without him even stepping on her toes.

The evening seemed to pass quite quickly without him realising it. When he looked on Secilia's wristwatch while dancing, the time showed nearly eleven o'clock.

He seemed to have all the luck; there was no other young man around apart from two younger children, which meant he had the two young ladies almost to himself and hardly missed a dance.

Returning to the table after the music stopped for a little while, Juliet asked, 'Would you like a glass of champagne each and a little rest?' which seemed a great idea as Secilia and himself agreed. Juliet called over the girl with the tray.

That was the first time in his life, even though he was still young, that he had ever tasted this so often talked about clear, cool, almost yellow, golden bubbling champagne and drank the first glass in almost one go, not realising that this should only be sipped and he helped himself to another quickly, hoping no one would have noticed.

Juliet and Secilia smiled, looking at him, and almost simultaneously said, 'you must be thirsty, Kiel. Carry on like this and you will end up on the floor.'

Not quite understanding what they meant by ending up on the floor, he asked, 'What do you mean by ending up on the floor? I have been on the floor nearly all evening.'

They both laughed and followed on by explaining, 'Laying drunk on the floor.'

He had never heard this before. He had heard of people ending up under the table when having too much to drink, but that was something quite new to him and they all had a good laugh.

It certainly was a good job that he had a good appetite and kept eating almost continually, but that was the first glass apart from a glass of wine, a beer and, to begin with, sherry he had all evening.

Although he was no real drinker, all of this seemed to flow down quite nicely and he sipped the second glass while chatting to the two young ladies and listening to the music, watching the others dancing on the floor.

After talking a little while he agreed to go and ask Secilia's mum, Her Ladyship, for a dance, to which she agreed.

He hadn't realised it was a quickstep, which she seemed to perform tremendously well, but he was not quite certain when or where to put his feet, but they managed to get to the end. Talking most of the time and watching others placing their feet, the lady was an extremely graceful and easy dancer to follow. Her slender body similar to Secilia's, just seemed to lie in his arm and every one of her body movements appeared to be transmitted to his. She was gorgeous, seemingly very friendly, and had a continuous beautiful smile; her hair and body perfume seemed to put me into some sort of trance, which made him follow her steps without feeling uncomfortable.

Returning the lady to the table, she thanked him and remarked on his flowing steps and good dancing, which made him feel great. He could hardly believe he was hearing this and thanked her for being an excellent dancer and a good teacher.

Kiel clicked his heels, slightly bowed to the lady and the rest of the people on the table, and returned to join Secilia and Juliet, who both clapped their hands and smiled with approval. Everybody looked and he became hot under the collar again.

'You were great, Kiel,' they both said and continued to praise him for his courage and performance, 'but you don't have to blush.'

'I am certain the Baroness enjoyed you asking and taking her for this dance,' Juliet remarked and said, 'you must do this again, Kiel. She loves dancing and the Colonel is not so keen; he prefers to have a drink, smoke and lots of talk.'

Kiel took Secilia and Juliet again for the next two dances and really began to enjoy the body movements of the young ladies, and slowly became more confident. Feeling the warm soft parts of their bodies against his, as well as the most beautiful scent from their hair and skin, felt like a dream come true.

They had so much to talk about, with lots of laughter and giggling, especially when he made the wrong foot movements occasionally and put them off balance for a step or two.

Returning with Secilia, she had noticed that his buttonhole flower had begun to drop its head and she went off to get him a new one.

This was a gorgeous smelling pink carnation and she replaced the half dead one with the newly picked one, when she remarked, 'You must be a real little flirt for these flowers to wilt on you so quickly.'

'What do you mean by that?' he asked. She gave him a completely unexpected peck on the cheek in front of all the guests, and remarked, 'Now you can carry on flirting.'

'I would love to flirt with you, my love,' Kiel said, in a very soft voice.

She blushed a little and said, 'Oh, would you now, I think you have been doing that all evening with Juliet and me: I have been watching you.'

This obviously turned the colour of his skin and it certainly warmed him up again, when he said, 'You don't think I have been flirting with Juliet, do you?'

'Well, it certainly looked like it,' she replied and continued. 'You do like her, don't you?'

'Yes, I like her. I like her a lot but I do love you and never forget it,' he replied.

'That is nice to hear from you, Kiel, and I do appreciate your remark,' she answered.

Time went by and he thought it a good idea to request another dance from the Baroness, and asked Secilia, while Juliet was dancing with someone else.

'Oh, I am sure she would love this, Kiel, especially now that you have already danced with mummy before and it will soon be time for the last dance,' Secilia replied.

He was beginning to feel quite at home, although most of these people seemed quite out of his circle of acquaintance, but all were very nice, friendly and cheerful.

The music started again and he walked across the floor requesting Her Ladyship for the next dance, which once again she delightfully accepted, placed her arm in his and they both walked to the floor.

This time it was a waltz, which he thought he was quite good at by that time, even being able to turn right and left to break the monotony and make it easier and more interesting.

Secilia's mum started talking straightaway with her lovely soft and seemingly sincere voice and smile. They got on to the floor and started to dance. He held her petite body fairly close to his, so that her gentle motions could be transformed into a mutual movement of exercise, which once again seemed to be a joint venture and went extremely well.

They continued talking while dancing, not taking any notice of feet or movements, and appeared to be floating across the floor without problems.

Her Ladyship suddenly asked him, 'Would you like to join us for supper one evening? What about Wednesday, while Juliet is still with us?'

He was taken completely by surprise and replied in a somewhat overcome manner, 'Yes please, if this suits your ladyship, but I have really nothing to wear.'

'Oh, but you must come in what you are wearing tonight, you are looking very smart,' she remarked.

'Oh, thank you, my lady,' he answered and returned her to the table, leaving with a slight bow and smile to the rest of the guests on her table.

The men were all well dressed, but in somewhat casual wear, the colonel in dark trousers and Scottish type tweed coat with pockets, while Juliet's dad also had dark trousers with a somewhat Bavarian style coat without collar, but both wearing ties.

There was a young man in army officer's uniform and another with open shirt and cravat, with just a cardigan, both of whom had been introduced as Juliet's brothers.

One brother with his wife and Juliet's father, who, he was informed, was a banker in the city of Dresden, not far from there, with Juliet's mother.

And there was the headmaster from the college, Dr Kohl, in a full light-coloured suit and tie, smiling at him, with his wife.

Most ladies wore some sort of silky flowery dresses, with shawls, this her Ladyship always left behind on the back of the chair when dancing, and most had small handbags and wore long-sleeved gloves.

The two children about eight to ten years of age, a boy and a girl, were Juliet's nephew and niece from her elder brother and wife. They were both quite cheeky and yet very friendly and well behaved, but wanted to know almost everything;

where he came from, to what he was doing here and both asked to dance with him, which he happily joined in with on occasions.

We all had a great laugh playing about. The children obviously enjoyed it more than Kiel did, since he wanted to be with the older girls.

He was completely overcome not knowing really where, or which way to look walking back to join Secilia and Juliet, who appeared to be sunk in a conversation and sipping their champagne.

After he sat himself down next to them, they stopped and said, 'Hello, Kiel,' almost together, which made him believe that they had been talking about him.

He asked them both to excuse him, giving them time to finish their conversation, when once again he had to retreat to the big house and the gents to relieve himself of some of the consumed drinks.

He noticed there was also a ladies just opposite, before the large solid wooden staircase in the entrance hall.

After his return, he asked what they both found so interesting to talk about him, and they almost simultaneously replied, 'We were not talking about you, Kiel. Well not directly.'

We were just talking in general about a small dinner party Mummy has arranged for Wednesday, when Juliet's parents are coming to collect her,' Secilia said.

'Oh, what a coincidence, your mum has just invited me to join you,' he announced.

They both laughed out and remarked, 'That is just what we were hoping to ask Mummy to do. Has she really?' Secilia asked.

'Oh, that is marvellous, we are pleased,' they both said as excitedly as obviously he had been, and they all had a good talk and laugh about it.

The music started again when Kiel asked Juliet for the next dance, leaving the last dance, which should be following soon, for him and Secilia and asked politely if that was fair. Both young ladies agreed.

Juliet, as before mentioned, was a superb dancer and slightly taller than himself, possibly only because of her high heel shoes, with his nose tickling her chest, but only when he looked down.

Dancing with her was a real pleasure and easy-going, with lots of talk, laughter and cuddling up close. She seemed very open minded and appreciated any small joke, replying with one of her own almost immediately following. 'You prefer a bird in your hand rather than two in the bush, do you?' she asked, when he preferred not to reply, and took it as a joke.

Juliet appeared to be a girl full of life and taking things as they came without any deep thought of what might happen or come tomorrow and an absolute treasure to have around, and yet she seemed very inquisitive.

The music stopped and he escorted the young lady to the table, while Secilia was still on the dance floor chatting to some other guest after dancing with one of her cousins.

Juliet made a remark and, without waiting for a reply, ordered some more champagne, 'Or would you rather have a cup of coffee, Kiel?' she asked.

'No, dear, that is fine, I would rather have a cool drink, thank you,' he replied.

'Oh, how lovely. I am your "dear" now; what have I done to deserve this?' she commented.

'This is just a matter of speech,' Kiel replied and carried on, 'you are both very dear to me and made me very welcome, which I had never expected, and you are a very fine upstanding young lady, who I respect tremendously.'

'Thank you, Kiel, that is very nice of you to say so, but we both like you and your outward easy-going approach and knowledge of most things. You never seem short of an answer or turn it to your own satisfaction in a delightful, cheerful manner,' she replied.

'Oh, thank you, Juliet, you are so kind. I have learned all this from you and Secilia, since I have been seeing you both,' he remarked and smilingly sipped from the champagne.

Secilia arrived, or rather had been returned by the gentleman she had been dancing with, and commented, while sipping from her glass, 'What have you two been up to? Hopefully not talking about me while I was away?' she asked.

'No, darling,' he whispered in her ear, which Juliet over heard and the talking began again in earnest, when Juliet told Secilia that he had called her 'dear' earlier on.

Kiel felt like hiding his face in shame, but managed to get out of this almost embarrassing situation with tiny excuses and they all had a laugh about his slip of the tongue.

The last dance was announced, and he got hold of Secilia quick, before any of the other guests had a chance to come and grab her, and accompanied her to the floor.

This, as hoped and expected, was a waltz and they had a great time talking and dancing, then about halfway through this last dance;

Juliet, who had been dancing with someone else, came to split us up and requested a short dance with Kiel, then she offered him to the Baroness and took the colonel for the last few steps. It had not turned out quite as Kiel hoped, but it was most certainly a surprise and all went extremely well.

He even managed to give Her Ladyship a peck on the cheek and thanked her for a lovely evening, which, to his amazement, she returned, and reminded him of Wednesday evening.

Kiel returned the Lady to her husband, the colonel, bowed slightly and requested Juliet to accompany him to meet Secilia, for a last quick chat and a goodnight peck on their cheeks.

Later, after a few more words and a giggle, they both took him to the garden gate to say goodbye with another peck on the cheeks, and followed on by waving their hands.

This Kiel returned, and he disappeared round the corner and through the yard back home.

## A Garden of Eden

This looked much like a self-created garden of Eden,
There are many from South Africa, to the north of Sweden.
In there he could see no apple to share,
Nor were there any females quite bare.

The serpent was surely the blonde-haired Juliet,
He was almost certain, she was out for him to get.
But he was not prepared to place his head into a noose,
And much preferred to be caught in a net.

This way he'd survive, avoiding temptation,
Without anyone, chosen for future creation.
Secilia's his type, although she's so calm,
He could hold her tight within his own palm.

K-WA

# CHAPTER 12

The clock had turned midnight and he was wondering if auntie and uncle would still be awake, or would he have to knock on the door to be let in?

The silvery moon was well up in the sky and although all lights were blacked out because of the war, it was plenty light enough to see. By the time he had walked across the yard and especially in his light coat and tie, they had seen him coming and opened the door for him to enter.

They were both as awake as he was and a cup of coffee with cake was already on the table, for them all to sit down and him tell them about the wonderful time they all had. He was not really hungry or thirsty, but could not possibly allow those two eager beavers to twist and turn all night not knowing what went on in the garden of the big house.

He told them all about having been taught to dance by Secilia and Juliet, and even managed to request Her Ladyship for two dances and had a short last waltz with the Baroness before the lights were switched off.

'You did not have the cheek to request Her Ladyship for a dance, did you?' auntie asked, with uncle listening and taking it all in with a grin on his face.

'Yes, I did, auntie,' he replied and continued. 'I should better say I was pushed into taking the first dance with the Baroness, by Secilia, and Juliet agreed. This turned out very well in the end and the Baroness thanked me for dancing with her. The second time I was quite willing to go and request Her Ladyship on my own, and she has asked me to come for dinner on Wednesday evening, so you had better not cook for me that day, auntie, or I will not be able to eat over there,' he said.

'You have never been asked for dinner at the big house for Wednesday! Have you, really?' Auntie wanted to know again.

'Yes, auntie, honestly, and when I pointed out to Her Ladyship that I had nothing to wear, I was requested to wear the same as I had on tonight, since the Lady and others thought I looked quite smart.

'And so you do, my boy. Does he not, auntie?' Uncle butted in.

'Yes, he certainly does,' she said, then turning to Kiel, asking, 'You better let me have your clothes in the morning so I can wash and clean them for you before Wednesday evening, my boy.'

'Okay, auntie,' he replied.

'Now you had better get up those stairs and have a good few hours sleep. It is nearly one o'clock and you have got to be up again by half past four,' auntie remarked.

Kiel kissed her and said goodnight to both, ran up those stairs as fast as his legs would allow him, threw everything on a chair and crawled under the covers quickly, without another thought.

He was not sure how uncle managed to get up again at half past three and help get in the fodder for the cows and other animals.

Those were hard times, but also pleasant, many years ago, when at that time one could leave all the doors unlocked in the daytime and no one would ever think of walking in or taking anything, which did not belong to them.

Uncle gave him a knock and Kiel replied, but turned over for another hour's sleep, when the alarm went off and auntie called him at almost the same time.

His eyes were very heavy indeed after all that drink and activity, but once he used cold water for washing they soon began to open and his body became mobile again.

Trotting down the stairs and across the yard that early in the morning, especially when by now it was beginning to cool down overnight, was a great help to wake up and shake an almost useless body back into shape.

By the time he got to the cowshed the headman was already waiting to see if Kiel was fit enough for work and handle the cows with respect, or he would have sent him straight back home again.

These animals meant a great deal to the headman and he would never, ever have allowed anyone to be cruel or rush them.

Time meant nothing to him and if a cow recognised her calf's cry and would not go outside, the calf had to be brought to the cow and be allowed the last few drops of milk to show her (who liked the calf) that it was well looked after.

He was a great deal more than just a head cowman, almost a veterinary surgeon, and performed many minor operations on the cows before and after calving, et cetera, with their help and would teach us all the while he was doing his job with great precision.

All of the headmen had to hold a master certificate before being allowed to train others, and he most certainly was a master at his job.

They all had to go to school or college training courses once a week to learn or be taught the more modern techniques of looking after and helping animals in need of assistance.

It was the same with headhorse or pigmen; every one had to have learned, passed their apprenticeships and carry on learning before they were given the master certificates, before they were allowed to teach others the same job, especially on large estates, where they had to have a number of people looking after the many individual animals.

These headmen all met with the estate manager and the colonel once a year to put their points of view, gathering in a large room at the big house over a few litres of beer and snacks no doubt, provided by the cook and staff.

The staff consisted of the cook, housemaid and cleaning lady, all living in the upper part of the big house at the rear, overlooking the large pond, or lake, and orchard adjoining the garden; and a gardener, of course, but he lived on the estate.

The Baron's, or colonel's, family had a small beach hut out near the river, near cleaner flowing waters, and only used this pond or lake very occasionally for boating or bathing, but the estate staff often used it through the summer.

There were all sorts of pretty ducks, geese and swans as waterbirds on the water and to take a walk round it was very pleasant, providing one watched almost every step, since the short grass around was soiled by bird droppings.

The water itself was quite clean and almost continually flowing in from a nearby brook, and was often used for the fruit and vegetable gardens.

Waterbirds of most varieties used this lake, which had a small boat to take one from the garden across to the orchard or just to the centre to a small island with a few trees upon.

It all looked, and no doubt was, very romantic when first dug out or built, but by this time it had been taken over by too many waterbirds and fish, and was not as desirable as one would have wished it to be.

Kiel saw it first from the garden, when he thought what a great idea to go for a romantic boat trip to the island in the centre. But when he looked again after partly walking round with Secilia and Juliet, that particular evening of the party and one had to watch every step, his great idea had reduced itself a little, although it would have been nice to take Secilia onto the island. It did not seem quite that glorious as at first thought, although the flowering bushes with short grass on the island and around the lake looked absolutely charming and most inviting in the setting sunlight, but not so inviting in daylight.

They all had to wash their shoes and soles, before returning and entering the garden, on a well and neatly constructed rotating brush wheel with bicycle chain and handle. This was over a trough of water with a water tap above to wash away the dirt, without taking it into the garden or house, and a great idea.

It was now Monday morning and since he had been informed by Her Ladyship that they would go out shopping today, to give their staff a rest, he did not expect to see anything of Secilia and was still quite worn out from the night before.

To his amazement, however, when getting ready to feed the little calves, who should come but both of them, Secilia and Juliet, asking the headman politely if they could both have a look at the calves, to which he agreed.

'Good morning, Kiel, how are you?' they both called out and came to give a hand with the buckets.

'Good morning to both of you. I am fine, but a little tired,' Kiel remarked and carried on. 'And how are you two? Have you had a good sleep?' he asked. 'I have been up since 4.30, but I slept really well. You must have worn me out completely last night.' he said.

'We have worn you out? Now that is a joke! We have been very good; you have worn us and yourself out,' replied Juliet, looking across to Secilia, who nodded her head in agreement.

'That is not fair,' Kiel replied and carried on to say, 'I only did my natural duties and some of the extras I was pushed or forced to do.'

'Oh, you little fibber. No one did, could push or force you to do anything you did not wish to do and we both knew and felt that you really enjoyed yourself,' came the reply from Secilia this time, who seemed a little quiet, or so he thought and nearly asked.

But all was well and they both had a good laugh with him, which did wake him up just that little more.

He asked, 'Are you both going out to town shopping with the colonel and Her Ladyship?'

'Yes, we are,' they both replied.

Juliet followed on by saying, 'We will probably go for a meal and most likely for an evening out as well.'

Secilia agreed and said, 'We might not see you again until tomorrow, Kiel. Will you manage without us for a day?'

This, the headman overheard and called across, 'I very much doubt it, you two seem to be on his mind all and every day.'

That must have turned Kiel a little red under the collar and face, and Juliet, who always seemed to be the first to reply, said, 'You don't have to blush, Kiel, we like to be on your mind, don't we, Secilia?'

They both smiled. Secilia replied, 'Yes, Kiel, and we shall both think and talk about you all the time we are in town shopping and enjoying ourselves, which we hope you will do, talk and think about us until we see each other again.'

'That is nice to hear,' he remarked and followed on by saying, I shall probably be asleep and dream about both of you and the lovely evening we had together until late last night, when I did not manage to go to bed before one o'clock in the morning.'

'Oh, you poor darling,' Juliet called out and followed on by asking, 'what did you do after you left the party, did you go somewhere else?'

'No, of course I did not, I went straight home, but had to tell uncle and auntie all about the lovely time we had over a cup of coffee,' he replied.

'Are you certain it was coffee, and not something stronger at that time of night?' Secilia asked.

'I am quite sure it was only coffee. I had enough of the stronger drinks, while with you. You can only thank your lucky stars I did not have any more or both of you might have got tangled up with me,' Kiel replied, with a smile on his face.

'Oh, Kiel, that sounds intriguingly inviting. What did you have in mind?' Juliet asked.

'Nothing, nothing at all, and I did say might; you are twisting my words and trying to confuse me,' he replied.

'Secilia knows me better than that. I don't do anything without being asked or invited,' he continued.

134

'Is that right?' Juliet asked Secilia or both of us, when the conversation got nearly out of hand and neither of them really knew what to answer and just shrugged their shoulders.

'It looks as if I shall have to find out a little more of this, since you are not prepared to tell me,' Juliet remarked.

'I think you are a little too inquisitive and too well informed at your slightly advanced age. You wait until I get you on my own one fine day, I'll show you what I might or might not do,' he said.

And Juliet replied in her cheeky way, with a broad smile on her face, 'Oh, that is nice, and surely well worth waiting for.'

Secilia did not seem at all interested in our conversation and said to Juliet, 'We had better be going, My parents will be waiting and we still have to wash and change.'

They both helped him to collect the empty buckets, before leaving then said, 'Bye-bye Kiel, hope to see you tomorrow.'

'I shall look forward to that,' he called after them as they disappeared across the yard and through the little gate into the garden.

Suddenly once again he was not certain if he had taken too much notice of Juliet, who appeared to be the outgoing one, and had he ignored Secilia in the process? They both seemed quite happy as they walked away, but one never knows what goes on within a certain person's mind. He was completely confused once again.

He liked Juliet's temperament, her cheerful and cheeky quick approach with answers to every question. She certainly a great deal more forthcoming and seemingly very much more advanced in life, but then she was about two to three years older than us two and already went to the University in Dresden, where they lived. That was a thought, which he unfortunately had to carry around in his head until tomorrow, when hopefully he would be able to see them again, to ask Secilia.

In the meantime we had to finish our work, which took quite another while, before we were allowed to go for our breakfast. By that time most of us were looking forward to it, and a short rest after four to five hours hard work.

Walking across the yard, he could smell the coffee and fried breakfasts from all the cottages at the far end, with the estate manager's house near the big house and lake in the far corner.

Kiel's eyes were looking towards the windows of the big house, but there was nothing to be seen. Perhaps the colonel and family had already left for town with the chauffeur, (the butler when not driving) the car.

After breakfast, Kiel once again put his head down for a few hours before lunch and he had hardly gone to bed when he was fast asleep and did not wake up until a call from auntie came up the stairs.

It was lunchtime already, and once again his stomach appeared to be ready for a refill. The lovely smell alone, coming up the stairs, made one peckish. Although he felt still very tired and not all that hungry at that time, he had no alternative or resistance but to get up and go downstairs and find out what was on the table. Food was one of his priorities in life, especially a well cooked, good smelling and appetising meal, and as usual it was once again most welcome.

It was a lovely day with the sun fairly high up in the sky, when after lunch Kiel thought of going for a bike ride down the river.

This time he took his swimming trunks and a towel in the hope of going into the water to wake himself up completely. There were several other youngsters already there, playing about in the water, which must have been warm enough to go in and have a swim. Taking off his clothes down to the trunks, which he had already put on, he jumped in and joined the others.

They all had a great time for a couple of hours, splashing and playing about. There were several boys and girls most of whom he knew now by name. Several came from the estate, and others from close by.

All of them asked about Secilia and tried to take the mickey, especially as some from the estate had found out or knew that he was invited to join the garden party yesterday.

The estate was similar to any small village or community and nothing could be kept secret for very long and all was discussed by most. But one must never forget that there were very few radios or papers, and most certainly no TV sets to keep people occupied at that time.

Neighbours were few, but most knew each other fairly well, and were friendly.

Gossip, however, has been an old inheritance handed down. This has been going on since time began and no doubt will continue while people are living on this globe.

It is nice when people talk to each other and discuss life or problems; it only gets out of hand when some take things too seriously. Sometimes jealousy sets in, but very seldom in these early days or years, although some of them thought it a bit rich for me to associate with the family in the big house. This Kiel presumed was only natural, especially since after all he was a complete newcomer and the only young male on the estate.

But they all had a great time and jokes as well as child's play took over from serious conversation.

Coming back from swimming and playing about Kiel could once again eat a horse, and the coffee and cake were already on the table. This time it was cheesecake, one of his favourites in those days and he managed three pieces quite easily. Auntie and uncle seemed more than delighted for him to have such a good appetite and only smiled, wondering where it all went.

Uncle was the first to speak out and said, 'Why don't you put a piece in your pocket for later?' Auntie remarked, 'Leave the boy alone, he can have another piece now.'

'Thank you that is very kind of both of you, but I am full up for now and have to try and work it off again, if I can still walk,' he said.

'Of course you can still walk, my boy; in a few minutes you will run about and will have forgotten all about this cake,' uncle replied.

His thoughts were still on Secilia, and how she had taken their previous conversation with Juliet, who was rather forthcoming and myself not the most shy of persons to reply. There was nothing that could be done until they met again, he just hoped that they had a great time together and we would all meet again in the morning.

Work always drags out when one had something else on one's mind and so did this afternoon; everything seemed to go so much slower, and it was one of those days. Even the headman and others asked him what was going through his mind, since it seemed he was not quite with it, or the situation around them.

One can never, or seem to be able quite to, explain and no doubt does not really want to, since one does not really know oneself and is just daydreaming, which unknowingly we all do at times.

But all problems pass and so it was the following morning, when both young ladies turned up again as bright and cheerful as ever, with a 'Hello, Kiel,' and helped him with the feeding of the calves and telling him all about their trip to town the previous day.

Juliet, as usual, spoke first and asked, 'Did you think of us while we were away? I bet you didn't and found better things to do.' This was a question he was at that time not prepared to go into and ignored it. Then she followed on saying, 'We have talked about you a lot and the lovely time we all had on Sunday evening.'

'I have been thinking about all of you all the time and even dreamed about you last night,' he told them.

'Oh, that must have been nice for you, Kiel. What have you been dreaming? Please tell us, as long as it was not a bad dream. Were we kind to you?' she asked.

Oh, lord, he thought he should not have mentioned anything about his dream, now he shall be questioned all day. 'No nothing bad. It was a lovely dream all about us dancing and talking together, getting very close at times, with little warning looks. I really enjoyed it,' he said.

'What did you enjoy most, the dancing or the dream?' Juliet wanted to know.

'I am not quite sure; both, the dancing and the dream,' he replied and left it there without going into further details.

'I would love to hear more about this lovely dream of yours. Will you tell me one day?' Juliet asked smiling and looking across to Secilia, who did not seem to be too interested.

'I might tell you one day when we are alone together, but you'll have to remind me,' he replied.

'Oh, if I have to remind you, Kiel, it cannot have been all that exiting, but I will do that just to find out how much you really like us,' she admonished.

'It certainly was exciting and satisfying, but not as much as being with you in the flesh, and not something one shouts about among others in a cowshed,' he remarked.

Secilia looked at me as if she seemed not over-pleased with the remarks and kept talking to Juliet, what could he do but answer Juliet's continual questions?

So he turned to Secilia and said, 'I will tell you as well one fine day when we are alone walking together. That reminds me, what are you going to do today? Shall we go for a swim after lunch if the sun is still out and shining? There are a few clouds about, but not many.' he asked.

'Yes, please,' Juliet answered quickly. Then, turning towards Secilia, asking, 'Shall we?'

'Yes,' Secilia replied quickly and continued, 'I would love to go for a swim with Kiel.'

'We have never had the opportunity to go for a swim together, have we, Kiel?' She said. 'Although he has been to the river with other boys and girls, or so I have heard,' Secilia remarked to Juliet.

'Yes, I went up there again yesterday afternoon and there were quite a number of young people swimming in the river,' he replied, and followed on, 'but there was no one as interesting as you two, and younger, but we had a great time.

'Oh, they were younger, were they?' Juliet wanted to know, and followed on, 'I hope you have behaved yourself.' That remark he allowed to flow like water off a duck's back.

'That is what we will do then, we'll meet you as usual in the yard, and don't forget to bring your swimming trunks and towel and not find any excuses,' Secilia pointed out.

'No, I won't, or try not to. Don't you forget your bathing costume either or I shall push you into the water in your dresses,' he promised.

'Oh that sounds romantic,' Juliet replied, 'but how can we get the dresses dry again, apart from lying down near the waterside with nothing on, which might scare you off, Kiel.'

'I am not that easily scared,' he replied and continued. 'I shall have to leave this decision to you both, and hope that you will do the right thing, but I shall close my eyes should you have to lie on the riverside with nothing on.'

'You are a spoilsport, Kiel, I thought perhaps you might want to do the same, so as not to shame us,' Juliet replied.

For a moment he just did not know what to say without this girl turning it all upside down and placing him in a difficult and compromising position.

They both said bye-bye and disappeared out of sight so quickly he could not reply, leaving him with all the clearing up to do. He did not know whether they had been in a hurry as Secilia had been once before, overexcited or had just forgotten that clearing up was as important as feeding.

That is the problem with high society girls, who never seem to have anything to do at home and have everything done for them by staff or parents. He would have to teach them not to run away again in future. But then he was always only too pleased to see them, even if only for just a few minutes and they nearly always helped. They must have just forgotten or perhaps were called, away, which he may not have heard.

After all the cleaning down and clearing up, they were all once again allowed to go for their own breakfast, and his stomach was rumbling already. Kiel certainly loved his food and nothing or no one would have stopped him from consuming a good breakfast after several early morning hours of hard work.

After that lovely mid-morning meal, he went up to lie down again for a couple of hours to make up for the early start and to be ready to go swimming after lunch. Swimming is always easier after something to eat, although not with a really full stomach. Just as one should never go onto a boat with an empty stomach, as one will surely be seasick, since the contents of a half empty stomach will float about inside similar to water, up and down.

On coming downstairs he had to have his lunch before even thinking of running away, which was a good thing or he might have been too early, since he was keen to go.

Even though no actual time had been discussed or remarked upon, he was just about finishing his lunch when auntie said, 'Look who's out there waiting for you.' And she asked, 'Are you going swimming? They seem to have got their towels with them.'

'Yes, auntie, if the water is warm enough and the sun is still shining. There are a few clouds in the sky, but they are quite high up and small,' he replied.

'You be careful and don't catch a cold. Wrap yourselves up with towels when coming out of the water, especially if there is a little cool breeze blowing near the river,' she advised, which was very nice.

Kiel said, 'Thank you, auntie, for your good advice, which we may not have thought of, but we will try and cuddle each other if we are cold,' he laughed.

'Don't you be so cheeky, or they will not take you swimming again and will tell their parents,' auntie remarked.

'I had better run or they will get cold waiting for me and we will have to have a little cuddle before we leave.' he teased and called out, 'Bye-bye, see you both later,' and he run across the yard to the two young ladies, who were patiently waiting and chatting to each other.

'Hello, my two precious birds,' Kiel said when he got there and continued, 'I am sorry but auntie held me up, giving me a lecture, about us wrapping up after getting out of the water if there is a cool wind, so as not to get a cold. I told her that I would look after you two and I was sure you would look after me by cuddling up together.'

'You didn't say that, did you?' Secilia questioned.

'You are naughty; you should not say such things or people will get the wrong idea, especially the older ones. We'll make sure you wrap up in your towel,' Secilia replied.

'Oh, you are two spoilsports,' he said. 'I had so hoped we could all cuddle up together if chilly?'

'What about all the other children and young people who might be there?' Secilia asked.

'They can do the same, if they so wish, but there might not be anyone else there, or at least I hope not,' he replied.

Both looked at each other, not knowing quite what to say as we walked along, then Secilia suddenly spoke and said, 'I brought along the key for the little hut for changing in, we can always sit in there for a minute if it should get chilly.'

'This is nice of you to think about that, which makes it easier. We can all go in and change,' he replied.

'No, we cannot,' came a quick answer. 'Well, yes, we can all go in and change, but only one at a time,' Juliet said.

'Why is that?' he asked. 'It seemed large enough for all of us to get in there at once the last time I saw it?'

'Yes, it is large enough for all of us to go and sit in there, but hardly big enough for all of us to change and, after all, you are a man and we are two ladies,' Secilia remarked.

'Oh, you are spoilsports. You have upset me now; I was full of hopes, expectations and surprises,' he replied.

'You can still be full of hopes and expectations, Kiel, that is what life is all about, but look how much nicer it might be just to wait and hope,' Juliet carried on saying.

'Perhaps you are right, Juliet. I'll just have to wait and see how things develop and continue to hope as you so kindly pointed out,' he agreed.

Walking along, which took about fifteen minutes they reached the river. There was not a soul to be seen anywhere, apart from the boats on the water.

The sun was still high up in the sky and Kiel reached in to feel the water, which seemed quite nice and warm, which he told the two ladies.

'Please take the key, Kiel, and you can change while we have a little stroll, and just leave the key in the open door when you have finished, so we can go and do the same after you,' Secilia said and handed him the key of the beach hut.

It was certainly quite comfortable in the little room or hut, with plenty of hooks to hang the clothes on, and a window, which looked out onto the river. He did not really need a changing room, since he had already put on his swimming trunks underneath the trousers, but it was nice to be able to hang everything up nice and tidy.

The cheeky young ladies came and peeped through the window, giggling, and gave a knock on the glass, but he had already undressed to his trunks and laughed back.

Going out to meet them, he told them both he would do the same to them in a little while when they were in there and they took notice and drew the curtains, which he could see while swimming in the water, which was very pleasant.

A large boat came upriver and made a massive swell, and he almost swallowed half the river, which was not too pleasing, but no harm was done.

In a little while, both of the shapely ladies came in their swimming costumes to join him and they all had a short swim upriver allowing the water to carry them downstream again after a while.

By that time they had all had enough for the first swim and climbed out onto the nice green grass covering the bank for a lie down.

All of them were breathing heavily and the young ladies' chests, moving up and down, was quite enjoyable to watch. Then they suddenly opened their eyes, looked at him and almost simultaneously said, 'What are you looking at, Kiel?'

He didn't know what to say for a second, then saw some birds flying in the air, and said, 'I was just looking at those birds and their lovely movements.'

'I am sure you were looking at lovely movements, Kiel, but not the birds; your eyes were on other things,' Juliet remarked.

'No, you must have got the sun in your eyes as you opened them, Juliet,' he replied, 'they were honestly going up and down just like fish in the water.'

She laughed, 'I don't believe you. Fish do not go up and down, they normally swim like people, in a straight line,' she said.

'Yes, normal fish do. I agree with you, but I meant the more exciting larger fish, like dolphins or whales,' he replied.

'I don't believe you, Kiel, but I must admire you for having an excuse for every question asked, and hope you enjoyed what you admired so much,' she said.

'I certainly did,' he answered by saying. 'What goes up must come down', and 'a bird in the hand is better than two in the bush.' But I have not been that lucky, although I would not have minded having two in my hand.

They both looked at him with some astonishment and a little smile on their faces, and he was not sure if he had said the right thing. They soon burst out laughing, obviously not expecting quite what he had expressed and both turned over on their tummies.

Secilia turned her head and spoke first, saying, 'Either you have another quick swim to cool down, or get changed before we do, since it is nearly time for all of us to return back home.'

'I will have another swim, to give you two beauties a chance to change in comfort. Give me a shout when you are ready; it will not take me long to dry and change,' he said.

'You had better be careful what you say or see next, you might get more of a surprise than you bargained for,' Juliet remarked.

'Oh, lovely,' he replied, and said, 'there is another old proverb: 'There is a lot of good in the worst of us, and a lot of bad in the best of us, so it does not behove any of us to speak ill of the rest of us.'

'Where do you get all these phrases from?' Secilia asked and followed by saying, 'You had better have another dip in the water, before you teach us any more.'

In he jumped, which seemed a little cooler than before, since they had been lying out in the warm sunshine, but it was delightful and refreshing.

He saw the two young ladies disappear into the hut with a little wave and smile. He almost got it into his head to get out and try to have a peep, but one must not be too forward or friendship could quickly turn into unfriendliness, and that he had to avoid.

After a short swim up and down, he saw both reappear fully dressed and calling him over. They once again looked charming with their silky dresses clinging somewhat tightly to their shapely bodies so that he had to have another short dip into the water to calm down.

'You had better hurry,' Secilia called out, 'it is time for all of us to go for coffee, or they will send out a search party.'

'I am coming,' he called back and after another short dip into the water and swim, he struggled out onto the bank, rushing quickly into the hut to dry himself up and change.

Oh, dear, he forgot to bring his pants, since he dressed into the swimming trunks earlier. It never occurred to him to bring them along. What could he do but slip into the trousers, with shirt tucked well around him, after a thorough drying? Luckily it was a fairly long shirt and all went well. He locked the door and joined the ladies for a slow stroll back to the estate.

'That was a lovely afternoon,' he said, and carried on 'I hope you have both enjoyed it as much as I did?'

'Yes, Kiel, we've had a great time,' said Juliet, turning her head, looking at Secilia, and both smiled in agreement.

'We shall have to do this again,' Secilia answered and asked at the same time, 'When will you have some more time off, Kiel?'

'I will have two hours again in the morning, if this suits you two best,' he replied.

'Right, tomorrow morning it is,' said Juliet. 'Hopefully it will not rain tomorrow. What about it, Secilia?'

'Yes, that is fine with me. We can always go again in the afternoon if the weather is still fine and warm,' she replied. 'What are you doing this evening, Kiel? Shall we all go for a little walk?' Secilia asked.

'Yes, that will be absolutely wonderful,' Juliet butted in and continued. 'If the weather is still fine it will be a great evening together.'

'That reminded him of another little phrase, that should always be remembered,' he remarked, 'which goes something like this, "Whether the weather is cold, or whether the weather is hot, we'll weather the weather, whatever the weather, whether it suits us or not!"

'You seem to be full of old proverbs or phrases. Where do you get them all from?' Juliet enquired.

'I don't really know,' he replied, and continued, 'it must have been my dear mum or dad, but many other people have come up with some on occasions. They just come into my head now and again.'

By that time they had reached the estate. We said goodbye to each other and went our own short way back home with a short wave.

Kiel could smell the lovely coffee before he even opened the door. He said 'Hello,' to his auntie and uncle and added, 'What a lovely aroma, auntie?'

'I hope you are hungry, boy; we are having your favourite cheesecake on the table again today. I hope you will like it reheated?' auntie enquired.

'Like it?' he answered and carried on, 'I love it, especially the way it looks and smells from where I am standing just now, auntie,' he replied, and sat down, beginning to stuff his face, or so it must have seemed to the two sitting opposite him. It was delicious and another piece was required to satisfy his appetite. 'Oh, that does taste good again, auntie, but then your baking and cooking always does,' he said, and continued. 'We have been swimming and walking, which made me really hungry.'

'We can see that, my boy,' uncle pronounced, 'but don't let that stop you. You go and enjoy yourself and have another.'

'No, thank you, two pieces are quite sufficient,' he replied, and washed it all down with some strong coffee, after which he had to go and change for work.

'Are you sure that is all you have been doing swimming and walking?' uncle enquired.

'Well, apart from a little lying down, talking and laughing, undressing and dressing again, that's all, uncle,' he replied.

'Dressing and undressing?' auntie spluttered out. 'I hope you have behaved yourself with these two young ladies around.'

'Yes, auntie, I must have done, since they have asked me to go out for a walk with them again after work and supper,' he remarked.

'Have they really?' uncle butted in, and carried on, 'You or they must be an extremely welcoming sight to be so keen?'

'Oh, they certainly are, uncle. You ought to come and have a look yourself; that will bring your eyesight back again,' Kiel replied.

'Don't you be so cheeky, my boy,' auntie commented, and continued, 'there is nothing wrong with your uncle's eyesight if he wants to see anything. You go and enjoy yourselves. That is something for the young; uncle would get too frustrated, not knowing how to handle the situation any more,' auntie said.

Kiel just remembered not having talked about a specific time for this evening, and he had no idea as to when they would be coming again, but with some luck he might see them later.

While he had some time on his hands, he helped auntie with the clearing and washing up, so that uncle could sit down to have his after coffee forty winks. Finishing that, he climbed the stairs to have a wash and change, put his pants underneath his trousers again, when auntie called, 'It's time for going to work. Are you ready?'

# CHAPTER 13

He shot down the stairs and out of the door and ran across the yard to work, carrying out the very same jobs day after day, when the two young ladies came round again to help.

They discussed the time to meet up again to go for an evening walk and they went off, while he, with others, had to carry on till finishing, before being allowed to go for supper.

Then, while still eating and drinking, auntie called out, 'There are your two ladies waiting already, you better rush,' and he did, across the yard.

'Were you not quite ready, Kiel, or are we too early?' Juliet requested to know and carried on. 'Have you had your supper?'

'Oh, yes, that was already waiting for me, before I arrived back from work,' he replied, 'but I was still eating and drinking when auntie told me that you were waiting.'

'You should not have rushed,' Secilia said. 'We would have waited or come and called for you.'

'That is nice of you,' he remarked and they carried on walking.

On the way through the yard, they just turned their heads and saw the net curtains in the little cottage move, and auntie's head disappearing.

'Your auntie is very interested in what you are getting up to, Kiel. She is a nice lady and certainly seems to look after you well,' Juliet remarked.

'Yes they both are very nice. I like them both and we get on well,' he replied.

Walking slowly along the little track, Juliet asked, 'Have you been here before and do you know them well?'

Kiel had to explain that he had never been here before, but they both knew him and the last time he had seen them was at his dear mum's funeral some years ago, but not since, until he turned up out of the blue in May this year.

'Oh, that was when I first met Kiel, and we have been friends ever since,' Secilia told Juliet.

'I hope we shall all remain friends for a very long time, now that we've all got to know each other so well,' Juliet interrupted.

'And I hope we shall remain friends,' Kiel said turning to Juliet, when he suddenly notice a slight change in Secilia's eyes, and he quickly butted in and said, 'I mean all of us.'

By that time we had reached the woods, with more and more animals around the edges, feeding and running around playing. They both sat down quietly, one either side of him, watching and talking or pointing at some different movements. It was a wonderful sight to see all the smaller animals playing around their parents, when the young were more interested in playing than feeding.

Later lying there side by side, with the golden sun beginning to settle behind the horizon, with both these soft warm bodies near him, he felt wrapped up in love and told them so.

They both seemed quite surprised to hear him say this, when Juliet asked, 'Are you in love, Kiel, and who with, we would like to know?'

'Both of you,' he replied and continued. 'You are both like sisters to me and keep me warm,' when they both looked at each other, not quite knowing what to say, but appeared to have liked what was said, and agreed.

After a while we got up and slowly returned once again, strolling along arm in arm in the silvery moonlight, discussing our next morning's meeting to go for a further swim.

We arrived at the gates, which were still open, said goodnight with a small peck on the cheeks and a little wave, when we all went our own way back home.

Meeting up again next morning feeding the calves, the girls arrived and, as always, gave him that soft smile which was worthwhile waiting for after a good night's sleep and early morning start.

After feeding the little calves, they returned for their breakfast, which Kiel or they all did after finishing the clearing and cleaning up jobs. He met up again with the two young ladies after breakfast and they all strolled up the farm track to near the river.

It was once again a beautiful late morning with the sun high up in the clear blue sky, with just one or two small white clouds around. They arrived near the river after a short walk.

'Shall I change first again?' he asked Secilia, who handed him the key for the beach hut.

'Don't be too long,' Juliet called out, 'We would like to follow you into the water to cool down a little after our walk.'

'You can go first,' he said, 'I am in no hurry. Or you can come with me, I won't mind.'

'No, perhaps you won't, Kiel,' Secilia suddenly spoke up in a quiet voice. 'But I would, and I would rather you go and then leave the key for us, please.'

'Don't be jealous, darling. I would love you to come as well, or should I have asked you first? I am sorry, I did not want to hurt you or leave you out. I hope you know that.'

'Please, Kiel, just go and get changed and disappear into the water, which will do you a lot of good,' Secilia spoke, seemingly a little concerned.

It appeared that he had upset poor Secilia. This was not his intention at all, but no doubt easily done if not very careful, which was difficult with Juliet around.

Without any further to-do, he took her advice and went along, changed quickly and dived into the river before any more damage could be done.

The water was quite warm but not as warm as the previous afternoon, since water in large rivers continually flowing and being turned over by large boats going up and down never really gets as warm as in a pool or pond.

While swimming, he saw them both going into the hut waving at him, so obviously he had not upset either of them, or at least he hoped not.

Soon after, they both came to join him for a swim and afterwards they lay on the riverbank on their towels in the short, fresh cut grass to dry off. While he was lying between them, we had a lot to talk about and both tried to take the mickey. Trying not to upset either one, he took great care in his answers.

Then they started tickling him and he had always been very ticklish. He had no alternative but to run away, something he never thought he would have to do from ladies. As much as he wanted to do similar to both of them, he thought better of it, since being overpowered by two girls can be a little embarrassing. He jumped back into the water with the threat that he would do the same to them when coming out. Although, he would have been a great deal more honourable and restrained his enthusiasm leaving this promised episode for some later date

They quickly went back into the hut to change, so as not to lose their bathing costumes in the process.

Kiel climbed out of the water again after a river crossing, which was not the easiest with boats about almost all the time.

After getting out of the water, he managed to get into the hut on his own, got himself dried up and changed for their return walk to the estate.

Walking back on the narrow driveway, he managed to get hold of both, one on each side and managed to do virtually the same to them as they had done to him earlier. They both shrieked out and took off like two shots from a gun.

They soon reunited after he promised not to do this again and they carried on talking while trotting slowly along under a gorgeous blue sky with the sun still high up.

Walking past the wood, the golden brown leaves came swirling down in a gentle breeze covering the ground. These were nice and soft to walk on, especially in bare feet, which they all three were at that time.

These two young ladies were made for each other and both seemed to understand his cheeky ways most of the time, but it sometimes seemed that a little jealousy would creep into Secilia. Or was this just his sensitivity? This they would have to wait for a while to find out after Juliet had returned home and they were once again on their own.

After getting back to the estate, he gave them both a peck on their cheeks and said, 'Goodbye, hope to see you later if you are allowed to come out again.'

They both did the same in return and wandered off toward the big house and garden gate, where they disappeared from sight after a brief wave.

He went across the yard to the little cottage for a nice lunch, which auntie had already placed on the table. She had been watching out for them to come home and saw him with both Secilia and Juliet, arriving and parting company at the gate.

'We saw you giving them both a peck on the cheek,' auntie remarked.

Uncle grinned all over his face, and said or asked, 'You seemed to be getting on quite well together; have you all had a great time?'

'Yes, uncle, we seem to understand each other quite well and they both got hold of me and gave me a really good tickle while lying down near the river,' he replied. 'We had a lovely time swimming and I ventured right across the river at one time while the girls went into the hut to change, but they both watched me, or so they mentioned,' he said. 'We have already provisionally arranged to meet up again this afternoon for another swim if the weather is still fine, and the sun shining. There are a few clouds in the sky,' he told them.

'Oh, are there, now?' auntie asked and carried on, 'You don't let the grass grow under your feet do you?'

Not really knowing quite what she meant, since he had never heard this saying before, he enquired, and she said, 'You don't waste any time getting to know each other do you?'

'Oh, no, auntie,' Kiel replied and continued. 'There isn't much time since Juliet is going home again tomorrow evening after the dinner party.'

'You haven't forgotten about this then?' auntie enquired to know and carried on. 'I hope you have behaved yourself with those two young ladies, or you will have to answer to the colonel and Her Ladyship, tomorrow evening.'

'You don't have to worry about that, auntie, I have been on my best behaviour all the time,' he replied. 'Well, part of the time at least, but I have so far not received any complaints from the two young ladies. 'I had better go upstairs and change a little. Will you excuse me, please?' Kiel asked.

Kiel was sure they loved the calves more than him and in return the calves seemed to like and lick them. Especially after Secilia asked earlier, 'Shall we go swimming again this afternoon, Kiel?' and looked across for Juliet's approval.

Kiel answered, 'Yes, please, I thought we had already agreed to go.'

'Well, yes, we had, but there is always a chance that you might have to change your plans, so I thought I had better ask, since we do not really want to go on our own. You are so much more fun to have around and make us laugh nearly all the time, apart from when you start tickling as you did this morning on our return walk.'

'That is nice of you two. You need a chaperone to look after you both and make you laugh; I am just the person who can do this well,' he replied. 'Yes, of course, I shall be happy to come along and look after you two beautifully blooming and smelling flowers,' he said.

'Oh, we are both flowers now,' Juliet remarked and carried on. 'As long as you remember to keep only smelling and not picking, we shall be happy to come.'

'But that is not fair. A gardener has to be allowed to do everything which he thinks necessary at certain times,' he replied.

'No, no, no, a gardener is supposed to do as he is told and to leave the best till last, not as he wishes to do,' Secilia pointed out.

'Oh, but that is not fair. Everything always tastes best when still young, firm and fresh,' he remarked with a laugh.

For once he seemed to have had the upper hand for a while, and they looked at each other, not quite knowing what to say.

But Juliet, as usual, found her tongue and spoke first, saying, 'A gardener should never have the right to taste fruits without having been given permission from the owner.'

This most certainly put Kiel in his place, for which smart remark he had no real answer and gave up trying.

They all returned to the house calling out, 'Goodbye, see you later, Kiel, and be good in the meantime.'

He looked up, called back, 'And the same to you two rose petals. I shall be ready and waiting for both of you.'

And he was, by the time they turned up to be seen from the window, when he ran out to meet them in the yard as usual.

Meeting up again, they slowly walked towards the river, hand in hand, but he was not quite sure why, although they had done this before. He thought it might be so as to keep his hands inside theirs and not allow them to wander into places they were not welcome, and he asked to be sure.

'Yes, you are a little free with your hands at times and they are better held tight,' Secilia remarked.

They had a wonderful time again, with several dips in the water and afterwards lying in the sunshine to dry off, but it was slightly more overcast by now.

They all changed, he having to go first again. They did not seem to trust him going with them and, to be quite honest, he was not sure if he could trust himself or Juliet, but she seemed a very friendly, open person, and not in the slightest concerned. At least that was the impression she always gave him, but one can never tell for sure.

Having had a great time in and near the water again, with lots of talk and laughter, they returned home once more with lots of chatter, departing at the gate as usual.

He was ready for a nice cup of coffee and a piece of auntie's gorgeous cake, which he could already smell before getting to the door.

Having had their snack, which was very welcome, Kiel changed and went back to work again as usual Luckily his two lady friends turned up again, calling out, 'Hello, Kiel,' and helped with the feeding.

He had just about time to go to work and as usual found the headman and the rest of the workforce waiting for him. He was almost certain this man had never been late or lost a few minutes in his life and was dedicated to his animals as no one else could ever possibly be.

It did not seem to matter what time one came to the premises; there the headman was waiting and nearly always smiling. He seemed to be Mr Patience himself with a smoking pipe continually between his teeth and making certain everything was in its right place at the right time. He also seemed to know almost everything, from repairing water pipes to electric fittings, and was happy to teach us all he knew.

After fetching in the cows, feeding and milking them, Kiel's usual job was, as always, to feed the little calves and look after them.

Later he met up with his two helping and talkative ladies.

Secilia spoke out first, 'What are you doing this evening, Kiel? We thought of going for a walk; are you coming?'

'Yes, please. I would be only too happy to come along; there is nothing I would rather do. I have nothing special on, thank you,' he replied.

'Nothing special on,' Juliet remarked. 'You look alright to me,' she joked.

'We'll see you later then, about the same time. Bye-bye,' and off they went, leaving him with all the clearing up to do.

This was not the most pleasant and he would have to tell them not to run away before all was cleared up in future, but how could he? After all, they were helping him without pay.

They met up again that evening after supper and had a long stroll virtually all round the estate, talking, laughing and watching out for wildlife most of the time.

They sat down in the wood at one stage, watching the little fox cubs playing with each other outside their parents' lair.

There were other animals and birds around, and they had a wonderful time lying there watching and whispering into each other's ears.

Every now and again Kiel would get just that little closer and nibble one or the other's ear lobes, when in return they would try to bite his.

Sitting there among the trees, with the autumn leaves fluttering down upon them in a slight breeze and covering the floor like a pretty carpet, they chatted very quietly so as not to disturb or chase away any timid creature. This, however, was a bit difficult, with all three of them trying to please the other and the animals at the same time.

After chatting for a little while, it suddenly came to light, from Secilia, that Juliet actually had a boyfriend in town and she was looking forward to going back home again the next night, after the dinner party.

This came as a little shock or surprise but, after all, she was slightly older than the two of them, and a very lively and beautiful looking creature. Juliet was a very pretty and outgoing girl and although Kiel was a little shocked to hear this news, it was not really unexpected, and after all he was in love with Secilia.

Juliet did not seem too keen to have this broadcasted, and made out that it was just a passing relationship with a boy from college whom she had met up with again in university. They teased her for a little while, and she did not really quite know what to say and even blushed once or twice, but Kiel made up by giving her a little cuddle and then had to do the same to Secilia, all of which he enjoyed.

After walking back, they reminded him not to be late in the morning. The weather was nice. They shook hands, said goodbye and goodnight with a little peck and wave, and they all returned to their respective homes with a smile.

Kiel was once again happy to know that all had turned out well, which he reported to auntie and uncle over coffee and late supper, which was ready, with the table and chair waiting for him to sit down.

Soon after, he climbed the stairs and went to bed for a good night's sleep, which he certainly needed after a full and hectic day out with those two and work in between.

He woke up again with uncle knocking on the door in the early morning; then he turned over again for another hour and climbed out after the alarm went off. Cold water would do the trick to open his eyes ready to go downstairs and to work.

Juliet and Secilia once again turned up to give him a helping hand, with their sparkling smile, saying 'Hello, Kiel, how are you this morning?' Secilia spoke first, followed by Juliet.

'Thank you, I am fine, and would love to do the same thing again as we did last night with the two of you,' he said.

'What is that then, lying among the leaves or nibbling each other's ears?' Juliet asked.

'No, silly, going to sleep with you,' he replied and they were both stunned for a moment, as everyone was listening. 'I thought I would teach you a lesson for continually taking the mickey,' he said.

'Yes, that is fine,' Secilia replied and carried on, 'but you must not speak too loud for everyone to hear and look.'

'Oh, I am sorry. I spoke a little loud, but that was intentional, since you both knew I meant going up into the woods for a walk last evening,' he replied.

'We both agree, don't we, Secilia?' Juliet answered, and continued, 'I did not enjoy going to bed on my own, so I cuddled my doll, thinking it might be Kiel.' She laughed and looked at Secilia.

Kiel did not know which way to look; not knowing what she really meant by this remark, and he must have got a little red under the collar.

'Don't worry about it, Kiel, I was only kidding, to teach you a lesson. Now we are quits again, I hope,' Juliet announced.

'Have you forgiven me? Are we still going swimming this morning after breakfast, Kiel?' Juliet asked.

'Yes, of course. I am all the more keen to pay you back for your cheek, humiliating me in front of all the others. I will tell them now that I normally sleep with you but I was too tired and worn out last night,' he replied.

'Don't you dare. I will never forgive you if you say anything like that and I shall hear of it,' Juliet remarked, not looking amused.

'No, of course I won't. I would not be that silly and would love to remain friends with both of you,' he replied, which seemed to bring back a smile on her face.

As previously agreed, they all three met up again later after breakfast. When the two girls came to look for him at the cottage this time, he must have been a little late again.

They both came along giggling or smiling, giving Kiel an indication that all was back to normal, and he greeted them with a handshake and a kiss on the cheeks.

After going to the river, once again having a wonderful time, chasing each other on the short green grass in the sunshine, they began to tease him again.

By the time they had to return they were all exhausted and all three of them starving hungry.

They reached the gate, him saying goodbye to the two sparkling beauties, and they returned their delight with a kiss on his cheeks. They all returned to their respective homes, with a wave.

Kiel could once again smell the lunch before entering. The lovely aroma was once again so strong and great, when he was waiting with eager eyes to see what was coming, sitting near the table and asking.

'This time we have *Wiener Schnitzel* (Pork chops rolled in breadcrumbs and deep-fried) with sauté potatoes and a freshly cut crisp salad. I hope you like it,' auntie replied.

'Like it? Yes, I love it,' Kiel replied, 'especially the way you dish it up with a lovely gravy, auntie,' he announced and began to eat this delicious meal. 'That tastes good, auntie,' he said and carried on, 'We have had a long walk and swim, which certainly made me hungry.'

Those two, as always were delighted to hear Kiel say this, including all the news, and wishing him the very best for the future. During and after lunch they always had a good old natter, when he told them all about their wonderful walk through the woods and a nice swim afterwards.

These two young ladies had completely turned his head and thoughts, to the point when he no longer knew exactly where he was or what he was doing at times.

After this lovely lunch Kiel went up stairs to lie down for a while and went off into a short deep sleep.

Uncle later knocked on his door to wake him, calling for him to get up and go for work, which gave him quite a shock.

He once again used cold water to wash and wake him completely, although they had no alternative. There was no such thing as hot water or a cistern in the house those days.

He was in good time and the headman was surprised to see him fully awake and remarked on it by stating, 'I would have thought those two young ladies would have worn you out by now with all their walks and talks?'

Not really knowing what he meant, Kiel carried on walking and talking, saying, 'No, not really, I enjoy their company and laughter. We had a great time up in the woods last evening, and again this morning while swimming.'

'Oh, did you now? You will have to tell me all about it one day when we are all alone,' he replied, as they both went out together to fetch in the cows for milking.

Kiel just ignored his remark and carried on with what he was doing as if he had not really heard, since it should have been of no importance to him or anyone else. He was just being nosy, like most people.

After milking Kiel did the usual thing of getting the food ready for the calves, and this time he knew he had to do it all himself since the girls would be getting ready for this evening.

'Oh, yes, you have been invited for dinner by Her Ladyship tonight, have you not? I hope you'll enjoy it,' the headman remarked?'

' Yes,' Kiel replied and carried on with his work.

After finishing he once again went home for supper and he began to feel a little uneasy about the dinner invitation later, and how to behave himself at the table with all other guests, Lady and Baron looking at him, and told auntie and uncle about it.

'Don't you worry,' auntie and uncle said. 'The knives, forks and spoons will all be laid out for you, just watch the others and follow suit.'

'Take it nice and easy and don't bolt your food, and you will be fine and enjoy yourself, you'll see,' auntie told him.

Following his little snack with auntie and uncle, he excused himself from the table, went upstairs and got changed. Luckily he did not have to shave at that time, but used a little aftershave lotion to make him smell refreshed.

He combed his hair, replacing that little wave at the front, of which he was very proud in those days, put on his jacket and walked downstairs.

'You look great again. I wish I could be at your side, going out somewhere,' auntie remarked, and uncle agreed, which made him feel a little easier.

He said, goodbye to both of them with a little peck on auntie's cheeks, which she appreciated and he walked out of the door, with all eyes following.

Shortly thereafter, he had only just arrived at the small garden gate when it opened, and both young ladies, looking very smart, were waiting for him. They guided him into the house and introduced him to everyone, which took some of the uneasiness away.

'Doesn't Kiel look smart again, just like the other night,' Juliet remarked and placed her arm into his, to lead him to the girl with a tray of glasses filled with drinks.

He once again took the clear, golden-looking sherry, which he liked at the garden party and they strolled over to Secilia, who later walked him to the already laid table. As he hoped, his seat was in between the two pretty young ladies, with whom he could converse easily and he could observe from them how to behave.

Her Ladyship sat almost opposite, and Juliet's mother next to her, with the two gentlemen sitting opposite each other at the table ends. It was, as mentioned, a small evening dinner party with only the two families and himself.

Kiel knew everyone from the previous garden party, and it was nice to meet all of them again, although he was still a little apprehensive.

However, with the two young ladies both side and the Sherry, he began to ease up to chat away with all the others.

Two serving ladies arrived with the butler and began to serve the starters, which he had never heard about and did not know what to have. There were two varieties and he picked pink watermelon, as did the ladies beside him. This he had heard a great deal about but never seen or tasted it before. He did not have a clue of how to eat or handle it until he watched the ladies either side; they never normally had starters at home. It was very tasty and refreshing, sweet and juicy and most welcome.

The dining room was quite large with a high, well-decorated ceiling and crystal chandelier, as were the walls and large floor-length curtains. All this was very different to what he had been used to, as were the serviettes on the table for hanging down one's front in case of spilling or wiping one's fingers or lips.

After the servants had cleared the starter dishes away, dinner was served, and the aroma as it came along was once again just fantastic.

It was wild boar, which he had heard of, but never eaten before; it was served with red cabbage and potato dumplings and, naturally, gravy, all of it standing in the centre of the table to be served as desired or self-service apart from the meat, which was brought in on hot plates and placed before each and everyone of them.

Kiel requested for just one dumpling like everyone else. The hot gravy, something he always liked with his dinners, was standing on the table to help themselves. The taste was something out of this world and although he wanted to keep digging in, he managed to restrain himself, eating slowly like the others.

Carefully watching everyone else with great care, and since they were continually talking and asking questions, they all took very small portions at a time, which was a good idea, and this he followed.

While at home he would have got stuck into it with gravy running down his chin, but it was just as well.

At home, as children, we were not allowed to talk while eating or over dinner. Here everyone talked, laughed or smiled almost all the time.

They seemed more interested in Kiel and where he came from, his upbringing and schooling. The questions were never ending and neither were the answers. Once he got used to someone, he could talk through the back of his head and had an answer to any question put to him, which may not have been in the most educated way, but talk he could, and everyone seemed to like listening.

He told them that he was born in a Dresden hospital before being brought home to Strehla just down the road, in which they seemed quite interested and curious.

The colonel seemed to know his grandad, who was a master builder, and his brother, who was a blacksmith.

The latter had seemingly shod his horses at times some years ago, which was also very interesting to him.

Then they asked about his dad and mum. When he told them that dad was a builder but not a master and mum's dad was a bank note printer for the Dresdener Bank in Leipzig. He told them of his mum's departure early in her life, but avoided further questioning in regard to this.

Luckily things became quite interesting and the conversation seemed to be going on and on, since everyone appeared to be interested in bank notes including himself. Although Kiel was interested in placing these in his pockets, the colonel was actually a bank note collector and showed him some of his collection later. This was very interesting indeed, although most came from the great German inflation period, of which there were many around but old and worn ones. His collections were all perfect, almost new coins and crisp notes with many from earlier years.

Kiel was glad he took only one dumpling at dinner, since after the main meal, there was a dessert course of ice cream, or black cherries with custard.

He once again followed the two ladies and had ice cream, one of his favourites, and then he had some cherries and custard to follow.

He had to admit his aunt's and mum's dinners were wonderful but what he had this evening overtook the lot. Obviously the company had a great deal to do with it, and this having been the very first dinner in well-educated and pleasant surroundings no doubt helped.

After dinner there were drinks, when the gentlemen retired into the smoking room, where they asked him to join them, but he declined, saying he would join them later for a while.

He was much happier in ladies' company and had a lot more to talk about among his own generation, nor did he want to be drawn too deeply into his poor mum's departure from life, which luckily the two young understood and seemed to keep away from the subject.

Juliet, as always, took him by the arm and asked, 'Would you like to have a look round the house with me and Secilia?'

Kiel was a little surprised that Juliet and not Secilia asked, but since they had obviously talked about it and both agreed, he was delighted, took their arms and followed, looking for Her Ladyship's approval, which came with a smile. No doubt he would have gone with Juliet, without any questions asked and probably enjoyed it more, but caution is of prime importance, especially in a situation like this.

They all walked through the dining room into the hall and climbed the massive staircase. They showed Kiel the gangway and window they had previously waved from, then on to the master bedroom with only just a glimpse through the door. This was very large, with adjoining bathroom or ensuite, looking out over the garden and lake.

There were more bedrooms, including Secilia's. We went inside this one, which was attractively laid out and well-decorated, with an adjoining door to the master bathroom, again looking out over the large garden at the rear of the house.

We sat on the bed, which was covered with a flowered silk bedspread, when Kiel got hold of Secilia and nearly took the chance of pulling her over, but thought better of it, and just gave her peck on the cheek of approval.

They chatted for a while, Juliet sitting in a chair by the bed, watching every move his hands made, smiling all the time, and looking very graceful with the light shining on her blonde hair.

They continued their walk and came to Juliet's bedroom, which was at the far end, still overlooking the garden at the rear; all other bedrooms facing the yard were seemingly guest rooms, into one of which he was shown later. Once again, Juliet's room was quite large, extremely well decorated with floor-length curtains, which every room seemed to have, and a crystal chandelier.

They sat on the bed for a short while, talking about various things. This time Secilia sat on the chair and Juliet on the bed close to Kiel, virtually rubbing shoulders.

He said, 'You have a lovely bed. I wish I had a bed like yours, then I would no longer have to sleep on the floor!'

They both laughed out loud and asked, 'Do you really sleep on the floor at home?'

'No, not really, that was just one of my jokes, although I have done occasionally.'

Juliet smelled divine sitting next to Kiel, just like Secilia, when her flowing hair once again tickled his face and he tried to brush it away.

Juliet laughingly grabbed hold of Kiel without any warning and laid him flat on the bed. She fell over as well and although he felt a little embarrassed, allowed her to kiss and cuddle him, virtually rolling on top. Her warm, soft breasts touching, and her arms around him, there was nothing much he could do but enjoy the moment, however short.

Secilia did not seem to be quite that amused with their cuddling and rolling on the bed, but smiled and said, 'You had both better get off there before something happens which you both might regret.'

They did that and, after straightening up, continued their walk, when they pointed out the staff quarters at the end of the corridor with an adjoining door, before going down again.

Kiel gave Secilia a gentle squeeze and a peck on the cheek to say, 'Thank you for showing me round and looking after me.'

Arriving at the bottom of the stairs, they ran into the two older ladies, who asked them if we wanted a drink, to which they all replied, 'Yes, please.'

The two young ladies joined their mums for a cup of coffee, while Kiel chose a glass of wine and went to join the gentlemen for a few more minutes in the smoking room.

There he had a really good look at the marvellous collection of bank notes mentioned earlier, which interested him almost as much as the two ladies

The colonel got up from the chair and explained that German banknotes existed only from 1874, while before that only coins or private country notes were used, of which he also had quite a collection, and Kiel's interest grew even larger. He had never heard of anyone collecting money and placing these in frames or drawers for future historical interest.

The smoke was getting too much for him and after chatting for quite a while, he excused himself and joined the ladies again, who in turn showed him the rest of the house, and introduced him to the staff. By that time he felt like one of the family and was completely at ease with everyone around him and himself.

It was a beautiful evening with the half moon and stars shining; there was no wind, but lots of fresh air, so he asked if they should have a short walk round the garden.

Her Ladyship was all for this and grabbed his arm, or rather placed hers into his and they both took the lead, with everyone, even the gentlemen, following.

'Have you enjoyed yourself, Kiel?' the lady asked politely.

'Oh, yes, my lady' Kiel replied, 'it was, or still is, wonderful and I have enjoyed the food, drink, company and every minute.'

'That is nice to hear,' Her Ladyship answered and added, 'We shall have to do this again one day and you can tell me all about your dear mum.'

'Yes, my lady, I will, but you must forgive me if I get moist eyes. I always seem to when I talk about Mum; she was such a delightfully kind and caring mother,' he said.

'I quite understand, my boy (she called me "my boy" which made me feel even better), it is difficult to talk about someone one loved after they have departed,' she replied.

By that time they had almost walked round this lovely garden full of sweet smelling flowers and shrubs, so they all retreated back indoors.

Looking at the clock, which stood at past eleven or 2300 hours, he remarked, 'I had better be going home so that Juliet and her parents can drive back to Dresden, which is quite a distance.'

'Oh, you don't have to worry about that,' Juliet remarked, and carried on. 'We have been later than this at times, haven't we, Daddy?' she asked.

'Yes, we have indeed, but it was usually weekends or Saturdays when we could lie in the next morning, but I have to go to work in the morning, so we do not want to be too late, honey,' he replied.

This was a good enough hint for Kiel, although they could have gone any time they wanted, but he knew he had to respect their feelings. Kiel said, 'Goodbye to everyone,' and kissed the lady's hand, to thank her once again for the lovely invitation and dinner.

Following our last minutes chatting, the two younger ones accompanied Kiel to the garden gate, holding him tight so he could not escape.

There he could not restrain his feelings any longer and cuddled both, especially Juliet, who said; 'I hope we shall see each other again, Kiel, it has been nice to meet you!'

He kissed both young ladies, then Secilia spoke and said, 'I will see you in the morning with the calves, and try to be good in the meantime.'

'Thank you, dear,' he said, kissed them both again and gave Juliet another extra handshake, cuddle and departed, calling back, 'Thank you both again for a lovely evening. Goodnight, and if I can't be good, I shall be like you two!'

Kiel felt like a little prince, leaving two lovely princesses behind and joyfully walked back home, where uncle and auntie were already waiting for him.

Naturally, he had to have another cup of coffee, but no cake, telling them both all about the evening meal et cetera, especially about the bank note and coin collection.

Uncle said, 'You had better not tell anyone else about this or the house might get broken into and you wouldn't want that to happen, would you, my boy?'

'No, most certainly not, uncle. I will be careful and would be ashamed of myself if this occurred. Thank you for mentioning it to me,' Kiel replied.

They were both overjoyed for Kiel having made such a good impression and for not overstaying or taking advantage of their kindness.

They all went off to bed after saying goodnight to each other when Kiel retired to his own little room.

After undressing and placing his clothes neatly on the chair, he rolled into bed without even looking out of the window again.

He was so happy and fell into a deep sleep until he heard the knock on the door from uncle and his footsteps downstairs. He replied and turned over for another hour, only to wake when the alarm went off.

# CHAPTER 14

Another day's work, an overcast sky with high clouds, which looked like clearing up soon again and, looking later, he was right. By the time they had finished the milking the sun had broken through, but not as bright as in previous days but it was still nice and dry.

Getting the calves' buckets and food ready, Secilia turned up as bright cheerful and beautiful as ever, with a big smile on her face, calling out 'Hello, Kiel, good morning,' and began to sing.

'Oh what a beautiful morning, oh, what a beautiful day, oh what a wonderful feeling, everything's going my way!'

Kiel was quite amazed at how she seemed to suddenly be so bright and cheerful and he said, 'Hello and good morning, Secilia, you look and sound full of life. Have you had a good night's sleep or perhaps a lovely dream?'

'I had a lovely night and dreamed about you and your constant cheekiness to Juliet. She is a lovely girl,' Secilia said and enquired, 'isn't she, Kiel?'

'Yes, she most certainly is. I would love to meet her again sometime,' he replied.

'Would you, really? Well, she went off with her parents last night and in the meantime you will have to put up with me alone. I hope you won't be too disappointed?' she remarked.

'No, I am sure I won't. What are you intending to do today, Secilia?' he asked politely.

'I would love to go for a walk after lunch, but want to have a short rest before, if that suits you, Kiel?' she enquired and looked sheepishly across with her usual little smile.

'Who could resist a lovely smile like this?' he said, and continued, 'Yes, that would suit me just fine, since I would like to have a short rest after work and breakfast, making up for the lack of sleep last night.

'Lack of sleep last night?' she enquired, and asked, 'Who have you been with after leaving us, which was still before midnight?'

'Yes, darling, it was, but only just before midnight, but I had to get up again at half past four, when you were still fast asleep and snoring,' he replied.

'I do not snore,' she said. 'I have never snored. What a cheeky accusation to make!'

'Oh, yes, you do, darling, I have heard you, when standing under your window at night,' he replied.

'You never stand under my window at night, do you?' she enquired.

'You did not even know which window belonged to my bedroom until last night, you tease,' she replied, laughing and pinched his arm.

'Ouch, that hurt. Sorry I should not have accused you of snoring and pretending to listen. I would not do that, I would come straight in,' he said.

'You had better not. Anyway my bedroom is upstairs, and you would need a ladder,' she remarked showing a little pink on her gorgeous neck.

'Yes, darling, you are absolutely right. I haven't got a ladder and would have to call on you to drop me a rope,' he said.

She suddenly realised he was kidding once more and smiled most invitingly, and said, 'I could not drop you a rope, since my bedroom is right above the conservatory and you would break the glass.'

'No, I would not do that; your parents' windows are right next to yours and that would wake them. I would be ever so careful,' he remarked.

'I think the best thing is to forget about all this and concentrate on your work for now,' Secilia replied.

She helped him with the clearing up and the cleaning of the bucket before she excused herself and left, calling out, 'Don't forget about this afternoon?'

'I won't forget and will be looking out for you, or you can call on me if I am a little late, thank you,' he called back.

After clearing up and cleaning everything, they all went for breakfast and he for a short lie down upstairs thereafter.

Kiel went off to sleep again in no time at all, only to wake when auntie called him for lunch.

He went downstairs with still sleepy eyes and yawning, when auntie said, 'You had better go back to bed again after lunch, my boy, you are only half awake.'

'Oh, no, I shall be fully awake by that time, after I've got my teeth into your once again deliciously smelling lunch,' he replied.

'It's only a sausage casserole, but it does smell nice I do agree with you, I just hope it will taste as good as it smells,' auntie remarked.

It was lovely with vegetables; carrots, cabbage and buttered baked potatoes, upon which he remarked, 'I would like to have this again.'

Uncle agreed, making auntie a happy woman, saying, 'Yes, I do agree we shall have to have this again another day; that tasted quite good.'

'Yes, auntie, that tastes lovely,' he said, when thereafter uncle and he had to have another helping to finish off the lot.

It always pleased auntie when we had a good appetite, since she loved cooking and baking, but was not too keen on housework, although everything looked sparkling to him.

Secilia turned up and, with his mouth half full, he ran outside to meet her, 'Hi, honey,' he shouted, 'I hope you have not been waiting long? We must have been busy eating and talking not to have seen you earlier,' he spluttered out.

'No, no it's all right. I have only just come. I have not been waiting, although I hoped you would soon be coming; I don't like standing around waiting for long, people might soon start talking,' she remarked.

Although we did not really mind what some might say, we liked each other and thought to be in love, when nothing else matters.

Kiel took her hand and off they walked up the small road or track towards the wood. The weather held out, with the sun still shining now and again, but it was not as warm as the previous few days.

Talking all the way about the night before and the previous few days with Juliet around, Secilia suddenly said, 'Have you missed my personal and private company?'

'Yes, dear. You are so very much quieter than Juliet, although I do like her. She is a girl full of fun, but I do love you,' he replied.

Seclia gripped his hand really tight, and he knew she had been a little resentful at times, when Juliet tried her best to needle him. That seemed her way of showing her friendship towards him and he had to respond, hoping to meet up with Juliet again.

Getting just inside the wood, they sat down, admiring all the wild animals feeding and running around with birds flying about and little fox cubs playing around once again on top of the dirt heaps scratched out of the burrows by their parents.

Lying there, just the two of them alone, quiet and peaceful, he realised what he had missed these last few days, having to respond to two of them. They had been very hectic, with quick responses having to be found, which was at times a little strenuous to say the least, albeit very satisfying at times.

Kiel pulled Secilia slightly towards him, inhaling her gorgeous fragrance and kissed her to thank her for a lovely restful and relaxing afternoon. After walking slowly back hand in hand he realised that the feeling was mutual since she responded by squeezing his hand every now and again.

Arriving near the entrance gate they once again gave each other the usual peck on the cheeks, shook hands and waved each other goodbye.

The afternoon and evening shift went well and Secilia came to give him a hand with the little calves again.

Secilia suddenly spoke and said, 'What are you going to do this evening? 'Shall we go swimming again?'

'Yes, I would love that,' he replied, and she returned home with a smile.

It had just started to rain or drizzle when she returned and said, 'I don't think we can go tonight, it is beginning to rain, we shall have to leave it till tomorrow.'

Kiel agreed and waved her goodbye although he would have loved to go, and so would Secilia, she looked a little disappointed after returning to tell him of the rain. But that is life and the weather decides all people's fates at times, sometimes for the better, since restraint was probably a better idea at this particular time.

An early night was on the cards. Although Kiel could not go to sleep very early, but slept well later, was no doubt the best thing, especially when he woke like a new man in the morning.

It was still drizzling and everything around seemed damp and dull, not at all like the lovely days they'd had lately. But, like the old saying, 'All good things come to an end one day', which once again seemed to be true.

Secilia came to assist Kiel once again but did not look at all happy, so he said, 'What is the matter, dear, you don't look your usual self. Where are all those lovely smiles?'

'It's the weather,' she announced and carried on 'I was so looking forward to going swimming with you today, since we could not go last night, and now look at it.'

'Don't worry, dear, there are several more days left to go swimming before you go back home to Berlin,' he replied.

'You never know with Daddy. We have been here a week and the war does seem to go on and on with no end in sight,' she remarked. 'With this in mind there is always a chance that Daddy will be recalled at a moment's notice and we shall all have to go with him,' Secilia said.

'You don't have to go, my dear. I will look after you if you stay behind. I shall even be happy to move in the big house with you,' he replied.

'Oh, would you now, Kiel?' she remarked and continued. 'That is very nice of you, but on what shall we live, fresh air?' Secilia questioned.

'You always look on the black side, my love,' Kiel replied and carried on. 'There is always a way and we would not want much. We could eat with auntie,' and Secilia smiled again.

'You know what I told you and Juliet about the weather: "Whether it's cold or hot, or we like it or not, we shall have to take it as it comes," he said, and she smiled again.

'If it is still raining after lunch, will you come round to see me? I would love to write those little phrases down.' Secilia asked and continued, 'I shall look out for you and meet you at the gate. But if it is fine and has dried up by then, I shall wait for you in the yard and we can go swimming,' she said.

'Okay my dear, your wish is my command, and I shall be only too happy to follow your wishes,' he replied.

After work and a good breakfast, he went upstairs to lie down for a couple of hours and went off to sleep, only to awake when auntie called for lunch.

It had stopped raining but everywhere was dull, wet and a little cool; no way could we go swimming.

Kiel told auntie and uncle, 'I have been invited to go to the house and see Secilia and the family for a couple of hours if it is still wet and we could not go swimming.'

'Oh, have you now? You will soon be living and having your meals there,' auntie commented.

'No, I don't think that will happen for a very long time, if ever, although I did mention it to Secilia only this morning,' he remarked.

'You have never been that cheeky, have you?' auntie said, and looked spellbound for a little while.

'Yes. I thought it would be nice if Secilia stayed behind in the big house if the colonel was to be called back suddenly, and I could go and look after her,' he mentioned.

'You cheeky little fellow,' auntie remarked, and continued. 'What would you be living on?'

'I told Secilia that you would be willing and able to cook for us both.

'You cheeky little monkey,' auntie called out.

'You seem to think of everything apart from where the money is likely to come from. That does not fall out of the sky you know,' she remarked.

He excused himself from the table with a smile, and asked, 'Can I help with the clearing and washing up, auntie?' Auntie replied, 'No, my boy, you take yourself off and behave yourself. Uncle can help for once.'

This Kiel did not need telling twice. Although he did not mind the washing up, he did not like the drying, in case something slipped out his hands, which has happened many times before at home, when most times he had to do it all himself.

He combed his hair and disappeared, walking through the yard, when he heard Secilia calling him from the garden gate.

He rushed and kissed her, took her hand and said, 'Hello, darling, how are you feeling now?'

'Oh, a lot better since you are here to see me after all. I thought perhaps that you would not be coming since it has stopped raining, but it is too wet and chilly to go swimming, and lie on the ground thereafter. You might as well come indoors and meet Mum and Dad,' she said.

Kiel did just that, and was offered a cup of coffee with them in the ladies' coffee room, with a large conservatory adjoining, both rooms with a view over the garden.

'I thought you would rather be in here than next door in that smoking room, since you do not seem to like the smoke too much,' Her Ladyship pronounced.

'Yes, thank you, my lady; the only thing I do like in there is the colonel's fine collections, and uncle has informed me not to mention it to anyone outside,' he said.

'That is very wise, my boy,' the colonel butted in, and continued, 'I should have told you this myself, but with all the talking I forgot,' he remarked. 'If ever you would like to see these collections again, please do not hesitate to ask, my boy, you will be very welcome,' he continued.

'Thank you, sir, that is very kind of you. I shall have to do similar when I get older and have the money,' he replied.

'Oh, you don't have to have a lot of money, boy, just collect what you can afford and when. You will find from small acorns large oak trees begin to grow,' the colonel replied.

That was quite a good phrase, which I shall have to remember, Kiel thought.

Secilia spoke and asked, 'Shall we go upstairs for a little while?'

'Yes, thank you,' he answered and got up from the chair.

The colonel had called him 'my boy' over this. He was quite surprised and took it personally, but it surely was only a general expression, and he could not hope for more, but was overwhelmed to hear him say that.

He excused himself and followed Secilia again like a little dog on the lead up the large staircase.

We went into her bedroom, and she asked, 'Would you like to see some of my collections of poetry books?'

'Yes, please,' Kiel replied and opened one.

She was very interested in poetry and had collected all the books she had ever seen, which were quite a few.

While he turned the leaves, she wanted him to repeat all the phrases he had used when they were on their own so that she could write them down, which took his concentration.

This collecting she had obviously inherited from her dad. It was a great idea, of which many people never think, until it is too late and it becomes very expensive.

He enjoyed reading some of these poems, but he was not the best of readers or writers since he had lost a lot of his early education with his dear mum's departure from life, which suddenly brought back memories with his eyes becoming moist.

Secilia asked, 'What's the matter, Kiel? You are crying.'

'No, its nothing, really. I just sudden thought of my dear Mum's agonies and her dying,' he replied.

'You must tell me all about your mum, which might help. It must have been quite a shock to you at that time?' she asked and put her arm around Kiel.

'Yes, I must. I remember when she had been to hospital several times for operations over a few years, one day she came home to rest.

'This was late in spring and very hot, with flies being around all over the place, her lying in bed and Dad having to go to work. It was a Saturday morning and I did not have to go to school. Dad asked me to look after mum and try to keep the flies away from her so she could go to sleep and have a good rest.

'Although we had fly strips hanging all over everywhere to catch them, the pests seemed to be around in millions and one settled on Mum's stomach. I found myself holding a fly swat to hit the poor little thing over the head, but I hit poor Mum's wound and she jumped, crying out. This burst the stitches and she began bleeding.

'I did not know what to do and ran away crying, but she called me back, cuddled me and asked to fetch a towel and go to the farmer Kirste to phone for the doctor quickly. This I did. When the doctor came to see, she was taken back into hospital and died a few days later, poor mum.

'This made me think (and I still do) that I had something to do with her dying and departure from life at such an early age. She was just thirty-three years old and myself seven.

Kiel carried on, 'She had stomach cancer, no doubt, by trying to feed us two growing boys and a working husband and starved herself in those terribly bad years in the 1930s.'

Telling Secilia all this and thinking back to those terrible years made him cry again, and Secilia took him in her arms and tried to convince him that it was not his fault, and he must never, ever think it was.

That was easily said; many other people had tried to tell him this before but he could never get it out of his mind. Especially when dad always thought and told him he should not have done that, killed that fly on their Mum's operated stomach.'

She was such a very kind and loving person, and mum to all of us. I shall never forget and always remember her and that day or time.

Secilia, however, tried her best to talk him out of it and held him even tighter in her arms, which he seemed to appreciate but it did not remove the guilt he felt.

He dried his eyes, had a few words with Secilia, then he suddenly found himself kissing her and holding her tight to him, which seemed to help.

Secilia responded and came even closer, with her tender breast touching his chest and her amazingly beautiful dark hair falling around his ears, which tickled when he held her head in both hands and kissed her passionately. He soon found himself beside and on top of her as they rolled around on the bed enjoying every moment of their togetherness.

### Tender Love

We laid there in the bright of light,
The sun was shining very bright.
Although we wished it would be night,
Since lying there, embraced quite tight.

We were in love, there was no doubt,
And of this both of us were proud.

We whispered in our ears, not shout,
And quietly we kissed, not loud.

We cherished our little time on bed,
When only tiny words were said.
Until there was a call, disguised,
And quickly, we got, up surprised.

K-WA


Suddenly a call from her mum, who was coming upstairs, maybe hearing the creaking of the bed. 'Secilia, are you all right dear? You are very quiet in there. Can I come in?'

'Yes, of course, Mummy. We have just been looking at some of my poem books. Kiel is very interested, just as he was with daddy's coin and bank note collections,' Secilia replied as the door opened and Her Ladyship appeared.

'Oh, you have been busy by the look of things around you. You had better tidy your bed before coming down. Daddy wants to know if you still want to go to Strehla with him,' she said.

'Oh, yes, of course. I had forgotten all about it. When is he going?' Secilia asked.

'In a little while dear, I think, but there is no great hurry, he will wait,' she replied and turned to go back outside and downstairs.

'I must be going as well, to change and get ready for my afternoon shift,' Kiel remarked.

'You don't have to run away, Kiel. There really is no hurry, but I thought that Secilia may have forgotten, with you two being so busy, and we have to have a cup of coffee first, before you go off,' Her Ladyship pointed out as she left them alone.

'That is kind of you, my lady,' he called after her.

Thereafter they both tidied up the room and bed as well as themselves, before they both went to joint Secilia's parents downstairs.

Coffee was brought along by one of the servants. This they once again took in the gentlemen's or smoke room, which had been thoroughly aired out and cleaned.

There was little or no smoke smell around; this gave Kiel another chance to look at the colonel's fine collections about which they talked and he showed him again.

Kiel suddenly thought of telling him that he had a few old silver three and five mark pieces given to him by his dad, 'But these are not as fine as yours, sir', he remarked. 'I also have a very nice, large nearly new four pfennig copper piece, which came out in 1934, but these were not liked by the people and no longer produced,' he continued.

'That is quite right,' the colonel remarked, and continued, 'I never managed to keep one of those. They will be quite rare one day. You have to keep this one in particular, and the others; they are still silver and worth a little more than they were in the days issued. You seem to have an eye for quality and no doubt will make a fine collector yourself one day,' he said smiling.

'Thank you, sir. I will try, but I will never come up to your fine standards,' he replied.

'Always remember, to buy and collect only the very best you can find, or can afford to buy, and exchange the others for better quality later,' he remarked.

This I shall never forget, he thought to himself. The colonel is a very good teacher and those things one has to take notice of in life.

The colonel was already dressed and seemed quite eager to go, so he said, 'Goodbye, sir, goodbye my lady, thank you both very much,' and Kiel turned to go.

The colonel suddenly spoke again and asked, 'Are you coming to the Strehla Feast tomorrow? I, or we, would like to see you there.'

Kiel replied to his request with, 'Thank you, sir, I will most certainly try if I can possibly get away in good time.'

Not knowing anything about it, he asked Secilia on the way out, when she replied, 'I was going to ask you to come along but we have not really had much time to talk about it. Will you come, please? I would love you to. However, I will see you later or in the morning. Thank you for the lovely afternoon; we shall have to do this again,' she said, and turned away with a smile on her face, giving him a peck on the cheek. Secilia appeared to be full of smiles when she brought him out through the garden and said goodbye.

'Thank you for asking me round. I really enjoyed it and agree with you wholeheartedly, we shall have to do this again,' Kiel replied, shut the gate behind him and ran off home.

Kiel was full of joy and enthusiasm; this afternoon certainly seemed to have been a breakthrough in their relationship, which appeared to develop in the right direction. He was glad he managed to get his dear Mum's death out in the open but in his heart, where she will always remain for as long as he lives, and with this, he seemed to have broken the ice. Secilia could from now on tell all the others without him getting moist eyes or him having to worry about feeling embarrassed in future. This certainly was a large stone lifted from his conscience and he seemed a great deal happier walking along.

# CHAPTER 15

This large Strehla Feast, on the bank of the great river Elbe, takes place every year. He could still remember it from his very early years now it had been mentioned again.

There were those great wheels, roundabouts with music, shooting galleries, ice cream and candyfloss stalls, et cetera, which was quite an excitement for the little boys and girls at that time, many years ago.

It seems that the colonel had been requested many times before, when available, to open this great festivity. Kiel mentioned it to auntie and uncle on his return. Both knew all about it but had not mentioned a word to him earlier. They hoped that Secilia would tell him all about it, since they no longer went, as it was too far to cycle at their age, or so they said.

Secilia just made it back before he finished feeding the calves and came to see him, asking to meet her for a little while this evening, when she could tell him all about it.

He naturally agreed. He could never be seeing too much of this attractive and smart little creature.

She later turned up and came to meet and collect him from the cottage after supper, since they had no time to talk earlier when she came to see him quickly near the calves. Secilia had only just returned from town with the colonel, her dad, only to say, 'See you later this evening,' and ran back home again.

The weather had settled again but it was still damp on the ground, so they went for a long walk, when she told him all about her dad being requested to open the great feast.

This would start the next morning at eleven o'clock, which would then go on right through the weekend, or longer if the weather kept fine.

Secilia asked if he could come along. There would be plenty of room in the car, which he would enjoy, especially arriving with Secilia at his side. But he had to be back again for lunch and afternoon shift, to look after the animals, so he promised he would go there on his bicycle and would come back in the evening after work to meet up again, which seemed quite a good idea.

Secilia butted in and said, 'You don't have to go home for lunch, there will be plenty to eat and drink at the feast and we could be together for quite a few hours.'

'This sounds great, but I shall have to talk this over with auntie first. She might want me to eat at home.'

'You don't have to do everything your auntie or uncle say; I don't. I should think Mum and Dad would come home for lunch, but I shall stay there and enjoy myself,' she replied.

Secilia looked quite a little charmer of self-determination at that time, which he would never have thought of her. He had never suspected this from her, and always thought she was completely following into Mum and Dad's footsteps and requests.

How wrong can one be at times, and one can learn every day, but then he was just a visitor in regard to auntie and uncle, who were not quite like his Mum and Dad.

After this long, slow, cuddly walk with Secilia, and back home, he requested to be allowed staying over at lunchtime. Auntie and uncle quite agreed, when auntie suddenly hugged him.

'The only thing is, you have to pay for everything there. So you better take some money with you.'

This, of course, was something he had not considered and there was little cash lying around in his place. He had no mum and dad to pay for everything. This got him worried again.

Uncle and auntie promised to help him out with a bit of change or a few Deutschmarks.

He could perhaps go to his other uncle, auntie and cousins, the latter of similar age to himself, who lived in the little town of Strehla and they might help out a little as well, but he had not been to see them since being around in the area.

Why is life always so complicated, especially when everything else seems to run so nice and smoothly?

But cheeky as Kiel was, he managed to get off quite early that next morning and cycled to uncle, auntie and his two cousins to Strehla, who were more than surprised to see him after so many years and he had to do a lot of explaining, in a short while.

He left his bicycle there for safety, and after asking uncle and auntie, they did give him some more money and after saying thank you, off he went with his two girl cousins, who were more than eager to see the colonel's young daughter.

On the way down through town, they ran into their granddad's brother and wife, or great auntie, who both still lived in town and once again a lot of talking had to be done, with time running by fast.

With his luck they helped out with some money and he seemed to have quite a pocketful by this time, and they all wanted him to come and see them again one day.

Almost running down the hill from the old Roman castle right at the very top, they did eventually reach the feast, and he was getting anxious to find Secilia.

Looking around through the crowd, all were listening to the colonel's opening speech with curiosity.

Eventually he spotted Secilia almost the same time as she saw him. She came over and said quietly, 'Hello, where have you been? I have been looking out for you for some time?'

'Yes, I guessed you had,' and he had to tell her the complete story, trying to introduce her to his two cousins at the same time, who had suddenly disappeared among the crowd, not to be seen anymore. They both listened to the colonel finishing his speech. The colonel, in uniform, stood on a small platform, Her Ladyship sitting beside him. She then got up and both waved to the crowd and declared the fair open.

Everyone cheered while the ladies waved their coloured handkerchiefs and children began to run around, then the music began to play and the roundabouts started to move.

They both went to shake hands with the colonel and Her Ladyship, when they spoke almost together and said, 'You both go enjoy yourselves; we shall see you later.'

Off they went, stopping first at a shooting gallery, when Secilia asked, 'Will you have a go and try to get me a little something to remember you by?'

Kiel thought he was quite a good shot from other previous feasts and said, 'Yes, dear, I will try my very best,' and asked the guy behind the counter for a gun and six shots.

Kiel was not very lucky since the gun no doubt had been fixed like most and the gun sight had to be aligned first. He apologised, and Secilia said, 'Never mind. Go on, have another go. I'll buy the next six shots,' which she did.

By then he had managed to sort out the gun's alignment and managed to knock down all six metal animals as they passed at the rear.

Secilia cheered loudly, placed her arms around him and gave him a peck on the cheek. They could either have a doll or a teddy bear, and she choose the teddy bear and said, 'Now I can call him Kiel and take him to bed with me every night.'

Kiel felt quite proud of himself and said, 'You could have saved your money and I would have willingly come to bed with you every night.'

She laughed and replied, 'I know that, Kiel, and would love you to come, but you will be here and we shall be back in Berlin soon. Maybe at some later time. This way I shall never forget you.'

'That means I shall have to have another go and get myself a doll and take to bed with me, so I shall never forget you,' he replied.

'I hope you will never forget me without taking another doll to bed with you every night,' she remarked, with a smile.

'No, of course I would never forget my little darling as long as I live, never mind just going to bed with you,' he pronounced, and she hit him with the teddy bear.

'Oh, poor little fellow,' Kiel said, and continued. 'If you treat him or me like this, he won't be too pleased to go to bed with you, and neither would I.'

'You should not make fun of me,' she replied, 'and I would not have to hit you,' and she cuddled the little bear.

'That is what I would do to you Kiel, if you behaved yourself,' she continued and gave Kiel another cuddle.

'What, only that? This you can do to me here and now, we don't have to go to bed for just a cuddle,' he said and ran away. She chased him, and caught up and they fell in to each other's arms for another little cuddle.

Kiel's girl cousins must have watched them, and came running. 'What are you two up to?' they said almost together. Kiel introduced them to Secilia and all of them had a little natter.

It must have been about lunchtime or later when Kiel felt a little peckish and asked, 'Shall we go and have a hot sausage with a roll? All agreed, apart from his pocket change.

Later they all got into a swinging boat soaring up and down, which shook up all the bits and pieces they had consumed and allowed the girls hair and skirts to blow.

After this they had another walk around, when they met up with uncle and auntie, his two cousins' parents from the town of Strehla, for a quick introduction and chat.

Kiel's pocket change was beginning to get a little light, so he asked uncle for another helping hand, which he agreed, 'But only for a loan, my boy, I want this paid back,' he said quietly and smiled.

'Oh, yes, uncle, I might not even need it, but I don't want to run out of money if anything needs paying for,' Kiel replied.

'You just be careful and don't spent what you haven't got,' he called out as they all four walked away, probably only too glad to get away from him.

'Why did you do that?' Secilia asked, and carried on 'I could have lent or given you some money, or paid if you got short, all you had to do is say or ask.'

'That's very kind of you, dear, but it's a common and recognised thing that the gentleman pays and that is what I would like to do,' he remarked.

'I respect you for this, Kiel, but you must not spend what you have not got. You are not a rich person and need money for many other things during the week. Please let me pay in future,' she appealed; looking at him with her gorgeous shining eyes and smile. Who could possibly refuse, especially when almost broke and destitute?

They decided to take a ride on the roundabout, sitting on a couple of horses next to each other. Who would they see but the colonel and Her Ladyship walking slowly arm in arm through the many stalls.

Secilia spotted them after Kiel pointed and she called out. When on our next turn round they had stopped and watched out for us to reappear and waved, we both returned the waving and carried on until the music and roundabout stopped, when we went to meet up with them.

They asked, 'Have you enjoyed yourselves?' To which we both replied, 'Yes, thank you,' almost simultaneously.

Secilia took over the talking, explaining that they had met up with Kiel's girl cousins who are around their age and their parents, his uncle and auntie who all live in Strehla, up the hill not far from the old castle, et cetera.

The colonel butted in and said, 'You had better not be too long, dear. We shall have to go back home and no doubt Kiel will very soon have to return to his work.'

Looking at Secilia's watch, Kiel realised he had only just about an hour and that included cycling back to the estate and getting changed.

'We'll have another short walk and meet you at the car in about fifteen minutes,' Kiel said.

'Yes, that is fine, Kiel. Look after Secilia and return her in a good mood,' the colonel replied and smiled, which he did not do too often.

Secilia gave both parents a kiss on the cheek and off they went picking up candyfloss on the way, for which Secilia paid and they disappeared among the stalls.

After a little while they embraced, when he said, 'Thank you for a lovely day. We'll have to come here again next year if you're around,' and kissed Secelia on the cheek.

She did the same in return and replied, 'Thank you, Kiel. You have made me proud, introducing me to some of your relations. I would like to meet them again.'

A few minutes later, they both returned hand in hand to find the car with chauffeur, the colonel and Her Ladyship not far way.

Secilia called out before they even got near and seemed so excited. She flung her arms round her mum and said, 'We've had a wonderful day mummy. Kiel is a real gentleman; he spent a lot of money and won me a teddy bear at the shooting gallery.'

'Oh, that is nice of you, Kiel, you will have to do the same for me sometime,' Her Ladyship replied, smiling.

'I'll try to get you one now, my lady, if we have a few more minutes,' he said and almost turned to go.

Her ladyship replied, 'No, thank you, Kiel, another time will do nicely. You are very kind.'

'We had better be off,' the colonel said, and began to walk towards the car. All stepped inside, then Secilia quickly stepped out again and gave Kiel a kiss on the cheek, saying, 'Thank you, Kiel, for a lovely day. See you later,' and returned to her seat.

They all waved and smiled, especially Secilia, who turned her head several times. Kiel returned the waves as they slowly drove away. After all this, he ran up the hill to get his bicycle and cycled down the hill along the road back to the estate.

Neither uncle, auntie or the girl cousins were anywhere to be seen, so he had to leave a quick note that he would come and see them again, took his bike and off he went as fast as his legs would allow, and he made it just about in time.

He looked for the car and Secilia on his way past the house and garden, but there was nothing to be seen, and he supposed they had gone into town for a bit of shopping.

Not thinking anymore about it, he went to the cottage said hello to uncle and auntie, who had a cup of coffee and cake on the table waiting for him. Knowing that he would not have eaten a lot at the fair, they had a good old natter, while drinking and eating.

After a while Kiel excused himself from the table and ran upstairs to change for work, where, as usual, the headman was already waiting for Kiel with a smile and smoking his pipe.

They both, as always, went out to the fields to collect the cows for milking and, after milking, his usual job of feeding the calves.

Returning and finishing the milking et cetera, Kiel looked out for Secilia to help him, but there was no one to be seen.

Amongst all the noise from these patiently waiting little animals, he had to go and get a couple more buckets to satisfy all of them and hand feed the smaller ones, which was quite a job all on his own.

Kiel kept looking but no one, only the headman, came and said, 'Secilia won't be coming today or anymore, they had to go back to Berlin in a hurry.'

Kiel was not sure if the headman was telling the truth and answered, 'It was not long ago when I saw them all at the feast in Strehla, but no one said a word about them going. I wish I had known.'

'Perhaps they did not want to tell you or Secilia, but the colonel knew just before lunch, when he had a message or orders to return,' the headman continued.

Kiel could have sat down and cried at that time. His legs seemed like rubber and about to give way from under him.

The headman said jokingly, 'Don't take it too hard, boy, those thing do happen in life and you will have bigger disappointments to get over before you get married.

This saying he had never heard before but it cheered him up just a little and he carried on with his work, but he could not get Secilia out of his head.

After work he returned for supper, which smelled delightful as ever. He rushed upstairs for changing and washing. When he came down, auntie said, 'I have got something for you.'

She went away and came back with a card from Juliet, which said, 'Thank you, Kiel, for a lovely time. I hope we shall meet up again,' and upon which she gave him her address and phone number.

This cheered him up no end. He grabbed auntie in his arms and kissed her on the cheek.

'Steady on, boy, whatever has got into you suddenly?' she asked.

Kiel told her that he had heard from the headman that, 'Secilia the colonel and Her Ladyship had left to return to Berlin; about this I am rather disappointed and miserable but now here out of the blue is this card from Juliet.'

This made everything all right again and he could at least get in touch with Secilia through Juliet, unless she writes to him herself first from Berlin.

'I am sure she will, my boy, especially since she obviously did not know herself that they were going straight back. You should not worry too much,' auntie said.

'You can always write to Juliet or go and see her. Dresden is not all that far from here and there is the train or bus from Riesa,' she continued.

This he had not even thought about but that all costs money, which he did not have.

'I still have the money uncle loaned me. I must take that back tomorrow and hand it over before I spend it on something else,' he told auntie.

'I have a card here, if you want to write back to Juliet. You can take it with you to post on your way, then go and see your uncle, aunt and cousins again perhaps over the weekend, as the fair is still on, and give them our best regards,' she remarked.

'Thank you, auntie, that is kind of you. Yes, I think I will write back to thank Juliet and tell her that I might go to Dresden one day and perhaps see her there,' he replied.

The days went by and with working and going to college every day there was little else to think about but the next day, apart from dreaming about Secilia and Juliet sometimes, remembering the lovely days we had together going swimming, et cetera. Hopefully they will come again, which made living all worthwhile.

He took the card upstairs after supper and sat down to write a few lines of thanks to Juliet, taking it with him on Saturday after breakfast.

He cycled back to Strehla to see uncle, auntie and his two young lady cousins, and posted the card on the way.

After handing over the money he had borrowed, to uncle, he pushed it back into his hand saying, 'You keep it, boy, you will need it one day. It was good of you to think of bringing it back,' he said.

Kiel thanked him by shaking his hand and auntie invited him to stay for lunch, which he accepted gratefully.

He remarked, however, that he had not mentioned anything about lunch to the other auntie before coming out.

This made him suddenly remember to hand over the good wishes from both of them, when auntie turned and said; 'Thank you, boy, but she will realise that I would invite you to stay and not think anything about it, so stop worrying.'

We all sat down for a cup of coffee and a long talk, and he told them all about Juliet, the garden party and the dinner he had been invited to. They also talked about all the previous years, as he had not seen them since his poor mum died, when they all came to the funeral.

They must have sat there for quite a while when auntie suddenly jumped up and called uncle.

Something had gone wrong in the kitchen and began to burn. It smelled wonderful, but auntie nearly cried and worried about her lovely dinner.

'Don't worry, auntie.' Kiel took her in his arms, which she obviously appreciated and he said, 'We all have good teeth and I am sure we all would have been glad to have even a burnt offering a few years ago.'

'Oh, you still remember those bad old days, do you?' uncle asked. 'Yes, indeed I do. We had hardly anything to eat or to put on our feet in the winter. I don't think I shall ever forget those years. That was no doubt why mum died, through not looking after herself,' he replied.

'You could be right there, boy. We have often talked about this between us; she was a very good mum to all of you,' uncle remarked.

After lunch the two girl cousins and himself were once again given a few Deutschmarks each and told to go down to the feast, to allow uncle and auntie a few minutes rest.

The younger of the two cousins was almost the same age and was born just a few months before him, while the other was two years older and both were great company. They had known each other virtually from birth and they all lived in the same big house together until grandad decided to take grandma to Bavaria and settle down in the hills dales and mountains.

This was a beautiful time and place, they later found out, and they both loved every minute or years out there, as they told Kiel in later years on visits.

Their granddad took over a smallholding from an old army comrade who took over his or their big house in Strehla, and our parents and the rest of the family, as well as others, had to find alternative accommodation.

Their grandparents' new place was beautiful with the little cottage on the mountainside with the sun getting up in the early mornings down the valley, rising over the mountaintops, shining right into the small windows and the front door if open.

We had several holidays there in winter and summer, with the gorgeous little flowers among the short green grass, with lots of birds and animals in and around their woods or forest. In the winter with the snow many feet deep and skiing down the hill, right over the low cottage roof and jumping down the other side, getting buried in the deep snow.

This was their dream wonderland, at least when still fairly young and they could enjoy themselves, working on the land, producing their own crops and everything they needed. That was when our mum and dad moved to Thüringen with us two boys, but Dad's brother, Kiel's uncle, stayed on in the town of Strehla, with his wife and two daughters.

Theirs was quite a large family in the early days, since dad had two sisters, one in America, and four brothers, plus grandad's brother; both were builders and blacksmith with wife, children and grandchildren.

This was quite a large house right in the centre of town, with plenty of building materials and sand around for all the children to play with.

Kiel could not remember a great deal about those early years, since he was not quite four years old when they moved.

# CHAPTER 16

They all had a great time together at the fair, when both cousins naturally wanted to know all about Secilia, who they had seen with Kiel at the weekend, the colonel and Her Ladyship, as well as Juliet he had send a card to.

Luckily there was not a great lot of time, since he had to get back to his afternoon shift, which was just as well since these two cousins of his began to get a little more inquisitive than previously expected or appreciated.

After they had been on the roundabout, swinging boats, and had an ice cream each, it was time for Kiel to say goodbye. He kissed them both on the cheek and returned to collect his bicycle, just managing to say goodbye to uncle and auntie, and return to the estate.

He was in good time to have a nice cup of coffee with more cake and tell this other uncle and auntie on the estate all about his visit. He handed over the return greetings from the family in Strehla, before he had to run upstairs to change and go back to work.

That was the Saturday gone, without even having had time to miss Secilia's lovely smile until it came to feeding the little calves again in the afternoon.

Later in the evening, he went for a walk alone through the woods, past all the animals and to the river.

Being Saturday, there were several young people there again for a splash and swim, but Kiel did not bring his trunks, so he had to settle for a natter, while lounging on the short green grass with the others. They had a great deal to talk about, and they all of them wanted Kiel to come back to the feast, but by that time it was too late for him to go and get changed again.

After a while Kiel returned to the small cottage to uncle and auntie; another cup of coffee and a lot of talking. He was ready for bed.

He had a long chat earlier over supper with them both, about Secilia, the colonel and Her Ladyship, when they said, 'Don't worry, my boy, they will be back some time next year. Secilia might even write.'

All this made things a little easier to bear and he went upstairs after saying goodnight to both of them, had another look through the window, before turning in to go to sleep.

# CHAPTER 17

It was now early September and college was soon to begin again, which would not leave Kiel a great deal of time for dreaming, but he could not get Secilia out of his mind.

He kept on thinking; did the colonel actually have an order to return to Berlin, because of the war cabinet meeting the following week, or did the parents perhaps think that Secilia and himself were getting a little to close for comfort? Although they both appeared to be very friendly and seemed encouraging, did they overstep the mark in their opinion?

Kiel doubted that the real truth would never be known by either of them two, especially himself, unless Secilia was prepared to let him know, if she ever knew herself? He would have to wait, there is nothing that he could do now but hope to see them all again the following year if this will be at all possible.

He tossed and turned from one side to the other for a very long time in his bed, when in the end he must have fallen asleep after all. He was so tired when uncle knocked on the door; he just turned over for another hour, and fell fast asleep again. He did not even hear the alarm when it went off, or he shut it up for the noise it was making and fell asleep once more.

Later auntie knocked on the door and called out to wake him, calling, 'You are going to be late, Kiel.'

At that time he must have known it was late, when he jumped out of bed, placed his hands into cold water and rubbed his eyes. They slowly began to open. He put his clothes on, ran downstairs and out of the door, across the yard as if someone was chasing him.

This time he was a little late and the headman had already asked someone else to go with him to collect the cows from the field for milking. He quickly helped spread the food on the gangways, making sure that all was clean and ready for the cows to be chained on, so that they could munch away in peace and quiet while being cleaned and milked.

It was now Sunday morning and college would start again tomorrow; oh, yes, of course, college. That, no doubt, is why they had to return to Berlin, which they had forgotten all about in their excitement. He was sure Secilia would have had to start the very same day as they in this area, but none of them had ever talked about having to go back to college.

That was no doubt why Juliet had to go back home, so that she was ready for university. Why didn't he think of that before?

This made things a great deal easier to understand and after breakfast, although he felt like lying down again, he thought he had better get his books and details checked out, so that all was ready for his return tomorrow morning.

He managed to get a short lie-down and fell off to sleep almost immediately; then a call came from auntie downstairs, calling out that lunch was ready to be served.

After lunch he checked over his bicycle tyres and wheels et cetera, gave the chain a good oiling and cleaned the whole thing down a little. The bicycle was now ready again and could be used for his daily journeys back and forth to town and college.

It was just as well; the next morning it was raining and the struggle of riding the bike was not the most pleasant. Luckily the rain was not too heavy and came straight down. Wearing a hat and coat was, although not the most comfortable and quite warm. By the time he had cycled for about twenty minutes and put his bike away at the college, he was almost sweating and his feet, like almost everyone else's, were drenched from the rain.

Life must go on and they all sat down for their next lesson, which was as boring as the weather, but they all managed to sit it out, only to return, by that time in brilliant sunshine.

Is it not amazing what the weather can do to one's own feelings and behaviour? Sunshine appears to bring out all the best in every one of us and smiles seem to be all round.

Like the old saying, 'Smile a while and while you smile another smile appears, and while you smile you wipe away the tears. This makes the world and us go round a great deal easier and happier.

The days and weeks went by without any special incidents, and by the time October arrived with, once again, fine clear weather, a much clearer mind appeared to be available.

Kiel thought of asking the headman for a weekend off to go to Dresden and visit his Mum's brother, his wife and family, another uncle and auntie, he had not seen for years.

'Oh, I don't know if we can manage that, we are a bit short-handed right now,' the headman said and carried on. 'I will let you know in a day or so. Is there a great hurry?' he asked.

'No, not really, but the weather appears to be holding out and I thought a rest will do me good,' Kiel replied.

Going back home for supper, he mentioned it to uncle and auntie, who thought it a great idea, and uncle said, 'You tell Franz the headman that I am quite happy to help out a little if necessary'.

This made his day and after a short walk and another cup of coffee with a nice piece of auntie's fine cake, he climbed the stairs and had a good night's sleep.

Waking up with the sun in his eyes, he had absolutely no problem in getting up and arrived for work in good time. This early rising and looking awake first thing in the morning even astounded uncle, auntie and the rest of the workforce.

On arrival, Kiel was ready to go or follow his usual job of collecting the cows from the field.

That morning, which was Wednesday, he told the headman all about his conversation with uncle, and the headman replied; 'I had thought about it and I think it will be okay for this weekend,' and asked, 'Will that suit you?'

'Yes, that's fine, since I cannot ring them anyway. I just hope that the weather will hold out; I have not been to Dresden for years,' he answered.

If uncle and auntie on his Mum's side are not at home, Kiel thought, he could always give Juliet a ring and see if she was available for a cup of coffee and a chat.

When Saturday morning came round, Kiel said goodbye to uncle and auntie, took his bike and cycled to town and the railway station. He bought a ticket and on the train he went, full of hopes and unexpected surprises.

It was an absolutely glorious morning or day, with the sun high in the clear blue sky and not a cloud to be seen anywhere.

The train, with the locomotive wheels first seemingly to skit, soon rolled noisily along the track through part of the town and following through the most beautiful countryside.

Sitting on the old wooden bench seats, which were common in those days but not very comfortable, he was able to look out the windows and admire the surroundings and villages as they passed by.

He viewed the landscape around as the train sped alongside a road, with the chimney blowing out the black smoke and people walking or cycling on the road nearby.

The journey took just about an hour, when Kiel arrived at the city's massive railway station, with no idea as to where or which way to go.

Following most others down stairs and along tunnels, he ended up in what he thought was the town centre with all the beautiful galleries and buildings around him.

Kiel stood there like a lemon hoping to be found and needing to be squeezed, not knowing what to do. Returning back into the station, he thought of having a sit down and have a cup of coffee to collect his thoughts.

He had no address and no idea where uncle and auntie of Mum's side lived, only the name, which may have been useful in a village, but was not a lot of help in a large city like this.

With all the luck in China, he had brought Juliet's card address and phone number along and after his coffee; he picked up the courage to phone.

As always when one does not want them to, the mother comes to the phone, which Kiel nearly put down again, but he managed to splutter out a few words, like 'Good morning, my lady. It is Kiel, could I possibly speak to Juliet, if available?'

'Oh, hello, Kiel, what a surprise. How are you?' she carried on, 'Hang on a second, there is Juliet,' without giving him a chance to reply, which was probably just as well, since he was already beginning to get red and hot under the collar, with nothing else to say.

'Hello, Kiel, where are you?' the voice came over the phone, which he recognised immediately as Juliet.

He answered, 'I am here in Dresden at the railway station and have come here for the day to visit my uncle and auntie, but I've forgotten the address and have no idea where they live,' he replied.

'Oh, I am pleased to hear your voice again. I am not quite ready to go out yet; would you like to go to the ferry and come over the river, please?' she asked and continued. 'This goes every few minutes and you can come across the river Elbe, where I shall pick you up in about half an hour.' Then we can talk,' she mumbled on.

'Yes, of course. I shall come and wait for you there,' he replied and put down the phone.

It was a good job he had brought a little money with him, or he would have been completely stuck in a large city to which he had never been all on his own.

Luckily there was a signpost for the ferry right outside the station, which he followed and this brought him right along to the massive river.

He had never been on a ferry before, which looked like a large boat to him. This was quite a new and exciting experience on its own.

There were two of them and as one crossed over, the other came the other way back, almost meeting in the centre of the river.

Upon these large ferries there were not only people going across, but horses and carts, one or two cars, which was still an unusual sight, at least for him, coming from the country.

There seemed to be quite a few cars and trams running around on the streets, especially army transport lorries, of which there were plenty going back and forth. One most certainly had to watch out with this continuous noise, which was quite overwhelming when not used to this, and completely new to Kiel.

Apart from one time he could remember, being very young and sitting on his mum's bicycle when they cycled through Leipzig, another very large town, but that was many years ago, and they both fell off the bike with the front wheel stuck in the tram rail lines. With him crying, the oncoming tram whistling, and mum in a real hustle, with dad and his brother not seeing or hearing what happened, carrying on well in front, but they somehow managed to get out of the way just in time to meet up with dad and brother again.

The scenery here was most attractive, being a mainly wooded area sloping gently down to the riverbank and its waters, with loads of green fir trees as well as golden coloured leaves in among, which looked most attractive with the sunlight upon them.

After a very pleasant ferry crossing, they slowly arrived near the other side of the river's landing stage and Kiel got off with all the other passengers.

Juliet was already waiting with two horses, sitting upon one and leading the other for him to climb upon, knowing that he was a good rider.

This, however, was completely unexpected and it was a good job he had no suitcase with him, which would have looked a little out of place.

'Hello, Juliet,' he called out just before he got near her.

She replied with, 'Hello, Kiel, it is nice to see you again. Come and join me.'

These most certainly were a couple of nice looking and kept horses, both black in colour, with dark brown saddles and leathers. They had been well looked after and were well brushed down, with their coats shining, and with hoofs and leathers well polished. They were a really lovely pair to see and ride. Juliet looked a picture with her black shining boots, hat, white scarf and cloves.

Kiel must have looked a sight for sore eyes, sitting on a horse in a suit, but they both enjoyed the ride through the woods.

Riding along, Juliet, with a lot of talking, took Kiel through the beautiful Dresdener heide (heather), which at that time was still in full bloom and was a great sight for any eyes to see. They took a gallop through the heather, then after a while she suddenly pulled up, got off the horse near a tree with a short grassy area around, tied up the horse, and asked him to come down and have a rest for a while.

'Have you had anything to eat earlier? I am sorry; I should have asked you before, but I never thought,' she enquired.

'Yes, thank you. I had a good breakfast before coming away from the estate and later a cup of coffee and a roll at the station on arrival. I am fine thank you,' Kiel replied.

'Oh, that is good, we shall not have to get back until lunch and it is only just about eleven o' clock,' she replied, looking at her watch.

Such fine luxuries, unfortunately he did not possess and had no idea of time, let alone the day, when he was overwhelmed to see this gorgeous young lady again after several weeks.

He got off the horse and tied it to the tree, took out the bits of each so that the horses could chew a branch or a little grass, before they both sat down in that lovely soft short mossy grass.

'Now you can tell me all about what you have been up to with Secilia, since I left?' she asked. 'We all had such a great time when I was there with Secilia and you, especially swimming in the river and teasing each other,' she remarked and continued.

'Then there was this lovely garden party and dinner. I really enjoyed your company. Can you remember?' she asked.

'I most certainly did enjoy your and Secilia's company. It was a shame that you had to leave, as did Secilia shortly thereafter. It has not been the same without you two,' he replied.

'Well, we are here together again now. How long have you got before going back?' Juliet enquired.

'I don't have to go back until Sunday evening. I managed to get the weekend off, but since I cannot go to my uncle and auntie overnight, I shall have to return later this evening,' he replied.

'I don't think you'll have to do that,' Juliet said, and carried on, 'I shall ask Mummy later; I think or hope we can put you up for one night.'

'But I have no nightclothes or washing material with me. I can't stay over,' he replied.

'Don't be so silly, we shall soon supply you with a pair of pyjamas and dressing gown from my brother who is in the army, and I will lend you a tooth brush et cetera,' she remarked.

'That is very kind of you, Juliet, but you should not put yourself out. Seeing you for just a few minutes, the whole trip has been worthwhile to me,' he said.

She gave a lovely soft smile, turned over to pull him close and gave him such a remarkable, enjoyable kiss, which he had no alternative but to return, while they both appeared to roll almost on top of each other.

Her soft tender body and gentle movements gave him quite a thrill, and his hands would have to be tied down, not to allow them to wander.

Juliet suddenly shrieked out loud, so much so that the two horses seemed scared and pricked up their ears. She rolled over; for a moment he thought he had done something wrong, when she called out, 'There's something in my blouse.'

'It's not my hands,' he said, 'they are both here.

'No, silly, there is something crawling about.' She opened her blouse and there it was: a tiny little field mouse, which had lost its way, obviously disturbed by them rolling around. The poor little thing fell out and ran off as fast as its little legs could carry it, back into the grass and heather.

Juliet was quite disturbed for a moment, but calmed down remarkably quickly and relaxed, lying back with her blouse still undone in the gorgeous sunshine, as if nothing had happened. She had a beautiful, slightly brown colour all over and obviously had enjoyed the sun on previous occasions, on which Kiel remarked and admired what he could see.

'Yes,' she said, 'we have a large balcony high up, overlooking the river and town, where we can lay and enjoy the sun all day long without being seen. I will show you when we get back.'

'When we get back,' he said. 'Why not show me now?'

They both enjoyed each other's company, and the glorious weather with sun overhead, so much that they almost forgot the time. He had no idea where they were living or how far they would have to ride to get to the house and meet her parents and whoever else might be living there.

Kiel looked at Juliet's watch and noticed it was nearly twelve o'clock. With lunch normally around twelve, they had little time left, which he pointed out.

Juliet did not seem to be greatly disturbed and said, 'We will just have to have lunch a little later, won't we?'

He certainly did not mind and enjoyed her close company and did not worry for one moment, when soon thereafter she remarked with another quick kiss, 'We had better be off. It is nearly an hour's ride from here and we do not want to be too late, do we?' she remarked.

We brushed each other down as best we could, got back to the horses, when he said, 'We shall have to come here again one fine day.'

'Oh, did you enjoy my company? I thought perhaps you were hungry for lunch,' she replied.

'No-no,' he remarked, 'I am hungry all right but not necessarily for lunch,' when she smacked him across the arm and smiled.

### In the shade of a Tree

In the shade of this tree, there were you and I,
Lying restful and completely free, under the sky,
Amongst flowering heather, in glorious weather,
Most happy and joyful just being together.

In the short grass, so soft and so green,
Remembering the past, as it has been,
With sun high up in the sky, we cuddled,
Since I seemed so in love, or quite muddled.

We embraced fairly tight, emotions we fight,
There's no better place right now to be,
Lying out in the wild, being quite free,
In the shade of this wonderful tree!

K-WA

After untying the horses and replacing their bits, they both got back onto them and slowly trotted along, still talking.

Juliet suddenly set her horse at a gallop, and Kiel followed like a dog on the lead, not knowing where they would go or end up. After a while she slowed her horse down beside him and pointed to their house, which was standing among large trees, with the river down below.

They both slowed down to a walk and rode into the yard, where a horseman was already waiting to take the horses from them. Handing over the horses with a stroke for appreciation on their necks, they thanked him and walked together inside the house, where they were greeted by her mum and dad, both of whom he had met earlier on the estate, with the colonel and Her Ladyship. They seemed pleased to meet him again.

Juliet showed him the bathroom for a wash and brush up, and cleaning down the trousers from the one or two horsehair remaining.

She had obviously returned to her bedroom. Then a little later she called out to him to come and join her to go downstairs, for lunch.

Juliet naturally had changed into a dress and looked even more divine and inviting than before, smelling fresh with her hair gleaming brightly and hanging down to near shoulder-length.

They both walked slowly down the stairs, when she asked him,

'What would you like to do after lunch? Shall we have another ride or would you like to go to *Sächsische Schweiz* (Saxon Switzerland) and *Schloss Königstein* (Castle Kingstone) with me?'

'Oh, I would love to do the latter, if we have time for it. I have heard a lot about it but have never ever been there. How far is this from here?' he asked.

'It is not very far by train, or we could take a riverboat and come back the same way, or go by train, whichever you prefer,' she replied.

That was when her mum, who had overheard their conversation stepped in and said, 'Why don't you go by train? It would be quicker than upriver by boat, and come back downriver by boat. This way you will have the best of both.'

This sounded a very good idea and they both agreed without any further discussion or mentioning of the matter. Since Kiel had not been on either in this region, he could not really comment and was looking forward to both journeys with great excitement.

After dinner, with a lot of conversation, Kiel was shown his room, since Juliet's request for him to stay had previously been discussed between the two ladies and the man of the house, without him knowing anything about it.

Juliet pointed out that he could use any of her younger brother's clothes; he was an officer in the army and about his size.

Kiel was naturally overwhelmed with the offer and was not really sure if that was the right thing to do without her brother's permission. He hardly knew him, by only seeing him once at the garden party, but had never really spoke to him apart from saying hello and goodbye.

Juliet, however, insisted and pointed out that he would love someone to use his clothes, which in a few years would only be thrown away, since he virtually lived in his uniform, even when at home on leave.

That was agreed and Juliet even picked out what she wanted him to wear, including shirt and coat in case it got chilly on the boat. This girl seems have thought of everything and showed him off to her parents before leaving, who thought he looked great and reminded them of their son.

They excused themselves, said goodbye to both Juliet's parents, went down to the ferry to cross the river and took the train as suggested.

The train journey along the river, through the forest covered hills the other side almost all the way with Juliet by Kiel's side, seemed more like a dream.

Juliet was chatting away, trying to explain as they went along, which was most interesting and the journey did not seem to take very long, although the train pulled up at almost every station on the way.

After crossing the river once again, they walked or climbed the hill on a cobblestone road all the way up to the massive *Schloss Königstein*. (Fortress)

There was a museum of the old weapons, uniforms and regalia; old cannons still well polished were displayed in the grounds, all of which were surrounded by a great wall. One could almost imagine or feel the old days, when this castle fortress was in use and defended from aggressors, trying to come across the river or surroundings with ancient weapons.

This certainly was a fantastic sight to see for the first time, with these massively thick stone walls all round and gangways just behind. Juliet took a few photos. Kiel was not that rich to own a camera, but she allowed him to use hers at times.

Later they both took a small steam train, driven along the road to the National Park, or the so-called, well-known *Sächsische Schweiz*.

There we had to do a lot of climbing on narrow gangways among the most beautiful rock formation, at times overlooking the river Elbe far below.

There were boats passing, with the ferry crossing in between and people walking back and forth to the railway the other side of the river, looking like small bees or beetles.

It was all forestry with some bare round rock tops; climbing was almost impossible, at least for any inexperienced climber like myself. In imagination, it was just like a miniature Switzerland as Kiel had heard of before, but again never seen at that time. Even on these narrow gangways through and across these mountains they both kept hold of each other so as not to stumble and roll down the steep sides or slopes.

There were a large number of small stalls, with all sorts of refreshments and undercover seating places amongst the trees and flowering shrubs.

Kiel chose to have a fried sausage and roll with a cup of coffee, while Juliet only wanted a coffee with a cream and jam bun. She gave him a bite of this jam bun after he had finished his sausage, of which she had to have a bite earlier as well, all of which they enjoyed to the full.

The time was getting on, having a fantastic time of sight seeing, holding hands and cuddling. Then they decided to climb down to the boat, to take them back home.

This was once again a most attractive return journey, overlooking both sides of the river, with road, railway and riverboat traffic as well as people walking past, on both sides of the river at times.

By the time they arrived back home it was just after six o'clock or 18.00 hours. They were both hungry again. A cold supper with sliced sausage, cheese and different salads was awaiting them with hot coffee, all of which looked very appetising.

They all sat round the table in a large well-decorated dining room overlooking the river and part of the city of Dresden next to a massive patio just outside the dining room.

Of this he had been informed earlier when both Juliet and himself were lying out in the heather, showing off her light brown colour, never to be forgotten.

Looking down along the hill among the trees and wood with the gleaming golden sun slowly settling down beyond the horizon, this was a most picturesque sight. Gently lightening up the very few clouds in the sky into a red golden glow, it began to disappear out of sight and the lights were being switched on in town down the far side of the river.

The house was every bit as large as the one on the estate, but in a very much more interesting position, adjoining a large, mainly wooded, estate with shooting and riding and this lovely river with boats and ferries, as well as the city down below.

After supper they had a short stroll round the large patio overlooking the river and city, the other side where the lights had already been switched on. Juliet asked, 'What would you like to do tonight, Kiel?'

He was not really sure what she had in mind and replied, 'Anything you wish, Juliet. I am quite willing to follow your ideas.'

She turned and said, 'Anything? Oh, that sounds interesting,' and laughed, gripping him by the arm, placing Kiel into a compromising situation once again and, with her parents around as well, what could he say?

'You have to explain yourself, Juliet. You are embarrassing Kiel with your cheeky remarks,' her mother admonished.

'Yes Mummy, you are quite right, but Kiel knows me by now,' she replied. 'I would love to go to town and maybe to a dance. Would you like that Kiel?'

She asked him politely, turning to her mum and dad, asking, 'What about you two? Would you like to join us?'

'I don't think so,' her mum replied, and followed on, 'You two go and enjoy yourselves, the day is still young.'

That is when Kiel suddenly remembered and realised that he could not go. He was too young and had to be off the streets by 9 p.m. or 21.00 hours and pointed this out to Juliet.

'Oh, that's no problem; you are in my company and I am old enough to be out,' of which the others approved and he was quite willing, perhaps even eager, and told Juliet.

'Right, that is agreed then, we had better go upstairs to tidy ourselves up and change.' Juliet grabbed him by the arm and, without a word or question to her mum and dad; she dragged him indoors and up the stairs.

It happened that his, or better said her younger brother's, bedroom was next to hers with a bathroom between, but adjoining.

Juliet said to Kiel, 'You go into the bathroom first, while I lay out some clothes for you to wear, and I will follow. There was no question as what would you like to do or wear. I am the boss and you just follow me.'

This was quite nice, and that is what he always admired about Juliet. It seemed obviously what she had to do or did with her younger brother and continued in the same way.

Since Kiel did not know anything about the family, the house, the city or set up, and never, ever having had a sister, he was quite willing to be led by the hand.

He had a quick shower (there was a wash basin in the bedroom for cleaning the teeth et cetera) and after finishing he gave Juliet a call so that she could use the bathroom. There was no real need to call anyone, since there was a switch at each door to switch on lights for red when occupied or green for being free to use, which was quite useful as long as everyone remembered to lock the door when inside, or look at the light.

After returning to the bedroom and cleaning his teeth, Kiel began to dress in what Juliet had laid out for him on the bed, from socks to underclothes, shirt and a suit.

By the time he had finished doing up the last buttons, who would arrive but Juliet? 'Are you all right? Does everything fit and suit?' she wanted to know.

'Yes, thank you,' he replied and continued, 'could you help me with this tie or bow? I have never worn one like this before.'

'You look absolutely stunning in that beautiful low-cut dress and stole over your shoulders. Come here, I could eat you,' he said.

'Thank you Kiel. That is nice of you; you really like it?' She requested to know and admired herself in the mirror again.

'Like it?' he replied, 'You look like a sugar princess I could begin to start chewing on you now,' which she seemed to like hearing and smilingly beamed with delight.

'Thank you, Kiel, I am glad, since we are going out together,' she said with a smile and continued, 'but I do not want to be chewed at or eaten, at least not before we go.'

In his own excitement, Kiel had also forgotten to place the studs into the cufflinks, not knowing how, which she did for him and said, 'You are as bad as my younger brother, I always had to help dress him.'

'How old is your younger brother?' Kiel asked.

'Oh, he is the same age as me. I call him my younger brother since I was the first to arrive, but we are actually twins,' she remarked. 'I think you are my younger brother now, since you are about three years younger than myself, or at least I'll adopt and look after you while you are here,' Juliet remarked.

'You are not the only one who is helping out; what about me having to rub both of your backs down with sun lotion near the river?' he asked.

'You did not rub it on our backs only; your hands kept slipping towards our fronts, you little tease,' she replied.

'Yes, but that was not intentional. They just slipped now and again. It is not easy to control one's greasy hands on beautiful curves like yours,' he said, admiring them now.

'Come on, you are teasing me. We had better go downstairs and say goodbye, before I leave you behind,' Juliet remarked full of smiles.

He could not take his eyes off her. He placed her arm into his and walked her down the stairs to meet up with her mum, who was the colonel's sister and her dad, who they told him worked for the bank, but Kiel thought he might own it.

They all shook hands. Kiel kissed Her Ladyship's hand and said goodbye and wished them a pleasant evening.

Her dad came close to Juliet and said quietly,

'Don't forget to book it all on me,' which Kiel overheard but did not know what he really meant at that time.

In turn they both wished us a good time and said,

'Don't be too late, but enjoy yourselves. We can all lie in. Tomorrow is Sunday.'

Waving hands, they both disappeared through the front door, which was closed and locked behind them by her dad, and they walked hand in hand, talking all the way down to the ferry, and crossed to the other side of the river to the city.

There they took a horse-drawn trap, which took them to wherever the young lady had chosen.

Luckily they both had a coat each to hang over the shoulders, since the autumn evening became a little chilly, especially on or near the water. Even later in town, with the traffic moving around and passing, causing a draft, it was a little cooler than before, maybe since there being a little space between both did not help.

Juliet paid the trap driver after they had arrived at what seemed to be more like a palace rather than a dance hall, when Juliet led Kiel inside.

There were gaming tables all round the ground floor, while the music and dancing was upstairs with a bar and provision for waiter service to the tables.

They both went to the bar first to meet some of Juliet's friends and she seemed to have many, with handshakes and kisses all round. One became thirsty by just looking and admiring. Juliet asked a couple of girlfriends to join them and they sat down at a table, with champagne ordered by one of the girls.

Kiel would have preferred a glass of beer to begin with, but water was on the table and that had to do, especially since he had very little money on him. But who would pay for the champagne? he thought to himself, getting a little worried, and there were four of us.

He was just hoping that they would not be too thirsty, since he could not have even paid for the entrance tickets. What could he do when the bill arrived?

Money had never entered his head until now. Even though Kiel thought he heard Juliet's dad say to her, 'book it down to me,' it did not ring a bell what her dad had meant at the time.

Kiel quickly asked Juliet for a dance just so that he could bring his predicament out in the open and told her all about his lack of finances.

She in return very quietly said, 'I thought you looked a little forlorn for a moment and not quite as cheerful as your usual self. Don't worry it is all arranged. Don't even mention it, and enjoy yourself.'

After this he certainly tried his very best and they had a lovely dance, or so he thought, but could not get this financial situation quite out of his mind until it was actually confirmed again by Juliet.

We returned to the table full of smiles, joining the others, had a sip of the champagne delivered in the meantime, with the part bottle placed back on ice next to his chair.

This started him to worry again. Why was this placed near him, when he had not even ordered it and could not possibly pay?

Luckily, the other two girls were asked to dance and the two of them remained seated, when once again he asked Juliet to make sure, so he would not be caught with his trousers down.

This time Juliet shrieked out laughing and explained that they knew very well that he could not possibly afford to take her out for a night dancing.

This they had discussed among themselves at home and, so she did not have to carry a lot of money around, all was booked on her dad's account. That sounded absolutely great and he was relieved from his worries and thought to himself, 'It is not what you know, but who you know that counts in this life', and have remembered it ever since.

After this they had the most marvellous evening with a snack for all of them halfway through. Kiel managed to dance with the girls who were sitting with them round the table and Juliet missed hardly one dance; everyone appeared to know her. Most of them were university students, she told him later as they walked along through the rooms and downstairs still shaking hands.

The music had stopped; it was midnight and time to take her young ladyship back home again.

After saying goodnight to everyone, with handshakes and kisses all round, they once again took a horse-drawn trap to the ferry. This was the last one for that night and on the other side they walked slowly arm in arm through the woods back to the house.

Kiel was not sure how many glasses of champagne he had drunk, or this young lady, but they both seemed a little light on their feet and had to support each other on the way.

Laughing, talking and giggling all the way, almost falling over at times, they made it home to the big house and inside.

Juliet requested some coffee, which one of the maids brought, along with some snacks, which they consumed while still talking and laughing.

They climbed the stairs, with Juliet trying to put Kiel to bed, just like an older sister or good friend would do.

Kiel must have gone off to sleep almost immediately, only to be woken by a gorgeous looking girl in a flimsy pink negligee, with short silky pyjamas underneath which he thought he had seen before, giving him a kiss.

'Good morning, Kiel, did you sleep well?' Juliet enquired, falling nearly on top of him with a kiss, or was this just a wish?

'What time is it?' Kiel asked pulling her close to him. 'I have slept very well indeed,' he replied, and asked, 'What about you, dear?'

'Oh, I had a good sleep,' she said and laughed. 'You should have slept well, with what you got up to last night, calling me darling. I shall have to tell Secilia all about it,' Juliet remarked.

She got him worried for a moment, until she said, 'Don't worry, my lips are sealed, since I enjoyed it as much as you did,' and she walked away. Juliet called out, 'See you soon; its time for you to have a shower and wake up ready for breakfast.'

Kiel soon thereafter jumped up out of bed and ran into the bathroom, not taking any notice of the light above the door and who would stand there under the shower but Juliet?

He didn't know what to say, but apologised. Then she turned to speak, 'Don't apologise. You have seen me like this before, only perhaps slightly covered and drunk.

Come and get under the warm water quickly before it gets cold and you end up with goose pimples like me.'

He was most surprised she said this, since what he could see were surely a great deal larger than goose pimples, unless he was mistaken.

Talk about Adam and Eve; the only thing missing was the apple, but this had presumably already been consumed.

What did she mean by saying, 'You have seen me like this before only slightly covered and drunk?' To have been or not have been, that is the question.

He knew he had a great night out with Juliet, and a beautiful dream following. He could see her in her silky pink nightgown and shapely figure or had this all been just a dream? He could not possibly ask and make himself look silly. Is it not amazing what champagne can do to one's brain or remembering capability?

One thing Kiel did know for sure, he slept like and angel and had a beautiful dream, until he was woken by a lovely looking young lady with a kiss and cuddle.

Juliet wrapped herself in a dressing gown and retreated to her room after giving Kiel a peck on the cheek to bring him back to normality.

He could not believe what he'd seen and what a graceful body there was standing right in front of him for a short while.

He had a quick shower, and returned to his room to get dressed, ready to go downstairs for breakfast.

The door opened once again after a knock and Juliet's head appeared round the corner, asking; 'Are you ready yet? You can come down with me.'

Juliet was more than just a sister to him he was sure. Why was there something he could feel deeply every time she came near or close to him?

What did they get up to last night after returning from dancing? He was not certain, but whatever it was, they both must have enjoyed it, since she seemed to be beaming of joy.

The lovely sun was shining again. Kiel took her arm, dressed in just trousers and shirt and walked downstairs, where they met up with her mum, obviously waiting.

Kiel spoke first, 'Good morning, my lady,' which greeting she returned with a gracious smile.

She said, 'Good morning, Kiel, how are you?'

Juliet and her mum had seemingly met before and we followed into the breakfast room over looking the river and city once again, with the sun gleaming down on these wonderful old large buildings in the distance.

'I am fine my lady,' Kiel replied and asked, 'Have you had a peaceful night, with us both being out and away?'

'Yes, thank you, Kiel; you have obviously enjoyed your night out with Juliet. Has she behaved herself?' she requested to know.

'Yes, my lady. We had a great time and quite a bit to drink with some fine friends, dancing and walking home from the ferry,' he replied.

This again was indeed a glorious sight to see, especially for the first time in the early or, better said, later morning, with the sun shining on to the city below.

Juliet's dad was already sitting there with a cup of coffee and the morning paper, no doubt studying the stocks and shares, about which Kiel knew nothing, but had heard a lot.

'Good morning, sir, what a lovely morning,' Kiel said. Juliet butted in, 'Good morning, Daddy. Any good news?'

'Nothing of interest to you two. Good morning. Did you have a great time last night? I hope you have not spent too much of my money?' he asked smiling.

'No, Daddy, we have been very good,' Juliet replied and asked. 'Haven't we, Kiel?'

To which he nodded his head.

Juliet continued. 'We just had two of my friends for company and we all enjoyed ourselves tremendously. All in all, we have had a wonderful time,' she remarked and requested my approval, 'haven't we, Kiel?'

He was more then willing or happy to provide and replied, 'Yes Juliet.'

'What would you like for breakfast, Kiel? Anything fried, or just cold?' came the request from Juliet's mum.

'Something fried, if that is not too much trouble?' he replied.

'No, not at all, we shall all have something fried, which won't be very long. Have a cup of coffee and a roll in the meantime,' the lady remarked.

He loved buttered rolls and started with one of those with his coffee, while Juliet and her dad was having a short conversation, no doubt about the bill of the night just gone. He could not really hear and was not particularly interested, unless he had to pay for it, which would have taken him a year at least out of the few coppers he was earning or got paid.

'I am really glad you had a good time. Juliet appears to have enjoyed herself, and I hope you did the same?' her dad said once again, turning to Kiel.

'Yes, sir, I most certainly did and thank you, sir,' Kiel replied.

'Nothing to thank me for, as long as you don't come here every weekend,' he said with a smile.

Kiel was not quite sure how to take this remark, until Juliet gave him a cuddle and said, 'You must not say that Daddy; I would love Kiel to come every weekend if he could.'

The breakfast arrived and was brought in steaming hot by the cook and assistant, on the already warmed-up plates.

Kiel had seen neither of the serving ladies before and both said, 'Good morning, sir,' to him.

They had obviously met up with the family earlier. He was quite taken in; never had anyone called him 'Sir' before, unless he had overheard it.

While we were all sitting round the table, Juliet asked him, 'What would you like to do after breakfast? Would you like to go for ride, or into town?'

Her mum intervened and said, 'Why don't you take Kiel to town and show him round, then you can have lunch in town and thereafter you can take him back to the station?'

'What a great idea. Would you like that, Kiel?' Juliet asked politely and remarked, 'It is a lovely day for a walk.'

'Yes, I would love to do that; I have never been to the city of Dresden, except for one day with Mum and Dad when still very young, and the day I was born here in hospital, but I don't remember a lot about that,' he replied.

'That is great,' Juliet said, and carried on. 'That is what we will do. I would love to show you part of our lovely city, so you had better put on your suit and take your few belongings with you, then we shall not have to come back.'

Going upstairs after breakfast, he was amazed to find all his clothes cleaned and pressed by the staff, lying there ready for him to put on.

That sort of life I shall have to try and enter into, where everything is done for you, but I doubt that anything like this will come my way a second time.

Juliet, as usual, popped in to make sure that everything was in order and he knew which leg to place into the trousers first, or which arm into which shirt sleeve. This may be a little overstated, but she was more like a wife or mum to him rather than a great friend.

That was what he liked about her most; she was always there when one needed her and very patient, never erratic or pushy.

After they both got ready, she loaned him the coat from her brother again, just in case it would be chilly or a spot of rain later, although the sky was crystal clear and blue with the sun still shining brightly.

Juliet once again looked a picture. She seemed to know exactly what to wear and when. With her gently wavy blonde hair glittering, her face and cheeks seemed like a fresh apple to bite into. With her beautiful bright blue eyes shining, who could resist?

After a peck on the cheek, they walked downstairs and said goodbye by shaking hands with her dad, and Kiel kissing her mum's hand, thanking her once again for all the kindness. They walked through the door.

They spoke almost together and said, 'Have a good time and allow yourselves a great day together. We hope to see you again, Kiel, and goodbye.'

Arm in arm we walked down to the ferry, which was not very far from this beautiful house, which was standing out among the fine large golden brown leaf covered trees and green firs, similar to a castle and obviously purpose-built into the hillside. Although it would have made a better picture in the late afternoon, when the sun would have been shining directly towards it from over part of the city and river. This time in the morning, the sun was shining upon the city and palaces, with the high and small buildings, which looked great from the distance, but mostly, disappeared once we moved further down among the trees.

Talking all the way, they soon got down and onto the ferry itself, with the water reflecting the clear blue sky. It did not take long to cross. Then they took a tram from there.

Juliet informed Kiel that she was to be the paymaster and he was to keep my hands out of his pockets for the day, which sounded great and relaxing, but not really him, although he had very little to put his hand into his pocket for.

He thanked Juliet for her kindness, but thought it not really right. He had been brought up that the male should pay and he informed her about this.

She smiled, cuddled him and said, 'You are old-fashioned and have to change with the times. Anyway, you haven't got any money, and I will allow you to pay for me another time.'

That was settled and not another word about it was spoken, but so he would not be embarrassed, she handed him the money. This he appreciated and placed it in a separate pocket, so as not to get it mixed with his few coppers. Kiel thanked her and promised to return all that would be left over with the change at the end of the day.

'You are a little softy, but I admire you for that,' she replied and gave him a peck on the cheek, and continued, 'You worry too much.'

Our first stop was the royal palace. Even though there were no more royals in Germany, the palace was still standing and what a magnificent place that was.

They walked all round the gardens and later went inside, which was just marvellous to see all these magnificently painted and decorated ceilings, walls and rooms with large windows and long beautiful curtains. The gold, silver and chinaware, the gorgeous large and small oil paintings on the walls of previous kings, queens and their children, all of it much too much to take in at once. They took their time, since there was nothing to rush for, and Juliet appeared as much interested as Kiel was, although she had seen it all before and tried to explain.

After that they went to see all the very fine architecture of the different beautiful galleries, museums, opera house, churches, et cetera, some of which they entered for a quick view.

It was lunchtime and Juliet took him to a smart restaurant-cum-hotel for lunch. Sitting down inside, she chose duck with orange and Kiel followed suit, since he had once again never heard of or eaten this, naturally with a bottle of wine to wash it all down.

Seeing all this stylish treatment, well-dressed people and waiters running around, it came to his mind to take up banking so he could use other people's money to do the same, but that was never likely to happen.

Everyone appeared to know Juliet and kept staring, or was it because of Kiel and our different ages, which, he would have thought would not have shown up too much. Kiel was convinced it was the beautiful lady sitting next to him.

It seemed that they had plenty to talk about ourselves and continually kept talking and laughing, enjoying our meal and wine.

Kiel felt like one of the gentry himself, although his attire did not appear to quite match the rest of the dining room's gentry. That could possibly have been why they all had the occasional glance across. He did not mind and neither did Juliet by the look of her, although she was dressed to perfection again, which was one of the great pleasures of being with her. She did not seem to mind what he was wearing.

They had a splendid lunch, but when Kiel received the bill he was almost knocked for six and showed it to Juliet, who did not seem to mind or care. Luckily, she had given him enough money to pay for it and it was she who chose the amount of tip to leave for the waiters and their service.

The tip alone was more than he would earn in a day's hard work, but she did not seem to be in the slightest worried, even though he could have lived on this one lunch for a week or more. Money seemed to be no object, especially for Juliet; she obviously had no idea where it all came from and how it had to be earned, which made Kiel think that it would be a fine thing to marry into money, but that was not likely happen either.

They enjoyed each other's company, which was the most important for now, and after they had coffee and paid the bill, they continued their walk.

Stepping slowly along the waterfront for a while was very pleasant especially with a pretty lady on one's arm.

It was a glorious day and after walking along the riverbank cuddling up close at times, they decided to go into the museum and have a look at ancient history and fine art.

The old uniforms and traditional clothing with all the glorious old furniture, crockery, fine china and glassware, massive paintings on leather hanging from some walls once again surpassed his fullest expectations.

When they came to the ancient coin and medal collections, he could hardly be dragged away. All this was something quite new to him, and the vast volume of cost to keep and look after these items must be colossal.

Time was getting on and Juliet reminded him that the next train was due in about half an hour, and not to leave it too late, as it was the rush hour when every one leaves off from work, or you might not get a seat. What rush hour? It was Sunday, but there was also a war going on and people had to work seven days a week, which one never thinks of living out on the land, although they always had to work seven days a week, war or no war. Kiel thanked Juliet for being so thoughtful and we slowly walked to the station, where he returned all the change and coat.

She took the notes and allowed him to keep the small change, for which he had to give her a last kiss and quick cuddle.

She went to the ticket counter, bought a first-class ticket for him to return, which he had not realised until she took him to the train herself and came in with him for a short sit-down.

The seats were all upholstered, not the wooden ones, which he had been used to. She was a little beauty.

They had a few more words, when thereafter she gave him a kiss and a cuddle, said, 'Goodbye, Kiel, I hope I shall see you again soon,' and left.

Kiel opened the window, followed her with his eyes and waved. This she returned with a smile, and then she disappeared out of sight.

He once again felt like a little prince and was completely over the moon, thinking this we shall have to do again, looking forward to the next time.

Several more people stepped into the train before it finally took off.

An elderly gentleman sat opposite. He obviously knew from Kiel's attire that he was not from the city and talked to him almost all the way back to Riesa.

He seemed to know all about Juliet's dad and his bank, as well as Dr Kohl, our head at the college and, lived in the town of Riesa, but worked in the city. This gentleman also mentioned his name, which had escaped Kiel, and asked for his. He had heard of the colonel and the lady as well as Secilia, but did not seem to know them personally. He seemed to know all about the estate, the town of Riesa and also the city of Dresden, and told Kiel a great deal about both.

After their arrival, Kiel collected his bicycle and cycled back to the estate for coffee and that marvellous cake of auntie's. Both of them were already waiting for him to hear the news.

There was a great deal to tell and they both listened with intense interest, asking many questions about his auntie and uncle in Dresden, some of which he could not answer, but he had to tell them that he had no address and could not visit them in the city.

They had a letter for him from his brother, which he had written since they could not or had not met up personally. He had been called up to join the German marines, and his employer had offered Kiel his job with quite a lot more money. Kiel had unfortunately missed his brother, but considered and talked over this new job offer with uncle and auntie.

They did not really want him to go, but said, 'You go and have a good look next weekend and if it is still available and you like it, we shall not stand in your way.' They continued, 'Please remember you will have to give at least one week's notice and not let the headman down, should you decide to leave, or he will not be very pleased.'

Kiel could hardly go to sleep for thinking about the weekend just gone, the company and the great time they all had, and now this wonderful news; but was it really wonderful?

That would mean leaving and perhaps never seeing Secilia or Juliet again and what could he possibly tell them? Would he hurt them, or only himself?

He was totally confused, but did go off to sleep in the end, after a lot of twisting and turning for quite a long while.

Kiel had done a lot of thinking with no actual answers coming his way, when suddenly the usual knock from uncle on the door woke him up, with very heavy eyes. He called out but had to turn over again for another hour, when he missed the alarm, and auntie had to give him another call.

He must have arrived a little heavy eyed, when he was confronted by the headman with the remark, 'You must have had a hectic weekend, you still look tired,' which he had to admit he still was, and told him all about it, including the letter from his brother.

He looked a little surprised about this and obviously had not expected anything of this sort to come his way on a Monday morning.

In the afternoon he came to see Kiel and they had a long talk about this new situation offered to him, when he said; 'I have looked at the books and could offer you a little more money, but nothing like the amount you can get there.' He continued, 'You will have to make up your own mind about this Kiel, although we would like to keep you on here.'

This made the situation even more difficult, when he never has had to make any of those difficult decisions on his own, but he had plenty of time.

By the time the weekend came along, Kiel decided at least to go to this little village or hamlet, but quite large farm, and have a look at the job and discuss things with the farmer, his wife and family together.

It was a late Saturday morning by the time Kiel managed to get there on his bike, which was not all that far, just the other side of the town of Riesa towards the east, the estate was laying in the south.

The farmer showed Kiel round the farm, pointed out his room and showed it to him, and invited him to stay for lunch, which he accepted.

That was when Kiel met the farmer's wife and family and shook hands and found out that they had two sons and two daughters; one looked a little older than himself but not a lot. One of the sons was older and had joined the army, and the other was much younger, about eleven or twelve, which happened to be right. There was also a little girl, who was only around eight or nine, but all seemed very pleasant to talk to.

They talked a lot about what Kiel had to do and how much they were prepared to pay and help. He would have his meals on the farm but every other thing else, like washing clothes, et cetera, would be his own concern or responsibility. They mentioned having a young house lady, who would probably be able to help him out.

They all seemed quite friendly and after lunch introduced him to the rest of the staff, but there were few.

Saturday as well as Sunday was still a working day on the farms and everyone was around if only to feed and clean the animals, especially in those days.

Kiel pointed out that he was still studying at college and needed that certain time off, which seemed no problem. They in fact seemed quite pleased to accommodate this and help out on those certain days or hours if necessary, which sounded good and made things easier all round.

He could even have the occasional weekend off, one every other month, and things seemed or sounded reasonably well, but would it all work out? He thought it best to discuss it with his uncle and auntie first before making a hasty decision, which all agreed as long as they would know within two weeks.

They realised that he would have or like to give notice, and not just running away, and they hoped that he would do the same, should he ever decide to leave them, in due course.

Everything seemed great; he got on his bike and cycled back to the estate for a cup of coffee before going back to work.

He gave uncle and auntie a brief outline and promised to discuss it all in detail over supper, with which short explanation they seemed quite happy.

Returning to work, Kiel did the very same to the headman and told him that he would make a final decision after he had talked it over and thought about it properly. Kiel promised to tell him in a day or so after a great deal of thought, which the headman seemed to appreciate as well.

A long discussion took place that night and both uncle and auntie seemed to agree that it would be right for Kiel to take this job, providing he was happy in his own mind.

Auntie naturally hoped Kiel would not go and leave them again, but she said,

'You are growing up and have to earn your own living. As much as we would like you stay, you must do what you think is right for you, my boy.' She came across the room with little tears in her eyes, grabbed him and gave him a cuddle.

They had a late evening drink on this before retiring to bed, when Kiel was once again lying there, turning and twisting to sort out the best solution.

This was not the easiest for any of them, especially him, since he had to leave a good home, good food, as well as auntie and uncle behind.

No one would or could advise Kiel and it was all down to him. Even dad and his brother had by now joined the army and could not be reached by phone. He had not seen his dad since he left home; they had, however, been in touch by letter correspondence for the last few months, which was of no help this time.

Small headaches pushed old thoughts out and allowed new ones to enter, but which of them were correct and which had to be retained or allowed to escape? Several days and nights were used up to come to the right decision, or would it be the right one in the end?

But money and finance are (even though not always thought to be correct) the most important, especially when young, and thus this new job had to be considered very carefully. Kiel still seemed to have the same opportunities to carry on his studies and the distance would not have been any greater. He would miss the many friends made, auntie and uncle and the lovely food she cooked and the delicious cakes baked. Secilia and Juliet, both of them he had grown so very fond, when he even thought he had fallen in love at times and the thought of leaving them was even harder than expected.

228

In the end he made up his mind, thinking that he had to try and stand on his own two feet sooner or later and decided to move on.

On his very last day a card arrived from Secilia, thanking him for the lovely time and knowing that he had been to see Juliet, but hoped they would meet up again soon. This nearly made him change his mind to stay. This card, however, arrived just one day too late; definite arrangements had by that time been made and the move to the farm would have to go on.

Saying good-bye to all was one of the hardest things and tears came to auntie's eyes and his, when they had to have a last little cuddle.

With a last message from her saying, 'Any problems, boy, you know where we are and let us know how you get on.'

He got on his bike with the few belongings he had, waved them all goodbye and cycled down the road a few miles.

There he met new friends who offered him a large bed and living room all to himself, but with no one to knock him awake in the mornings.

Oh, Lord, that was something he had never thought about; what would he do if he did not hear the alarm going off? Kiel suddenly became somewhat concerned, or even afraid, until he suddenly realised that there was another, older farm worker living in a room right next to him who would surely help to wake him.

The farmer's daughter and her friend, the housemaid, who went dancing almost every Saturday evening, very soon befriended Kiel.

In the meantime he took motorcycle riding lessons, passed the test and bought himself a small motorbike.

This made going to college and out in the evenings so much easier and quicker. After this he could even take a passenger on the rear seat and felt like a little king in his own rights.

That way he thought he could go over to see Secilia any time when she came to the estate and he could even ride to Dresden to see Juliet, but neither of this was to become true.

In May 1941, he had to go to Berlin for a medical, only to be called up in August to join the army or, rather, air ground defence forces, and later joined the paratroops.

With the war continuing, he was posted from pillar to post and in the end landed up in St Denis, France just outside Paris, from where later, in June 1944, they were forced to retreat.

They managed to get as far as Mons, in Belgium, whereby the most unfortunate bad luck, Kiel, with all the others was blasted with shellfire from the American tanks, which had overtaken and encircled them without noticing.

After being shot through both legs, et cetera, he was taken prisoner and later transported to England and from there, after months of hospital treatment, shipped out to the United States of America.

Arriving after a tumultuous ocean crossing with German U-boat attacks and massive storms, in New York on December 10th 1944, travelling down to Fort Mead, Baltimore, the first camp and plenty of American food et cetera, which put them back on their feet. From there down to Texas and following Arizona, Idaho, Utah Oregon, Montana, back to Arizona and later, in 1946 back to England.

While working with the sun blazing down in the cotton fields of Arizona, he often thought of the poor chaps who did not make it that far.

He sometimes thought how lucky they were, not to have to do this dirty, filthy, backbreaking job, with over a 100° Fahrenheit of sun and clear blue skies above and no shade whatsoever. Nor were they ever allowed to write or receive any correspondence.

They spent almost two years in various camps travelling all around most of the States, from officer to working camps, mostly along the Great West. Travelling for days on end in trains through the icy cold of the north, they again reached the sunny hot desert sand in the south, details in a previous book, '75 Years of Sunshine'.

He sat down on a fine hot Sunday while the sandstorms swept through the desert sands and whirlwinds with cones rising up to the sky, rushing through the camp, and almost taking them with it. Chewing more sand than sandwich and writing a little story, 'The Long Awaited Meeting', as below, thinking what the others lost in the war, would have felt like sitting here with them. They were here in the sand and dust filled tent without female companionship among all male Prisoners of War, with heads full of thoughts from the past.

Since he had, with great fortune, managed to survive and was allowed to stay on in England, it is with great pleasure that he told this story of bygone years before departing himself. Many who may have fallen, on all sides, never having had the chance to return to their loved ones or old sweethearts and for what, but selfishness and greed?

**The Long Awaited Meeting**
*(Written in 1945, Arizona, USA)*

After a very long frustrating time and years of anticipation, I saw her once again here today, right in the middle of nowhere. In one of the most southern states of America, in the sandy, dusty plains called Arizona.

My knees shaking, feeling like rubbery jelly and her sudden appearance, there she was, as from outer space or fallen out of heaven. The blood rushed through my veins, raising my blood pressure to the point of boiling, speeding up the heartbeat.

Just seeing her placed me in a state of near exhaustion. I had to try and steady myself as well as my shaking legs, finally trying to master self-control.

After a reasonably long time, I managed to pull myself together and relaxed, somewhat regaining my regular breathing.

It was such a long time of going without, that the pleasure of seeing her again completely unbalanced my thoughts and brain.

Noticing her most slender, sweet, inviting, beautifully shapely figure, just like a present come down from the angels of heaven.

Here she was, right in front of me, a Prisoner of War, behind high barbed wire fencing, among the cotton fields of the Deep South.

I was naturally overcome and speechless; very tenderly, just like a piece of china, I touched her, softly and with gentle, inviting hands and steps, I began to lead her to my, or better said our, large canvas tent.

She came with me, without resistance; holding her in my tender shaking hands, I accompanied her.

Jealously, with all eyes upon us, my fellow prisoners disappeared. After giving them a slight wink, we were alone, quite alone, and now closer than ever.

It was very quiet and quite still outside and all around us; the sun was high up in a clear blue sky, shining laughingly through the only very small open gap in the tent.

Every little sound or smell was followed with my wide open and tense but keen ears and nose, trying not to miss a thing. Outside, the steps of a soldier on guard duty came near and then disappeared again in the distant surroundings of tents, huts and sandstorms.

I was still listening, but turning my head in her direction, smilingly and full of fear of being found out, I admired her, lying there fully covered and wrapped up on my bunk.

The torment of having her here with me all alone was most overwhelming and very exciting to say the least. This I cannot and must not miss or spoil, I have to try and make the most of this wonderfully handed to me opportunity. This I would love to taste and enjoy to the full, I thought quietly to myself, trying not to allow my impatience and desire to run away with me.

It was now beginning to get twilight; I lit the only small candle we had in the tent, with trembling, shaking hands. In the soft glimmering of the gently shining candlelight, she was and looked even sweeter and more desirable, tempting and inviting as before.

I could hardly restrain my emotions or myself and moved just that little closer, without giving her any inkling that I might be too forward or fast.

A battle began to start up inside me. I was trembling once again; shall I or shall I not get nearer to her, grab her, take her in my arms and hands as she lay there with her marvellous, deliciously sweet scented smell?

On tenterhooks, shaking from head to foot with raving emotions and full of enthusiasm, I thought 'no', trying once again to relax, restraining myself, holding back the excitement.

Knowing that specific timing and patience was of vital importance not to spoil or unbalance the entire evening, I lay there right beside her with my head full of thoughts and being restless.

Seconds later, I could no longer stand the impatience, strain, or prolong the waiting. Slowly and quietly I turned, facing her as gently and softly as my hands and body would allow, even though I was still shaking or trembling with little control.

I began to undo, take off and slide down just a little of her first covering and gently placing same to one side. Very slowly and gingerly, cover after cover would follow to come off, putting them within easy reach next to us.

Not a word was spoken, all was very still and quiet, in as well as outside. Darkness had begun to set in with no one in sight or hearing distance as we both naturally hoped.

Quite willingly and without resistance or seeming discomfort, she bends slightly, lying within my eager restless hands.

I was completely beyond self-control and very frustrated, quite taken in by her overwhelming sweetness, softness and warmth. She lay there in her natural state and charm, completely undressed, delicious and beautiful before me.

No longer could I stop or restrain my passion, innermost emotions and sense of self-control.

Placing myself upon her softness, almost squashing her beneath my heavy breathing, my teeth biting gently and softly into her.

I am touching her tenderly with my fingers. Slowly and very gently I withdrew my hand, my fingers covered with a sweet, most exciting moist sticky substance.

After enjoying every minute of this exercise and excitement, I began to relax, once again gently opening my eyes.

Waking up having enjoyed this exhausting work of consumption, some time later, she had gone. Just as expected she had completely disappeared out of sight forever. This so long awaited and looked forward to, so sweetly tasting bar of chocolate!

Yours forever and ever in thought and expected anticipation.
*Karl-Werner Antrack*

## Don't Cry, Just Kneel

I am the sunlight on the ripened grain;
I am the gentle autumn rain.
When waking in the morning's hush,
I am the swift uplifting thrush.

Quiet birds in circling flight,
For all of you a star that only shines at night.
I am underground, of this fine so-called Earth,
Remembering and treasure, all our love's been worth.
We've never had the chance to meet again,
In sunshine, or heavy rain.

But don't forget we were so near,
Without the slightest sign of fear.
We held each other close and tight,
In daylight or the dark of night.

I won't forget the happy times we've had,
With you around, I've been so glad.
These good times, which were surely real,
Don't cry, just kneel; I am still your good friend Kiel.

Written by Karl-Werner Antrack.

Printed in the United Kingdom
by Lightning Source UK Ltd.
101449UKS00001B/70-108